LOVE MOVES WILDLY
THROUGH THE PAGES OF
WILD SPENDERS

That night he made love to her ~~savagely, with~~
almost loss of ~~c~~
frightened.

"Will? Please

He looked dow

the air. He mo
shoulders hunc
he was close to the edge, it was like watching
him grow old. In the dim light his lips went
slack, his face muscles dragged, and his eyes
shrunk. Then he collapsed on her.

"Don't you see, Sybil?" he breathed. "Don't
you see? I want to be everything for you—
friend, father, lover. I want to be enough."

WILD SPENDERS

WILD SPENDERS

DIANA DAVENPORT

AVON
PUBLISHERS OF BARD, CAMELOT, DISCUS AND FLARE BOOKS

AVON BOOKS
A division of
The Hearst Corporation
1790 Broadway
New York, New York 10019

The Macmillan edition contains the following Library of
Congress Cataloging in Publication Data:

Davenport, Diana.
  Wild spenders.
  I. Title.
PS3554.A8598W5   1984   813'.54   84-5762

First Avon Printing, May 1985

For
Becky Young, Lorraine Dusky, Bettina Moë
and
Bernard Jennings

Acknowledgments

For continuing support, special thanks to Hillel Black, my editor and publisher, and to my agent, Sterling Lord.

I have lived in the village of East Hampton, Long Island, for several summers and would like to thank the local people of that town for their patience, humor, and unflagging generosity while I was writing this book.

WILD SPENDERS

Chapter
1

It was a day in early June when the summer was so new, sunlight seemed raw and trees still had the greenness of spring. Two women in bikinis lounged on the lawn of a summer house in Maidscott, a beach hamlet nestled between the more resorty villages of Bridgehampton and East Hampton, Long Island, jutting ninety miles east of New York City into the Atlantic Ocean.

The women were of that indeterminate age when looks begin to lack youth. Yet their movements were quick and charged, like the movements of young girls who believe life's largest surprises still lie ahead. Sybil Wade, dark-haired, with a long, lean body that traced sharp angles in the air, rolled over on her stomach.

"Funny," she said, "I never *meant* to be an older woman."

Beside her, Blair Heywood tugged at a blonde pigtail and frowned. "You say it like it's an award."

"How am I supposed to sound?"

"Well, try for a little less exuberance." Blair studied the young man polishing the car in the driveway. "Or try older men."

1

Sybil threw a wedge of lime at her. "You should talk."

It landed on Blair's stomach, a stomach firm yet of a certain ripeness. Her whole body was that, mature but arrested at the perfect point. She swiped at the lime, shifted in her bikini, and sat up.

"OK, OK, Tom's five years younger than I am," Blair argued. "But at least we're both over the thirty hump." She nodded toward the young man. "He's still a kid."

Sybil arched her neck, watching beach towels drying on the clothesline, moving in the breeze as if, like migrating birds, in response to some polar ordination. Then she looked toward the driveway.

"Will's old for twenty-two," she said. "I'm not, by the way, hurting anyone."

Blair looked at her affectionately. "You're new at this, Sybil. Young men make you risk things. You get silly."

She squeezed a worm of Piz Buin on her leg and rubbed vigorously, thinking how she needed the silliness. Before Will entered her life she had felt like something in a winding sheet. They gazed across the lawn at him, sandy-haired, bare-chested, ferociously bronzed.

"I'm in love with him, Blair. Is that sick?"

"Considering you're thirty-eight, it's not exactly sick. It's . . . gaudy."

The car shone frantically under his rag. The job was done, but Will kept rubbing. They were discussing him, he knew it, and felt larval, as if his bones were still developing. This bothered him because he was mature for his age, usually confident with older women. Of course most older women he knew near Sybil's age—his mother, for instance—didn't wear bikinis or cowboy boots. They had settled into life, resigned you might say. There was nothing settled about Sybil; even in sleep, she assumed the posture of motion.

"Will." She waved from the lawn.

He walked over slowly, smelling their lotions, their perfumes. Slim, long-muscled, two inches over six feet, from the neck down he could have been five years older. But his face had the big-eyed hunger of a young man impatient for experience.

"How'd I do?" He pointed to the car.

"Like glass."

He blushed, looking at Sybil for cues. He circled her slowly, she the center, he the orbit. It was always like that: She smiled, he laughed; she was silent, he brooded. Now she moved to the house for fresh drinks, and left alone with Blair, Will froze, wanting to be fascinating. She had blonde pigtails and soft, brown eyes, like a teacher he followed home when he was a boy.

"That's some car." He nodded toward the driveway. "How old did you say it was?"

Blair stared at the yellow Jaguar, so bright it seemed lit from within. "It was made before you were born, Will. A '54."

"Oh, wowww." His eyes grew huge. "Your boyfriend must be crazy about it. Do you let him drive it?"

She laughed. "It's really his. I just wheel it around to keep the battery charged."

She had closed three real-estate deals before she could afford to buy the Jaguar.

"What does your boyfriend do?" Will leaned closer. "I mean, while you keep the battery charged?"

Blair cleared her throat. "I think of Tom primarily as a . . . consumer. He sails a boat, plays the stock market, and wants to write novels like Sybil. I come in fourth. When I can get in."

3

He stood, embarrassed, studying cloud formations as if deciphering code.

"Sit down, Will." Blair gestured wearily. "What I told you isn't bad news. It's just old news."

He sat down and studied his feet.

Sybil put down the phone and stared at them from the kitchen window, heads hanging like they had swapped mantras. She came out of the house balancing drinks.

"That was Lu on the horn. She's flying in from Boston to East Hampton Airport tomorrow."

Blair looked up. "Is her cargo warm or cold?"

"Cold."

"Who's Lu?" Will asked.

"Another old college friend, like Blair." Sybil sat down, smelling the sun on his hair. "You'll like her, Will. She's a pilot."

"A pilot!" His eyes sparked. "You mean she owns a plane?"

"Yep. People hire her to get places fast."

Blair laughed. "Tell him the rest."

"She also transports corpses."

"Huh?"

"People die, and Lu flies them home to be buried."

"Corpses," Will cried. "Oh, wowww."

Blair's eyes closed. Oh, wowww?

It was going to be that kind of summer. Puissant.

A small, exuberant cumulus sat on her left; otherwise the day was flawlessly blue. Leaving Massachusetts and Connecticut behind, Lutheria Campbell hummed over Long Island Sound, passing Orient Point and beyond that Gardiner's Bay. Descending over the South Fork of Long Island, she made radio contact with East Hampton UNICOM.

"Yeah, this is Cherokee five-two-four-eight-eight. What's your active runway?"

Below her in the pattern, Lu saw two small planes, student pilots doing "touch-and-go's," takeoffs and landings. She got clearance for runway twenty-two and, keeping the other aircraft in sight, banked over the airfield. Nose down, power back, the Cherokee Six began descending one thousand feet a minute.

"Cherokee downwind runway twenty-two, East Hampton."

Aligned with the runway, Lu pulled back a little, slowing air speed to sixty-five knots, continuing her descent. Then, turning base, she made her final approach.

"Cherokee on final. Runway twenty-two, East Hampton."

Pulling up her nose, she leveled off above the runway and flared to a gentle landing. As the engines hummed down to the rollout, she exited at the first taxiway.

"Cherokee off the active. Request tie-down space."

Sybil was draped along the fence, waving. Behind her a man in an alarmingly ill-fitting red wig backed a hearse up to the gate. Lu parked the Cherokee, waved to Sybil, cut across the field to the small flight-service office, and stuck her head in the door.

"Hi, Rick! Can anyone give me a hand? I've got a cold one."

"Hey, how ya' doing?"

He whistled to two mechanics hosing down a Piper Cub. They looked at Lu and moved fast.

She shook hands, jerking her thumb at the Cherokee. "Can you guys help me move a coffin over to that man wearing the veal parmigiana?"

The mechanics cracked up. They were young, muscled, as if they worked on the stun-line of a slaughterhouse. "You got it!"

With a freight dolly, they loaded the coffin on the

hearse while Lu concentrated on the undertaker's wig and his Jewish inversion of speech.

"A female pilot I didn't expect." He signed her receipt and handed it back, frowning. "A male I expected."

"So did my father." She smiled, shook hands, and ran to Sybil.

They hugged, jumping up and down like kids because it had been a year. The mechanics backed off, watching them. The pilot fair-skinned, freckled, with wild, terra-cotta hair and nice breasts; her friend dark-haired, tall, a lot of leg.

"I'll take the pilot."

"Nah. The tall one. Skinny women are always hot."

Rick, the older man, piped up behind them. "All right. All right. Quit flogging your dongs. They're only broads." But he watched too. "Imagine. A looker like that flying dead bodies for a living." He shook his head. "Women. Today."

It was a short drive from the East Hampton Airport to Maidscott. Within minutes Sybil turned her rumbling old Dodge off the highway and down Seth Lane, headed for the ocean.

"Christ." Lu looked out at hedged estates. "I thought your last book rolled over and died. How'd you afford a summer place here in the Smarthamptons?"

Sybil hit the brakes. "My last book didn't die. It was bludgeoned to death." She narrowed her eyes at Lu. "You sound like all you read were the reviews."

"I'm sorry." Lu took her hand. "I read it."

"And?"

"Your characters were unkind, Sybil. The novel was one bad mood."

Easing up on the brake, accelerating slowly, Sybil

shook her head. "Amazing. Everyone kept telling me to write a funny novel, that I had this *sense* of humor."

"Your first two books were funnier. You didn't flog the reader."

"They were vapid," Sybil argued. "Throwaways."

"They were funny."

"Yeah, well maybe next book."

They pulled into a long, pebbled driveway, past a faded brick manor on the left, and stopped before a small, gray-shingle carriage house set off behind hedges. The carriage entrance had been walled up years ago so that, approaching the house from the driveway, there seemed to be no door, only windows. The entrance was on the side of the house, off the lawn. Beyond the lawn, the hedges, and then the dunes, the sea.

"Say." Lu stared. "Are you being kept?"

Sybil laughed. "It's Blair's real-estate client. The place is on the market for nine hundred grand. They're in Europe for the summer and thought it would be droll to have an author-in-residence as caretaker."

"Well, maybe this makes up for the bad reviews."

She reached in back for her suitcase, and Sybil caught her arm.

"Uhh . . . there's someone else in-residence."

Lu smiled. "Hit me."

"I've been seeing this guy since last October. You might be shocked. He's—"

"Let me guess. A Haitian Rastafarian."

"No. He's just young."

"Oh, that. Hell, I've been fooling around with twenty-eight-year-olds."

"Lu, he's younger."

Will dragged a garden hose around the corner of

7

the house, looked toward the car, and waved. Lu's jaw dropped slowly, as though hinged.

"Good God, Sybil. I've got underwear older than that."

Inside the carriage house, Lu toured the near-empty first floor, seeing only an old Empire sofa and a ratty, hanging tapestry, unraveling the weave of a satyr's chase.

"This place looks like a struck set." She frowned. "Where do you people sit?"

"We drag in the patio tables and chairs," Will said. "They put the good stuff in storage. Don't worry, there're enough beds." He followed her upstairs with her suitcase. "Besides, Sybil likes it empty this way."

Lu smiled. "She would."

"Why do you say that?" He suddenly sounded defensive, territorial.

"Sybil always had this approach." She shrugged. "Afraid comfort might corrode her artistic . . . integrity."

Will looked down thoughtfully. "Eastern philosophies consider space a spiritual imperative."

Lu's eyes sought the roof of her head. She turned to him slowly, folding her arms across her chest. "I bet you're into alfalfa sprouts and TM and Castaneda, right?"

He moved closer and shook his head. "Red meat. And Robert Stone. And I'm not intimidated by rude women who fly planes." After Lu unpacked, she and Sybil sat over drinks on the patio, catching up on the past year.

"How's Blair?" Lu asked. "Still in bondage?"

Sybil frowned. "Tom's getting better. He remembered her birthday this year."

8

"With a salad spinner. Remember what he gave her for Christmas? A meat thermometer."

Will banged the screen door, coming out of the house with a bowl of nuts. "This guy sounds like a shit," he said. "Why does Blair put up with him?"

Sybil looked at Will with infinite patience. "Because Tom's steady. He stays in one place, and he doesn't chase other women. After a certain age, that's important."

"But does he love Blair?" he persisted.

The two women traded glances, making Will feel young and tired.

"In Tom's words," Sybil said, "he does not *not* love her." She glanced at Lu again, then sat back thinking how no one but the very old and the very innocent touched that word anymore. It was like a fossil from a fussier stage in human evolution.

Later in the day Will sat on a dune watching Sybil and Lu walk the beach, wary like pirates walking the horizon. They knew things it would take him years to learn. The odds in life. He smiled, studying their silhouettes; at certain angles they looked more frail than girls his age. Then, thoughtfully, he strolled back to the house, clipped at rose bushes, and carried a big bouquet to Lu's room, a truce.

Dinner was the wreckage of a roast duck and spinach salad speckled with grit. But the wine was cool, the night was balmy, and from the patio they watched the constellations.

"Hit me again." Lu held out her glass for the fourth time.

Will poured, forehead glistening, a beacon light of anxiety, to be charming, mature.

"So." She looked at him. "What's all this flexing about red meat and Robert Stone?"

"I like his writing. And Jim Harrison. Pat Conroy." Will grinned. "You know, grunts."

Sybil leaned back, high. "My god. Where are the grunts of yesteryear?"

"We weren't interested in grunts, remember?" Lu swilled the wine in her glass. "While Will here was being weaned, we were reading Hesse and Gibran and the Baghavad-Gita."

"I was." Sybil argued. "You were reading *Fortune* magazine."

"That's right." Lu smiled. "Everyone was getting it up for Dylan and Krishnamurti, and I was trying to get a date with Armand Hammer."

"Armand Hammer?" Will asked.

"Uh huh. Like baking soda."

"You mean like millionaire industralists. I read the papers too. So," he studied Lu, "you were a power fucker. Is that how you got your plane?"

In the silence, an insect of feverish luster strolled across the duck.

"You know," she smiled, but barely, "at first glance you look about sixteen. But as you talk, Will, you get older."

He relaxed, and his tone was softer. "The flowers were a truce, remember? So let's forget the weaning bit. Seriously, how did you get into flying?"

Lu held up her glass. "Here's to the memory of Alfred Chase, my first big-time lover. I was fresh out of college. He was forty, he said. And rich. One night we drank too many martinis, and he started singing college songs."

Sybil bent over laughing, because she knew the story by heart.

"Funny thing," Lu went on. "These college songs sounded like tunes from World War One. The more Al drank, the older the songs got. I finally pinned him down. He said he'd sung in the chorus at Yale. With Rudy Vallee."

Will looked at his plate, subtracting World War One from now.

"The next day I called the public library. They told me Rudy Vallee was sixty-three years old." She shook her head slowly. "Dear Al. He died a year later, a heart attack. He left me his Piper Cub. I learned to fly it and discovered piloting was a bigger power trip than sleeping with powerful men. So I decided to become a commercial airline pilot."

"Wowww." Will sat up. "Did you?"

The women exchanged looks.

"No."

"But that," Sybil stood, yawning, "is another story for another day."

On Monday morning at first light Sybil drove Will to the Hampton Jitney stop. He would be in Manhattan in two and a half hours. As the bus pulled up they embraced.

"See you Thursday night," she said. "Lu will be gone. We'll have the weekend to ourselves."

"Tell her I think she's hot stuff." He smiled. "You're all hot stuff."

"Is that good or bad?" Sybil asked.

"It's scary."

Will boarded. Passengers studied him, then stared out at Sybil with the wide-eyed dementia of strangers needing to know. The man he sat next to grinned.

"That's sure a good-looking mother you've got there."

"Thank you." Will smiled ingenuously. "She's an elegant cocksucker too." He leaned at the window, waving. "Bye, Mom!"

* * *

The two women were stretched out on the beach, gulls deploying overhead, while Sybil talked about Will.

"He's Irish Catholic from the Bronx. Graduated from a Jesuit high school with honors. Turned down a college scholarship to be an actor. He's got a day-time job in a bookstore and takes acting courses at night. He's already done some TV commercials."

She stabbed a sand crab with her toe, then asked nervously, "What do you think of him, Lu?"

"Well, he's bright. Mature. Confident. And I think you've lost your senses."

Sybil dropped her head to her towel. "There wasn't anyone else."

"In all of New York City?"

"Maybe it's my attitude." She shrugged. "My agent says I look inaccessible."

"Except to Boy Scouts," Lu cracked.

Sybil hit the towel with her fist. "Look, I didn't seduce Will. I'm in his store a lot. He read my book and invited me for a drink. No one had asked me out for six months."

Lu sat up, giving her voice more impact. "That's no excuse, kiddo. Twenty-two is still embryonic." Then she threw her hands up in the air. "Oh, who am I kidding? I probably envy you. You know, one day last spring I figured out it's been seven years since I slept all night with a man. That's two thousand five hundred and fifty-five nights of sliding into the vortex alone."

Sybil reached out and touched her arm, as if in reassurance. "What about all your one-night stands? A guy in every airfield?"

"Hah." Lu laughed, but it was more the sound of a loud cough. "Saloon jocks. Frogs that suddenly look like princes at closing time. As soon as the sex is over, I shove them out the door."

"Why?"

She smiled. "I guess all these years I've felt it was OK to get laid, but to sleep all night with a strange male body, to go all needy and cozy-cakes was weak, subversive to Sisterhood."

"Sisterhood! There's a wistful word. The age of vibrators and female hard hats. The death of underwear. And marriage."

They laughed and were thoughtful for a while.

"Speaking of marriage, how's your ex?" Lu asked.

"Stewart's fine. He's married to a very attractive woman in public relations. They have a little boy."

Wind tossed Sybil's rich, dark hair. Stewart had always said her hair had presence. The woman turned their profiles to the sea, and yet they watched each other.

"How's yours, Lu?"

"Terrific, I understand. George married his secretary last year."

A teenager furthering the cause for Clearasil dragged a kite nearby, eyeballing them in their little triangle bikinis while they studied his muscled thighs.

"Do you ever miss George?" Sybil asked.

Lu pursed her lips, forgetting the kite flyer. "I miss his adversity. His humor. We'd fight, and then he'd laugh me back into bed."

"I miss things too." Sybil closed her eyes. "While I was writing the first book, if I couldn't sleep, Stewart would sit up and talk to me all night. In a way he helped me discover what I wanted more than marriage. I didn't deserve him. I . . ."

Lu jumped up, straddling the towel, the ocean a whitecap between her legs. "Act your height, Sybil. 'Deserve' has nothing to do with it. We all have exactly what we intended for ourselves. You, me, our ex-husbands. Maybe we don't always like it, but the trick, it seems to me, is to like it most of the time."

They sat still for a while remembering their ex-husbands and their former lives. Then they stood, gathering towels, their bodies burnished and sleek.

Sybil squinted in the sun. "Jesus. Look at us. Gorgeous, accomplished, available." She pirouetted, yelling, "So where are the legions of men? Where are the knights on white chargers?"

Lu laughed. "Haven't you caught on yet? They don't come with the territory."

Chapter
2

WILL LAY beside her, snoreless. In the dark, Sybil turned to him, but he was curled, foetal and silent, so unmanlike she pulled the sheets up around his chin and backed off. Sometimes she woke with her arms around him, his face mashed into the pillow behind her shoulder, as if she were burping a large, muscled child. He fed on sleep ten, twelve hours, a still-growing human. It was the time she felt most guilty. Most old.

Yet when they made love, he was potent, brooding over her with his incessant, careful pounding, attentive in the way of a young man already wise who sensed all the tenderness he would ever learn derived from this woman. Once when they were both so exhausted, so sweaty their bodies made two outlines on the sheets, Sybil told him how through the years she would freeze just before making love, so dry that men could not enter her for a long time.

"I was afraid to respond. I thought it meant they controlled me."

"Did that happen when you were married?" Will asked.

"Toward the end."

.* * *

She didn't remember much from that period of the mid-seventies, just before her divorce. She didn't remember much of the year following either, because she spent most of it sleeping. A failed marriage seemed to impose on Sybil the slowed gait of an invalid; when she wasn't sleeping she walked with her head down, as if looking for clues to how the marriage should have been.

Some nights were sleepless, and she lay in the dark hearing water drip, her world so empty the sound was magnified, like small wet animal pelts slapping together. On such nights she thought of Stewart and their marriage, the way he had brooded over their antiques, moving them back and forth, polishing veneers, tightening knobs, babying them like a man who wanted a child.

Why had they married in the first place? Because, she remembered, he wanted it more than she did not. She had needed a refuge, and playing protector gave Stewart a mission; it seemed a fair exchange—until, in their third or fourth year, this thing occurred. He started coming home from racquetball or jogging and leaning over her work, dripping, *dripping* on her manuscript. One day he used a page of her notes to wipe up spilled coffee. Sybil walked out of the apartment, wishing him dead, and spent hours in the Metropolitan Museum, imagining the peace and solitude of marble statues in the storerooms below.

Well, she had finally achieved that solitude. But as a divorced woman, there were handicaps. To have food she had to shop, which meant facing people. She was tall, attractive, and they stared, and Sybil felt they knew this was a failed human being, a woman who had blown a good marriage. She quit shopping and lived off a backlog of canned goods. One night, finding a big, meaty hambone in the trash outside her kitchen door, she cut up some vegetables and made a soup. Afterwards, she threw up, not from the ham but from the image of herself brooding over garbage cans, the fact that she was rowing perilously close to strange waters.

With the analgesic of time, Sybil revived a little. She stopped going all day without brushing her teeth or combing her hair, stopped wearing sweaters and jog pants inside out, pulled on blindly from a drawer. And she stopped eating out of cans.

One day she bought a six-hundred-dollar black-linen suit with wide 1940s shoulders. She couldn't afford it and had no place to wear it, but from time to time she put it on and stood in front of the mirror. It fit her perfectly, giving her a certain Crawford aggressiveness, a menacing confidence, as if she knew exactly where she was going.

For a while she, Blair, and Lu, one divorced after the other, closed ranks against the world, replacing their husbands with each other. Blair's divorce came eight months after Sybil's, and they commiserated in out-of-the-way places like sushi bars favored by laundry workers and fluttering roaches, where they didn't have to pretend.

"You spent six hundred dollars just to stand in front of a mirror?" Blair shook her head. "And I've been staring at the same slice of pizza beside my bed for three weeks. It's a very definitive gesture, not throwing it out. It means I'm no longer an anal domestic wife."

They laughed, but by rote. For there was something deeply disturbing about two intelligent women surviving the way they were, like crash victims groping in the wrong direction for safe ground.

Sometime in that period Sybil's first novel, *The Chocolate Legacy,* was published, a metropolitan love story with small sales and scant reviews. As she started outlining her second novel, slowly writing out the breakup of her marriage, she saw that divorce had given her her first sense of internal aging, but it wasn't fatal.

In comparison, she looked around at real tragedies. Her editor, a man of gravelled gentleness, was rushed into emergency surgery, surviving but only on tubes. One day a friend she was meeting for lunch burned to death. A high-school crush was shot by terrorists. Compared to real tragedy, it seemed divorce was just a change of mind. And she would think of it that way, that simplistically, until solitude, through the bleak alchemy of time, became loneliness.

A year or two passed, and life was even occasionally salvaged by humor again. All of the following, for instance, took place in one day. Sybil flunked her second driving test. Her accountant told her she owed the IRS an additional thousand dollars. Her agent called to say the book club she was addressing in Cleveland in two days was an audience of six hundred, not sixty. And by the way did she know Angus Foote, the black author her agent had seen her with, was a regular at Plato's Retreat, the sport-fucking emporium on the west side of town?

At first she lay down and cried. Then she rolled over on her back and thought of Foote and laughed out loud. She had never even made it to his address book. Women worked their way slowly, he explained, from a slip of paper to his Rolodex to, finally, his permanent address book. She was somewhere between the slip of paper and the Rolodex when she blew it.

One night in bed, kneading her hips like dough, he murmured, "Ooooh, get down."

Sybil looked at him, confused. "Do you mean that literally or in the Negro sense?"

18

The whites of his eyes took over. He ejaculated on her new sheets, drank her best brandy, and left. She was still waiting for him to call. Ooooh, get down.

A month later she flew to Paris with her next-door neighbor to celebrate his divorce. The first night she woke with an effigy man beside her in bed. She nudged the form. Pillows. Her neighbor spent four nights in their bathroom at the France & Choiseul off the Place Vendôme, talking transatlantic to his ex-wife. On the fifth night he calypsoed into primal screams, and by the sixth night they were winging over the Atlantic in reverse, Sybil's neighbor a gelatinous mound of Valium. She was sad, for she had liked him.

His ex-wife met them at Kennedy Airport. "He happens to be a Harvard graduate!" she wailed and dragged him away.

Sybil stood there, groping for the subtext.

She wrote, she traveled, researching magazine articles that financed the writing of her novels, freighting her luggage with writers she admired: Colette, Lessing, and especially the ancient Victoria Grant, one of America's doyennes of letters. Over a period of fifty years Grant's literary output—novels, histories, criticisms, essays—had been staggering. Through the years Sybil had written to her what amounted to gush notes, as had many young writers influenced by Grant's thinking since their college days. More and more Sybil found herself brooding over Grant's works and her biography, looking for clues on how to write and live in isolation without feeling the combination was fatal.

In 1980, her second book, *Wild in Granite,* was published, a romancy *danse macabre* set in Manhattan, with florid treatments of the city's architecture as giant fenestrated tombstones. As in the first book there were tragic overtones, with lovers dropping like flies. But both books, though female tracts, turned out to be funny because the characters were inherent fuckups. Sales were better but still modest; reviews were lukewarm.

A few more years passed. Or, rather, time seemed to stand still; it was the men who passed through her life. Good men but broody, confused by New Women like Sybil who wanted freedom but not always, who wanted the luxury of lovers without the responsibility of marriage. Women who said their demands were small but, like Dobermans, one false move and they bared their teeth. It seemed to Sybil, when she and her friends tried to figure out what was wrong, that they were living in an era of impasse because the women were as confused as the men.

And then she met a sculptor, Chuck Abbott. Short, thick, in his late forties, he stood behind her at a gallery opening and whispered into her shoulder blades.

"Hey there, you're a woman I could go up on."

She turned around laughing, disarmed the way tall women can be by wise-cracking little Mickey Rooneys. He was a transplanted midwesterner who sounded as though he'd been raised around staple crops, a knee-slapping, four-letter man who liked Johnny Cash, the New York Knicks, boilermakers, and handguns. Sybil became a hockey fan, a drinker of rye, a crooner of country and western songs, and adequate on the draw.

For months her typewriter sat like the disused part of a car while she noodled on a fantasy. She and Chuck in the country, a shaded hutch, he sculpting, she writing, their passion intensified by the daily withdrawal from each other into creation, struggle. The fantasy never extended to marriage, just the animal comfort of a good man beside her at night. One evening, magnanimous on rye, she shared this idea with him.

Then something began attracting her notice. He had a sudden courtesy. And a fastidiousness about Sybil touching him too much, as if her hands were thieving. Sex, which had been rollicking and bawdy, was now tame, neutered. Maybe he was tired or his work was not going well; maybe he was homesick for Iowa. She went on and on, off in the rough with her theories, until she realized Chuck had dropped her. After a week of disbelief she called him.

A woman answered, screech-voiced, like the E string on a violin. "Chuck's . . . er . . . at the dentist. Who's calling?"

Number one, he was too conceited to go to a dentist. And number two, his dentist was in Iowa. Sybil called Lu in Boston.

"Keep calling him," Lu advised. "You deserve an explanation."

Two days later she called Lu back, crying. "He said it didn't have anything to do with me. He just needs to expand."

"What did you say?"

Sybil cried harder, then stopped. "I told him he was supposed to be a man, not a fucking loaf of bread."

Laugher at the other end.

"Float me a philosophy, will you, Lu?"

"Expand. It means he got bored, Sybil. It means you're too tall, too clever, maybe the competition's prettier. It means there are more women around than men."

"That's what I figured. The bastard."

They listened to long-distance wires singing between them.

"Lu, you've been divorced longer than me. How do you deal with this new territory. What are the guidelines?"

"Guidelines? I just steer by my instrument panel, kiddo."

This was not to say men had gone bad, only that in the game of love and chance all the rules had changed; no one got to score. Sybil sat down to think it over, and when she looked up six months of her life had gone by. Life before Will.

He must have been working at the bookstore for a while, because one day when he finally spoke to her, Sybil looked at him with vague recognition: the sketch of a beard on his pink cheeks, deep-set blue eyes, long, muscled arms, his neck a strong white stalk.

He blushed, and his glasses slid down his nose. "That book you ordered," he waved it, "came in."

While she paid he stared at her, the way they do before they learn how to hide it. Later, as she browsed through the stacks, Will went over her body, his eyes round as if looking at something beyond his means. She turned and caught him.

"You read a lot, don't you?" He was trying so hard.

"Well, yes."

"What do you do besides read?"

"I write fiction." Sybil smiled. "Novels."

"An author. Wow. You sure don't look like an author."

She was afraid to ask him what she looked like.

Her book was not in stock, so he asked to buy a copy from her. The next time she came in she gave him one, signed. A week later they spent six hours over drinks talking about his reaction to the book and about books in general. Then he walked her to her building and took her up in the elevator.

"Can I take you to lunch tomorrow?"

"Wait a minute, wait a minute, Will."

She unlocked the front door, drawing him into her apartment, and he folded his arms, ready. Nervous, she leaned over and flipped on the stereo, then looked at him.

"How old are you?"

He took off his glasses. "Twenty-one. But I think older."

"That's not the point." She smelled his sebum, like a young athlete. "How old do you think I am?"

"Thirty? Thirty-two?"

"I'm thirty-seven. Divorced."

He shrugged.

"I can't go out with you, Will. It's ridiculous."

He breathed in patiently. "We just talked nonstop for six hours. Is that ridiculous?"

"No, but—"

"Then why are you uptight?"

"I'm not. I'm just sane." She opened the front door.

An old number came on the stereo, and Will drew her to him, slow-dancing. She struggled, but he was taller and strong. As they moved around the floor, she kept a stubborn distance, her hand hovering awkwardly just over his shoulder. When the song was finished, he held on.

"Will, I don't . . . I've never gone out with a younger man."

"I won't hurt you. Maybe we'll learn something from each other."

"What?"

"I don't know yet. I've never been out with an older woman."

She stood still, feeling unaccountably shy, and

23

he looked around her bare, rugless living room. A couch, a few chairs.

"Are you moving in or out?"

She laughed. "I just pass through here. This," leading him to her study, "is where I spend all my time."

It was a small room cluttered wall to wall with books, a big worktable full of research papers, a typewriter. A large charcoal drawing on one wall showed the head of a werewolf, with pen points for incisors. Will laughed. The room seemed right for her. Then he kissed her lightly on the cheek.

"Well, I'll see you tomorrow."

He walked down the hall to the elevator, and she leaned from the front door, her mouth still working on a response.

"You won't be sorry." He smiled and stepped into the elevator like someone stepping out of a frame.

She looked in the bathroom mirror for a long time, her cheeks flushed, her eyes shifty.

"What," she wondered, "is the point?"

After lunch the next day Will and Sybil took snapshots in Central Park and, sitting on a bench, he drew his old leather jacket over their heads while she changed film in her camera. It took a long time because she was nervous. Suddenly someone tapped her knee.

"Hey, what are you kids doing under there?"

In the dark they giggled.

"Snorting coke!" Will shouted.

Her knee was tapped again. "Hey, I asked you kids, what's going on?"

They pulled the jacket off their heads. The cop looked at her, then at him, then at the camera.

"Oh. Sorry, ma'am."

They walked on again, and people turned, watching him hold her hand. She wondered how much older she looked.

The next time they had lunch, it turned into dinner and then an affair. That night when he undressed he shook, whether from anticipation or fear she wasn't sure. Then he slid into her bed, his eyes hugely blue and virginal.

"Will, you're not, are you?"

"For Christ' sake." He laughed softly. "Give me a break."

He was not a virgin; he knew so surely what he was doing. Still, he made love to her slowly, as if memorizing each movement. The first time he came she thought he was having a heart attack. He bucked and screamed as though someone were stabbing him from behind, then melted down beside her.

"Thank you," he whispered.

"Oh, Will, you were so . . ."

Before she could finish, he was out. A vessel of primary sensations, sleep called and he fainted. She smiled in the dark. So much for afterplay. During the night he got up and walked into a wall; she sat up frightened, then remembered it was Will. He rummaged in the refrigerator for a while, drank half a quart of milk, then came back and knelt beside the bed, the moon on his hair, his hands smelling of mayonnaise.

"You're so beautiful," he whispered. "I could love you all night."

Sybil thought just getting him to stay awake would be good for starters. He climbed back into bed and made love to her again, new sweat on old sweat, and she smelled the innocence of him, his hair like wheat after rain, his semen sweet like clover, his member fresh-burst like a newly exposed nerve, so taut inside her she was chafed. Something deeply maternal flooded out of her then, and she wrapped herself around him protectively.

This time he stayed awake and pulled her to him, bracing himself against the headboard. "I used to see you and forget what I was doing. One day you came in the store in jeans and cowboy boots. Man, I was so rattled I was giving books away!"

He chattered on and on, and Sybil dropped her head against his chest, disappointed, horny, for what? Late-night elegaics on mortality, love, human need, not this babbling cretinism about the cut of her jeans. It would dawn on her again and again how much living he needed to catch up with her.

At such times she longed for an older man and thought of Stewart and the beginning of the end of the marriage. They made love, then she would roll over, not wanting to talk. Stewart would get quietly out of bed, roam the apartment, come back and stand there, looking down at her; she could feel it though her eyes were closed. Sometimes he touched her hair lightly, and she feigned sleep, thinking he wanted sex again. But what he wanted was company, to talk. He had been lonely afterwards, and realizing it now made her incredibly sad.

One evening Will was waiting with flowers outside her building.

"Why didn't you call first?" She was touched and half-annoyed.

"I keep getting that damned answering machine of yours. I gotta get used to it."

"Will, you can't just show up here. Suppose I was with a date?"

He looked at her a long time. "Why would you do that? You're with me now."

He radiated confidence, but lying alone at night in his Village walk-up, Will was frightened, afraid she would tire of him fast and look for another lover. She was a grown woman with a body and experience. He was just a neophyte, stunned with hormones and ambition. How tragic it would be, he thought, if she left him, leaving behind their mental and physical potential.

He talked about her in classes, acting out how Sybil would desert him, how he would spend his life looking for another woman like her and would in desperation marry the wrong woman. It would be a lousy marriage and a sordid divorce. He would never duplicate her. He had watched her for four months before they even talked, and believed this was the woman he would love most comprehensively in his life. He just needed a few years with her to mature, to prove himself.

"Except," his drama coach reminded him after class, "by the time you mature, she'll be middle-aged. Why not just lie back and enjoy it, Will?"

He removed his glasses and thought of hitting the man.

He took her to rock concerts at Madison Square Garden where, in crowds of twenty thousand rock fans, she was sure she was the oldest one there. Once during a YES concert she jumped to her feet moving to the music and heard two boys behind her.

"Go, big mama, go!"

"Motha', move those hips."

She sat down, feeling old and deviant. Afterwards, when they went somewhere for beers, the bartender looked at Sybil, then Will.

"Got some ID, sonny?"

He flashed his driver's license, cursing softly, and

in the mirror behind the bar Sybil watched the reflection of staring customers, the women amused, the men hostile.

In turn she took him to Broadway shows, where his reactions were pure, unchecked. When he laughed it was loud and deep, spontaneity not yet bred out of him. Once at intermission, coming back from the ladies room, she watched him across the lobby. He swayed back and forth, Irishly handsome and primal, wondering what to do with his hands, rolling, unrolling his *Playbill.* Sometimes his arm shot out in front of him, out of control. Yet when he saw her approaching, he became very still.

Occasionally Will went home to the Bronx for dinner, and his folks started smelling her perfume in his clothes.

"My dad teases me," he smiled. "My mom says the perfume's too heavy for a young girl."

Sybil looked at him. His mother was forty.

"What do you say?" she asked.

"Last night I told her you were a little older than me. She hit the roof. Said she didn't want me running around Manhattan with any wild twenty-five-year-olds!"

She bent over laughing, but it was half-forced.

For Christmas Sybil gave him his first pair of Tony Lama cowboy boots, and when he opened the box he was silent. Embarrassed, she put her arms around him.

"Will, please. I wanted to."

He pulled out a small present, a silver cross and chain. As he struggled with the clasp at her neck, he whispered, "Next Christmas I'll give you gold."

Next Christmas. She burst into tears.

New Year's Eve was a bust. She was too embarrassed to take him out with her friends, and she refused to go out with his. They spent the night alone with cheap champagne, getting morosely drunk.

"When are you going to bring me out of the closet, Syb?"

She envisioned him as a small boy baying in the dark and thought of many answers, each of which would hurt.

For breakfast she tried to make it up to him by squeezing fresh orange juice, peeling his soft-boiled eggs the way he said his mother had. But the eggs were blisteringly hot; she threw them down and walked out of the kitchen.

"I'm not your mother. If you want someone to peel your damned eggs, go home!"

He left silently. Two days later he arrived with a stack of discounted books from the store: Dalton Trumbo, Ken Kesey, Arthur Conan Doyle. "You should read some of these guys instead of all those humorless intellectuals." He was still angry, hurt.

"Why? Why didn't you bring any women writers?" She frowned.

"You've read the best of them. And you're beginning to sound like the worst of them."

Sybil sat down as if he'd hit her in the stomach, and then unexpectedly laughed.

"Will, you've got balls. I apologize for the eggs."

It wasn't what he wanted.

"And . . . no more closet."

Finally she introduced him to her friends at a dinner party. Mostly writers and artists, even *their* reactions were limited, and when Will asked the bartender for something naive called a Tequila Sunrise, faces expanded like blowfish, trying to suppress laughter. Jason Jenkins, her agent, took one look at

Will and dragged Sybil into the bathroom. He was a bookish, overly slim man who had left his wife for a young graduate student, who then left him.

"Are you out of your damned mind?" He shook her arm.

She pulled away. "Jason, please. You traffic in youth."

"I'm supposed to. I'm old and deviant."

"Then let me live *my* life," she shouted.

"I'm fond of you, Sybil, and I hate to see you look foolish. I could handle the black supremacist, and the Greek god in the motorized wheelchair who turned out to be a heroin addict, even that redneck Chuck. But this. How old is he?"

"Twenty-two. Almost."

He looked her up and down. "Is this supposed to be some sort of coup?"

"No." Sybil's voice grew soft. "I'm serious about him."

"How long has it been going on?" Jenkins asked.

"Five or six months."

He moved back from her as if aware of an unhealthiness, then sat on the edge of the tub, shaking his head. She sat down beside him.

"Jason, how old was your wife when you met her?"

"Twenty-three."

"And you were thirty-five."

He frowned. "As you see, the marriage didn't work."

"Look, I love Will. But I'm not planning to marry him."

"Exactly. You're just going to suck his veins for a while."

"Oh, come on, Jason. Men have been doing this for . . ."

He suddenly jumped up and waved his arms

around. "Look, don't give me a lot of crap about double standards. You think one little woman's decade is going to change the way things have been since we crawled out of the prebiotic soup?"

She looked up at him as if asking for help. "Somehow I thought you'd be happy for me."

"Happy? Let me tell you from experience, screwing a youngster is nowhere, Sybil."

"Well," she sighed, "if I'm headed for oblivion, at least I'm on schedule."

A few friends stopped calling, and she consoled herself with the fact they were probably never friends. Still, it hurt.

"When you're older," she told Will, "you'll see how losing a friend is like a death. You never quite replace that person because there isn't that much time in life."

Whatever losses she felt, Will made up for them. But there were times when she wondered if she could deal with his stamina, his almost violent impatience about life, and still get on with her work. She would sit in her study trying to clear her brain, wanting it uncluttered like an Oriental room, and just when she felt her mind achieving that calm, Will came crashing in with news of an audition or a TV spot. She nodded dumbly at her typewriter, feeling the long-gone atavistic hairs on the back of her neck rise, and suddenly he would stop.

"Christ! I interrupted your work." And be gone.

Later, feeling guilty, she would buy him something, a silk scarf, leather gloves, a way of celebrating a generosity she hadn't felt before in her life. With Stewart she had played the courtesan role, the taker, because he wanted the role of provider. Now the roles were reversed, and Sybil took the lead. Or did she? Will could show the toughness of a street youth when he was angry, and he was unswervingly persistent when he wanted his way.

One night in bed he moved down to her thighs, long deprived, and she resisted. The head, the mouth, the mind, all that intelligence concentrated down there on her genitals didn't appeal to her. It was too complicated to analyze. Will simply waited. When his prick was throbbing and chafed from overuse, and Sybil lay exhausted, he took her by surprise.

"No!"

She tried to sit up; gently he pushed her back down. Still fighting him, she stretched her legs taut, head turned aside, eyes locked on a BACH T-shirt, Bach's eyes locked on her. Then, too tired to resist, she gave in to the gentle tugging of his lips, her organ swelling as he aggravated it until she felt the freeze climb her legs and moved back and forth with his tongue until she, quite simply, came.

He unfolded her in other ways. She had become so hurried in her life, her career, so busy milking each minute, she had lost touch with everyday life, avoiding stores and traffic and crowds, as if anything breathing got in the way of her craft. Will broke through her invisible shield and made her react to the city again.

Some days he'd burst into her apartment, look at her, and be able to tell by her posture that she'd pushed herself to the point of witlessness. He'd hoist her up from the typewriter, wrap a coat around her, and push her to the door, with her fighting him all the way. Outside he'd hold her hand like a child and walk her up and down the city streets, pointing at ice-shagged winter trees electric in the sun, muggers and muggees grappling in the snow—anything to get her mind off the punishing blank page and back on humanity.

One day they weaved in and out of rush-hour crowds in the rain, following the panther-tread of a black with a huge Afro hairdo. Raindrops sat intact on his oil bush, so it resembled a fabulous pearl-studded headdress and gave him the look of a chieftain. Sybil had always thought of Central Park after dark as a wilderness of rape, murder, and rites of perversion, but they followed the black into the park until he evaporated in the night. For the first time in all the years she'd lived there she saw the Manhattan skyline wrapped around the park, with the sky a lid of fireballs and tapers. Both the chieftain and the prehistoric night sky would recur as dreams in her next novel.

On the first day of spring Will woke her at dawn and sleepwalked her down to the Fulton Fishmarket just to touch up, he said, her sense of smell. Then they hiked across the Brooklyn Bridge, saluting the day with a breakfast of things ethnic and pickled that parched her lips. And dozing beside him on the subway ride home on this spring day, the beginning of their third season together, it seemed to Sybil, Will had returned to her the gift of her senses.

In return she gave him time and patience, coaching him for auditions, waiting for him on cold sidewalks during acting classes, riding subways to his one-room walk-up where they cooked on hot plates. She could afford cabs but Will could not and once when she offered him money he looked at her as if she had struck him.

But another time he gave in and let her spring for a three-star meal at a restaurant with an overstarched maître d'. He met her there in a suit, slightly disheveled from acting class, carrying a gym bag, with a big blue Calypso Comb sticking out of his jacket pocket.

As Will hugged Sybil, then checked his bag, the maître d' suggested drolly, "Perhaps your son would like to check his comb."

She felt Will tense and gripped his arm, and the moment passed. Hardly tasting the rich food, she watched his long neck bent over his plate; he ate slowly, almost devoutly, as if memorizing each bite. Maybe it was the heavy wine or overeating or a combination of both, but by dessert Will's eyes drooped like an aging man's.

His head nodded dangerously close to his plate, and she reached over and nudged him on the shoulder. In response he shot back against his chair and let out a loud, resounding belch like a farm animal. People paused over their dinners. The maître d' stiffened as if with electric shock, then came at them full gallop with the bill. Sybil managed to hold back her laughter until they were out on the street.

Mostly he liked the food of children—sugar, starches, and meats—not the finicky health foods of Sybil's generation. One day she ran into a neighbor in the supermarket, and he looked down at her shopping cart full of cookies, milk, ice cream, cold cuts, white bread.

"Looks like you're expecting company." He smiled. "Young company."

He was a celebrated playwright who lived in the penthouse over her apartment, a virile, attractive man of sixty-six, three times divorced and living with a twenty-nine-year-old model who had been with him eight years.

"I hear you're robbing the cradle these days, Sybil."

34

She gave him a smile like gin splashed on hot coals. "It's not exactly a new trend, is it?"

"Tell me" he leaned close, "is he that good in bed?"

He had made passes at her on his terrace, but she considered him married.

"Better than good. He's faithful."

In late spring of that year her third novel, *Live Burials,* was published, and one day Will arrived at her apartment, morose. He sat staring at the floor, and she knelt in front of him.

"What is it?"

"*Live Burials* is part of our window display at the store."

"Yes?" She was bewildered.

"It just sort of hit me. I'm nothing, just starting. And you're a published author."

She waved her hand. "Forget it. The reviewers are already burying the book."

"I don't mean that, Sybil. I mean, I wonder why you're with *me.*"

"Oh, Will." She slid down to the floor, and they sat there, lost. "It just happened, didn't it? We met. And we didn't stop."

"But why were you alone? Why weren't you with some incredible guy your age?"

She smiled. "Most incredible men my age are married. Or else with incredible girls your age."

"I just don't get it, a woman like you." He frowned. "What happened? I mean, with people?"

Sybil thought of her marriage and divorce. "Maybe we got too greedy."

A photographer who came for publicity shots saw a blowup of Will in her study.

"Oh, you have a son," he said. "How handsome!"

Something about the way Sybil did not react made him look at her.

"He's not your son? Your brother?" The man was asking for help, embarrassed.

She stoked her gaze with inner vows of truth, breathed deep, and answered, "He's my friend. My lover."

The man bent over his camera silently and focused on her. In the lens he saw a good-looking woman in a room as grim and cluttered as Oblomov's bedroom, with a picture of a lover who looked like a teenager. If this was the fallout of women's emancipation, he thought, he was damned glad to be a man.

"Now a smile, please, Miss Wade."

One night Will looked at her over a meal.

"I saw a review today. Pretty negative."

"They're all like that. They say my characters are too vain. You don't care what happens to them."

"I care." He took her hand across the table. "I know you. The people you write about are arrogant because they're frightened. We're all frightened. Even those damned reviewers."

She shrugged, too beaten to want to discuss it.

"Please talk about it, Sybil. I want you to lean on me."

"There's nothing to say. The book cover's bad, or the reviews kill you, or the ads don't appear. Something's always wrong."

"Why do you keep at it? Where's the gratification?"

She sighed. "In the actual writing, pulling it out of me. I must love it. I can't seem to stop."

That night he made love to her savagely, with almost loss of control. His mouth to her, he seemed to be trying to swallow her, to crawl up inside of her. Then, hoisting her thighs, he went down deeply into her, moving until they were both so wet they held their breath listening, the sound like animals at a trough. For a moment she was frightened.

"Will? Please. We'll kill each other."

He looked down, lost, his body shimmying in the air, sweat and saliva spraying her. He moved now with blind drive, his shoulders hunched high and hard. And when he was close to the edge, it was like watching him grow old. In the dim light his lips went slack, his face muscles dragged, and his eyes shrunk. And when he climaxed it was like a slow-motion seizure. Then he collapsed on her.

"Don't you see? I want to be everything for you— friend, father, lover. I want to be enough."

He wanted to be all these things for her because it was two months after publication of *Live Burials*, and on that day they had moved her book from the front shelf with new fiction and bestsellers to the back of the store. In a week unsold copies would be returned to the publisher for refunds. When Will saw the manager moving them, he was furious.

"What are you doing? Give it a chance!"

The man looked at him.

"Will, I know the author is your . . . friend. But we're trying to sell books, remember? No one's buying this. It died."

Will helped him carry her books to the rear. As conspicuously as possible he had arranged four copies on the top shelf.

In May, Blair called from the Hamptons with the offer of the free carriage house, and Sybil jumped at it.

"By the way," she asked, "how's the book doing?"

37

"It self-destructed, Blair. I don't know anymore. Maybe I should do something else for a living."

"You mean drop out like I did?" Blair laughed. "Then what would you do with all that spleen? Come on out to the beach and rejuvenate, and bring the wonder boy. I have to see this to believe it."

At the end of May, Sybil moved out to Maidscott for the summer, where Will joined her almost every weekend.

Chapter
3

ONE DAY in the third week of June, Sybil sat reading
on the lawn of the carriage house. Pebbles popped in
the driveway like things deep-frying, probably a car
pulling in to turn around. She turned a page and
dozed off. Across the lawn a woman approached so
slowly, her shadow impositioned itself, inch by inch,
across Sybil's torso.

The woman was black-haired, violet-eyed, with
full lips and flawless skin set in a perfect, oval face.
Her figure was reminiscent of a turn-of-the-century
hourglass figuration: astonishingly small waist, full
breasts and hips, and shapely legs. Her name was
Kate Castaldi, and her beauty was remarkable, almost excessive, and seemed to call for self-abuse.

She looked down at Sybil and whispered, "Hi. It's
me."

Sybil started. Her eyes climbed the side of Kate's
body. Then she shot to her feet, throwing her arms
around her. "Kate! What are you . . . Where . . ."

"Your agent in New York told me where you were.
I took a cab out from Kennedy."

"Why didn't you call and warn me?"

Kate inhaled deeply, as if for a good punch line,

then answered, "I was moving fast. The cops are looking for me in LA."

Alarmed, Sybil snapped her head around at the cab in the driveway, then looked back at Kate. "What happened?"

"Wife kills husband and kids." She laughed and squeezed Sybil's waist. "Only joking. Can I have a drink first? And can I hide out here for a while?"

Sybil nodded dumbly and waved toward the cab.

As the young driver pulled luggage from the back seat, Kate's eyes followed him. "Cute, isn't he? He offered to take me surfing."

She paid the driver, walked him back to the cab, then lounged against the kitchen sink making small talk while Sybil poured drinks. Then they sat on the patio facing each other, Kate raw-looking around the eyes.

"All right, what happened?" Sybil asked.

"Walter's having an affair. I took a little revenge."

Sybil waited. With Kate there would be no frills. She would tell the facts with the deadly precision of tracer bullets.

"How do you know he's cheating?"

"I had him followed. He's set up a love nest off Sunset with a teenage starlet."

"Oh, Kate. What did you do?"

"Yesterday I infiltrated the love nest. The bimbo was in bed alone. I woke her up with a carving knife." Kate's thick, black, perfectly shaped eyebrows lifted, as if in sympathy for the starlet. "I didn't hurt her, just identified myself and kept waving it at her. Then I locked her in the bathroom and sort of redistributed the love nest." She giggled. "Lot of feathers floating around."

"Christ." Sybil shook her head. "Why didn't you just confront Walter?"

"I did. When he got home last night I met him at the door with the knife. Told him if he tried to come in, he'd get it in the sweetbreads. He took off."

Sybil sat back, relieved. "Doesn't sound like you did too much damage."

"There's more," Kate whispered.

Sybil groaned.

"You know the prize-winning koi fish he has, the one worth a hundred and ten grand? I debrained it with a revolver. Also, he now has an open-air view of Mandeville Canyon. I took a few potshots here and there, including the picture window."

Sybil dropped her head to her hands.

"And on the way out I torched the cabriolets."

"Oh, my God." Sybil remembered two vintage Mercedes coupes Walter had had restored. "How badly did they burn?"

"I dunno." Kate looked off toward the dunes. "I poured gasoline around the garage, dropped a match, and took off. A squad car and fire engines passed me headed up Canyon Road. I got the first plane out of town."

"Kate, Kate. Where were the twins?"

"Who knows? Nora doesn't even come home at night. She's running around with a Third World type named Trinidad Jesus. Justin's been kicked out of school in his senior year for scoring Quaaludes." She looked at Sybil. "I want a divorce. From all three of them."

"Take it easy." Sybil put her hands on Kate's shoulders. "Just relax."

"You're damned right, relax. I gave it all I had for eighteen years, Sybil. There just isn't any more." She took a long pull on her drink. "You know how Walter introduces me to people? 'How do you do? I'm Walter Castaldi, and this is my support system.' Nobody in Beverly Hills knows my name. Even the kids

41

picked it up. Their mother the support system. I've been going around for years feeling like a damned kidney machine."

"That's not you, Kate. How did that happen?"

"I don't know." She looked at Sybil, confused. "Remember me in college?"

Sybil nodded, remembering Kate twenty years back, beautiful, swearing like a trooper, smoking nonfilter Camels like a steam engine, and at the age of eighteen or nineteen with a steady boyfriend over twenty-five, wise in the ways of the flesh. Kate was pragmatic to the core, following the ground rules of Bryn Mawr to the letter, maintaining a 9.2 average, yet somehow doing just what she wanted to do.

"You had impact, Kate. We all knew you'd be something."

"And I was something. Superwife. Supermom. But somehow," her voice grew soft, "I dropped the ball."

Sybil shook her head, astonished. "Every time I visited you in LA you seemed so happy. A home, a family. We thought you had it all."

"All?" Kate laughed. "Do you know I joined a prayer group just to have people to talk to? I knew one day I was going to blow."

"Couldn't Walter see what was happening?"

She nodded. "Since last summer he's been sleeping with his face toward me. I thought, you know, he was feeling affectionate again, second honeymoon stuff. Then, during a fight, he tells me he's afraid to turn his back on me in his sleep."

Sybil poured them a second round of drinks, then cleared her throat. "Did you still . . . have sex?"

"Now and then." Kate looked down at her lap. "Anyway, after eighteen years it wasn't sex, it was missionary work. For both of us." She looked up, crying. "But my God, adultery! It's such a cruel act, and it's not even a misdemeanor." She cried harder.

Sybil jumped up and drew Kate to her feet, hugging her until she calmed down.

"That's nice," Kate hiccuped. "No one's done that for a long time."

"I'm glad you're here, Kate. It'll be good for all of us."

Hours later Sybil climbed the stairs of the carriage house and looked in on her. Kate was spread across the bed in a deep Seconal sleep, hair a blue-black cloud against the white sheet following her body like a shoreline. Mistress dimensions was how Lu had described Kate's body in college, when the rest of them were built like cigarillos. With a temperament to match, they had called her El Shrew.

Sybil leaned against the doorway now, studying the Irish-Italian face of heart-stopping beauty. Unsettling beauty, though, there had always been a look of secret, intelligent plans. Kate was the anarchist in the group, always tearing away, never sharing. What she had she kept, even her misery.

Back in the seventies, when everyone's life was disintegrating—marriages, careers—Blair and then Sybil and Lu had all taken turns hanging up on Kate for a few years. Living in Beverly Hills, perennially plighting her troth, they felt she didn't deserve their grief. Now here she was, and for the first time in twenty years, since their college days, the four of them would all be together at once, exposed to the opposite of what they had chosen in life.

Blair Heywood sat in her posh, sundecked little A-frame, set back in the pines about two miles from Sybil's carriage house on Seth Lane. The A-frame was as unsuited to Blair as the yellow Jaguar, but she had rented the house to be near Tom Fairmont, hoping eventually to move in with him in his old saltbox wedged in the dunes about six miles away in

43

East Hampton. After three years, six miles away was still the closest Blair had come to living with Tom.

The phone rang, and Blair sat there, braiding a blonde pigtail while Sybil filled her in on Kate's arrival from LA.

"Funny," Blair mused. "I was just sitting here reading about this woman acquitted of first-degree murder on the grounds of premenstrual tension."

Sybil's voice came across distinct and concerned. "Yeah, well, I think Kate's situation is more complex than that."

Blair exhaled sharply. "Let's not dramatize things, kiddo. We've all been through broken marriages. It's simply Kate's turn."

Sybil pulled the receiver away from her head momentarily, detecting an uncharacteristic bitchiness in Blair. "What's eating you?"

"Like I said, a little jungle rot in Lotusland, that's all. Is Kate listening in?"

"No. As a matter of fact," Sybil frowned, "I haven't seen her since last night. She went out with the cab driver who brought her out from Kennedy."

"Oh." Blair laughed sarcastically. "That's cute."

"Hey, I thought you and Kate buried the hatchet a long time ago."

Blair closed her eyes, fighting for control. The subject of Kate had always put her on edge, maybe because Kate's life represented all the things Blair had never achieved—a loving husband, a home, kids. It had all come too easily for Kate.

She picked nervously at little hearts embroidered on her ankle socks. "Sybil, you never knew the details of our last encounter. Kate flew into New York for my play three years back. Remember?"

Sybil sat back, remembering Blair's last produced play before she dropped out of New York and left playwriting for real estate in the Hamptons. "Yeah, *Beast with Two Backs.*"

"Well, Kate spent the night in my apartment afterward. But we didn't talk about the play, the performances, any of it." Blair's usually soft voice grew hard. "All she did was grill me on that last abortion. How was it possible to have one at four months, the exact process of amnioinfusion, how long the needle had to be to reach the uterine cavity . . . on and on."

"Forget it. That's just Kate."

"She was like a ghoul," Blair protested. "When I woke up the next morning she'd left me a long note about self-flagellation and a check for fifteen hundred dollars."

Sybil laughed. "Which you, you dope, never cashed."

"Would you?" Blair sighed. "She just never had the sensitivity."

"Look, I'm not saying Kate's changed or that you have to hold her hand. I'm just saying come over to the house for dinner." While she talked into the phone, Sybil studied her reflection in a wall mirror. "Blair, we're getting older. We've got to hold on to each other."

She resisted. "You'll take Kate's side."

Sybil groaned, on the verge of impatience. "I said dinner. Not a competition. Besides, Lu's coming. She's starting to fly these equestrian types in and out of East Hampton for the Labor Day horse show. She's planning to stay here for a few days. Come on, Blair. Remember the four of us in college?"

"OK. OK. What about Will?"

"I asked him not to come this weekend. I didn't think he could handle a reunion; anyway he's coming out next weekend for the Fourth."

"One thing," Blair added. "If Kate gets on any bandwagons about the right-to-life or any other visions of the uterus, it's going to be an unfortunate evening."

"I'll warn her. Now, how should we dress? Up?"

"Down. You said it's not a competition."

"Tomorrow around seven, then." Sybil grinned. "This is going to be incredible!"

She hung up, wondering when Blair would tire of dressing, as she put it, down, which meant pigtails and ankle socks. For the past few years she'd been decking herself out like she was being graded on cuteness.

Sybil drifted through the carriage house, spacing flowers strategically, making up for the absence of furniture. The dining area was empty, so she pulled in the big glass table from the patio. There were three bedrooms upstairs, each with a bed, a bureau, and linen. If Kate didn't like the austerity, she could move in with Blair two miles down the road.

"Hah," Sybil laughed out loud.

Throwing those two together would be a violation of logic. The problem between them, she realized, was that whatever they shared would always be complicated by the fact that a lot of the time Kate would rather have been Blair, and Blair would gladly have exchanged places with Kate.

She remembered watching Kate at a performance of one of Blair's plays a few years back. She was bowled over by the dialogue, the actors, the sets, by Blair causing all these things to come together. And at the final curtain, the Off-Broadway audience shouting Author! Author! Kate's eyes had unswervingly followed Blair, her talk, her laughter, how she handled the applause. The look on Kate's face had not been envy so much as longing.

Yet Blair had always said her greatest ovation would come in the form of a husband and kids and a home. Looking back, there were times when Sybil had envied them both. Kate had a family and security, or so it had seemed, and Blair got live gratification from her work: She could see people reacting in the flesh to what she had written.

Sybil thought of Blair now and of the man named Tom she had left New York to be near, a man who could take her or leave her, it seemed. Blair argued that he was worth it because he wasn't sadistic or unfaithful, ignoring the fact that he was also not terribly available.

But then she was a pro at ignoring facts. From first-generation Slavs, coal miners near Pittsburgh, Blair had ignored the odds when she applied for and won a scholarship to Bryn Mawr. In New York after college, she married a stockbroker, ignoring the fact that he was perverse and weak. When the marriage went bust, she refused alimony or loans from friends, despite the fact that she was living on a poverty level and her plays weren't getting rave reviews.

Then she met an actor, and while she was carrying his child, he met someone else. Blair had ignored that too, until he left her. Then the abortion, the big one, when it was almost too late to have it. After that she met Tom Fairmont, took a real-estate exam, and moved out of the city to Maidscott.

Sybil suddenly sat down with no sense of it, a thing that happened whenever she remembered Blair's abortion. For Blair, it was a vaguely remembered nightmare, something she chose to ignore like the rest of her past. But it was a day Sybil would remember with melancholy horror, each little atrocity etched indelibly in her mind, for she had not only witnessed the abortion, she had assisted in it.

When Sybil picked her up in a cab that day, Blair had reverted to a student look: angora sweater, ankle socks, and pigtails. At thirty-five she was still lovely, not in the hard, windswept way of modern blondes but like the soft-eyed soda-fountain blondes of Norman Rockwell. In the college clothes she looked ten years younger. Sybil remembered so clearly what she wore that day because three years later she still wore the same look.

At the hospital the two of them were calm through the preliminaries and the blood-typing in the abortion-unit admissions. They expected the amnioinfusion for advanced pregnancies to be the same procedure as earlier abortions: anesthesia, a quick suck with a vacuum aspirator, a few cramps, and presto! it was over. No one had told Blair differently.

In the prep room she squeezed Sybil's hand. "Just make sure they knock me out."

A small Oriental nurse came in and swabbed Blair's stomach with alcohol. The doctor arrived, and Sybil started moving out to the hall.

"Stay," he said across the bed. "You're tall. We might need you."

Sybil looked at him, feeling sweat form at the base of her pores. She looked down at Blair and stayed. The doctor gave a hammed-up briefing of what would occur, but both women were beyond hearing, transfixed by the length of the needle the nurse had filled with Novocain. It was injected an inch below Blair's navel.

"But I thought I was getting general. I want to be knocked out."

The doctor looked at Blair as if she were dim-witted. "I need you conscious so you can tell me what you're feeling. I thought they explained that to you before you decided to do this."

Blair shook her head helplessly. Sybil squeezed her hand as the nurse tied a mask over Sybil's mouth and nose. When Blair's stomach felt completely

48

numb, a hypodermic needle of astonishing length, at least six or seven inches, was swabbed by the nurse. The doctor held it like a wisdom scepter for a moment, looking down at Blair's stomach.

"You're sure you're numb already?" he asked.

She nodded, squeezing her eyes shut. Very delicately, with lapidary care, he inserted the needle through her stomach into the uterine cavity. Sybil watched it sink into flesh; she could not pull her eyes away. And then she swayed, feeling sweat drip down her back and legs. The doctor looked at her over his mask.

"Be cool," he commanded.

Amniotic fluid from Blair's uterus shot up into the needle.

"You see," he explained, as if they were medical students, "we extract a certain amount of fluid surrounding the fetus and replace it with the saline prostaglandin, a salt solution that brings on the miscarriage."

The nurse attached tubing to the same needle now deep in Blair's belly. From a jar, the salt solution flowed through the needle, and into her. The jar was suspended from one of those trolley arrangements, but the short nurse kept leaping up to adjust it so that the flow into the tubing was even. The doctor shook his head, watching.

"Jar's not high enough. We're getting uneven flow." He looked at Sybil. "Take it off the hook, will you? Hold it over your head with both hands."

Sybil froze. "No one told me I would have to—"

"We're short-staffed on this ward," he barked. "Just hold it. If you start feeling dizzy, tell me."

Sybil lifted the jar from the hook and with both hands held it over her head, watching the solution flow down from the jar into the tubing and into Blair. Blair opened her eyes once, looked at Sybil, then at the needle disappearing into her, and her eyes rolled, becoming whites.

Sybil heard a buzzing in her head; she tilted, nauseated, and made a mini-wave in the jar, thinking how the almost five-month-old fetus inside Blair would already be cranky, noticing a change in the currents of its fluid world. She went abstract and thought of Egyptian temple women, immortalized in marble, holding jars.

"Higher, hold it higher," the doctor shouted.

Sybil felt a gummy, slidy business in her mouth that usually presaged vomiting, and swayed toward the bed, watching Blair writhe.

"Easy." The doctor patted her shoulder. "Easy, Blair. These are just cramps. It'll be hours before the main event."

"Oh, my God," she moaned.

Sybil leaned on the Oriental nurse as the woman supported her out to the corridor. An orderly rushed into the room to hold the jar as Sybil folded, her head between her legs.

"We thought it would be just a regular abortion," she whimpered.

The nurse snorted. "You must be joking. At this stage of pregnancy what you're dealing with is a baby, not a fetus. These things can blink and cry. You couldn't pay me to have this kind of abortion."

She stuck something under Sybil's nose that jolted her, then helped her to her feet, handing her a paper cup of water.

"This is what we marched for, honey. Welcome to Liberation."

Steady, Sybil returned to the room and replaced the orderly, who was on his way to another patient. Blair's sheets were twisted around her ankles. The doctor struggled to keep her from bunching herself into a ball against the cramps.

"Lie straight," he said softly. "You tilt that needle, we'll botch the job."

The jar over her head had the dead weight of solid metal. Sybil stared at the depleting contents, imagining it swelling up Blair's uterus like a blowfish, an almost-formed thing surprised within.

"When the jar's empty, that's it," the doctor whispered.

Sybil swayed again. The room went black. The nurse caught the jar as she slid to the floor.

"Just stay there." The doctor looked at her. "Take deep breaths. That part's almost over anyway."

Blair's voice came from far away. "What's happening to me?"

"Your uterus is expanding. The salt solution will kill the placenta, cutting off oxygen and food to the fetus." He rattled it off mechanically. "After a while it'll be expelled."

"How long?" she asked.

"Could be up to thirty hours. Depends on your body."

As he talked, he turned to look at a man who'd been sucked, seemingly, into the room.

The man's eyes were riveted on Blair. "No!" he shouted.

"Get out of here," the doctor said. "Who the hell—"

Sybil struggled to her feet. "The father."

Blair opened her eyes. "Alan."

The doctor stared at him. "Too late. You're too late."

Alan bent over as if struck by darts. "No!"

"Out," the doctor repeated.

The nurse pushed him through the door. An orderly half-dragged Alan down the corridor, but he collapsed, crying, and they led him to an alcove with chairs. Sybil sat down beside him.

"Why did you come?" she asked.

"Fuckin' murderers," he cried, an actor with good bones.

She studied the floor tiles for a while, then asked again. "Why did you come? How did you know where?"

He cried harder, blew his nose, and studied the open handkerchief. "Her landlady told me. I wanted the baby."

"But you didn't want Blair."

"I'm the father. I have a right!"

"But you didn't want Blair."

He sat back and tried to explain it. "I thought I did. She seemed so together, so independent when we met, but then she started smothering me, always needing affection."

Alan suddenly looked at Sybil, big-eyed, as if realizing that needing affection was a good human quality.

"Then when she said she was pregnant," he continued, "I said OK, keep the baby, don't have an abortion. Give me a month or two to get some money together, and we'll get married. I thought a kid would change my feelings. I like children. Then I met this other woman and *really* fell in love."

"And you expected Blair to go ahead and have the baby without you?" Sybil asked.

He looked at her for a while. "Didn't she tell you? I wanted to adopt it right from the hospital. I'm getting married. My fiancée's willing to raise it."

Sybil's head moved back from him. Her lip slowly curled as if a foul, oozing thing had slid into her field of vision. It was an awful, ugly look, and his head jerked, as if from a sideways blow.

"Do you know what it's like," she whispered, "for a woman to carry a child inside her for nine months?"

He shook his head, showing real pain. "I wish I could have carried the child inside me. It was my kid too. Don't I have some kind of right?"

"Yes." Sybil felt sorry for him, and suddenly very tired. "But I'm not sure what it is. The rules keep changing."

"How could she do this? How could she kill it?"

Sybil stood. "She couldn't raise it alone. She couldn't give it away. Go home, Alan. It's too late."

He looked up at her, defeated, like a boxer felled by his own punch. Sybil walked down the hall so slowly, the movement had inordinate grace. She stopped and stared through a window, having her own moment of grief, remembering the fathers of children she had never had and how they never knew.

Thirty-eight hours later, Blair expelled the fetus and passed out. In those awful hours Sybil stayed by her side in the expulsion unit, a small ward of eight beds. Behind each curtain women from four to six months pregnant, injected with salt, waited. For a day and a night she sat there, listening to them suffer.

Blair recovered in time to attend the Off-Broadway opening night of her last play, *Beast with Two Backs*. Reviews were good, but it didn't run long enough to pay one month's rent. By then she had left New York for good.

Three years later Sybil was still trying to assess the impact of that experience. Sometimes months would go by without a thought, then that day would suddenly flood over her, and she would examine what transpired in that hospital room, what she had helped perform. Other times the day would be there, tapping on her skull, but she wouldn't let it in. Where she drew back varied.

Once she tried to discuss the abortion with Blair, but Blair tossed it off. Sybil had provided her with moral support and given the doctor a hand, that was all. But Sybil had to deal with the fact that the doctor had not forced her to stay in that room or forced her to assist him.

She remembered with sickening clarity how part of her had wanted to leave, but at the same time another part of her detached itself and stepped forward with the ghoulish eagerness of a professional observer. Deeply, physically and emotionally, in the thick of each moment of that day—the jar, Alan, the expulsion unit, women screaming, and, once, the sound of something expelled half-alive—Sybil had been aware that she was *recording* it.

Yet she had never been able to write anything down, not a word, refusing to give that day tangibility, so it floated around like a fog outside a pane. Write about it? She could hardly bear to remember it. The abortion would become a metaphor for that point where a writer draws back, observing some moral boundary so that human feeling can remain intact.

In time Sybil would see that in the observing of, and participation in, the tampering with another person's body, in the constricting of vessels and the rearranging of cells, the plucking and playing with an actual existence, affecting its nonexistence, she had recorded that day more than she wanted to know.

Now she looked down at her watch and at the flowers spilled at her feet and realized she had been in a daze for almost half an hour, replaying Blair's abortion. Sybil looked up and saw Kate strolling across the lawn toward the house. Her black hair was wild like a gypsy's, her clothes were wrinkled, and her lips looked swollen as if they had been misused. At closer range Kate smelled of beer and stale cigarettes.

"Good God," Sybil whispered. "Where were you all night?"

"None of your beeswax." Kate grinned, eyes glassy with fatigue.

Sybil studied her, then shrugged. Kate would tell it in her own time. They made motions in the kitchen fixing lunch, then sat down on the patio, sliding cheese and melon balls around their plates.

"Dinner's set for tomorrow night." Sybil hesitated a second. "Blair said she'd come."

Kate beamed and clapped her hands involuntarily.

"Oh, and Walter called my agent from LA, looking for you." Sybil glanced at her. "My agent said I was out of town. He knew not where."

"I hope Walter gets irreversible clap." Kate's violet eyes blazed. "I hope his cock falls off. I hope I never see him again."

Sybil watched her for a while. "Tell me, were you faithful to Walter all these years?"

"What do you think?" A Kate answer, a nonanswer. "Ever have an affair with a married man, Sybil?"

"Once. For two nights. When he told me he was married, I threw all his clothes out of a ten-story window."

"Hmm. When did you get so moral?"

"Listen, Kate, as far as I was concerned Liberation never meant acquiring a taste for other women's husbands." Sybil sat back smiling. "I used to sit in the dark in the evening waiting for Stewart to come home. Even though our marriage was breaking up, it made me sick to think he was with another woman. Once I found dental floss in his coat pocket. I built a whole scenario on that dental floss."

"Was he ever unfaithful?" Kate asked.

"No. Not until we separated."

"Stewart Thornton." Kate sighed. "Uptight Yalie, always smoothing his hair, shooting his cuffs. But my God, he loved you, Sybil. He could just never get the hang of you."

Unexpectedly Sybil stood and cleared plates. "Why don't you nap, Kate? You look like you've been had."

She went sloe-eyed, distant, and headed up to her room.

Sybil followed her to the foot of the stairs. "By the way, how old is he?"

"Who?"

"The cab driver."

There was no response from above.

"Come on, Kate."

Kate hesitated, then shouted down, "Twenty-five."

Sybil shook her head. "This place is beginning to sound like a cross between 'The Gong Show' and *The Graduate.*" She called upstairs again. "Well? Was he good?"

In front of the bedroom mirror Kate undid her bra, staring at teethmarks in her shoulder, wondering if brutal was the same as good.

Chapter

4

SYBIL MOVED around the patio of the carriage house, lighting candles. The three of them were on their third round of margaritas, and Sybil felt lopsided, as if the drinks had gone to her middle ear. She looked down at the drink already spilled on her T-shirt and shorts, and wondered if it was the alcohol or the excitement. Lu had flown in to East Hampton Airport in khakis and stayed that way. Kate strolled around in high heels, in purple-jumpsuit overkill.

"Christ," Lu cried, hugging Kate when she arrived. "Is this a reunion or an audition!"

Kate had pushed her pelvis at her, pointing at the jumpsuit. "This is Rodeo Drive, mama."

She was nervous and kept clicking her high heels. Hearing Blair's car in the driveway, she sat down, then jumped up, cheeks glowing like fanned coals.

Sybil waved a finger at her. "Now behave, Kate."

"Yoo-hoo?" Seeing candles flicker on the patio, Blair came around the corner of the house.

In her pigtails, pink-linen shorts and halter, and pink flats, she looked like one of those blonde debs from the forties. Kate tried to hold back, then ran to Blair, hugging her. They held on to each other, and after a while pulled back, both sniffing, embarrassed. Then, smelling of four perfumes and summer drinks, the women moved close, all gabbing at full throttle.

Lu stood on the lawn unsteadily and raised her fourth margarita, red hair flashing in the dusk. She nodded to each of the women. "My fellow fellatrices . . ."

Snorts and raspberries from the patio.

"We're gathered here tonight to revise the past, indict our lovers, forge our friendship, and simulate youth. *Santé!*"

"Salud!"

Sybil carried her glass to the edge of the patio. "I want to make a very sober toast."

She looked down affectionately at her friends, pale nodes glowing in the candlelight. Then she lifted her glass and looked up at the sky.

"I drink to four girls. Wild spenders, they were. Each a destined fuckup at one thing or another in her life, but each believing that in the shopping center of her soul, thrift sucks. I drink to those four girls who mothered the sodden, sorry-assed quartet gathered here tonight. Cheers!"

Sybil drowned her drink and threw the glass high across the hedges. It shattered on a macadam tennis court next door. The other three sat still, amazed.

"Sober? She's not sober at all."

They were drinking hard and fast. Through the years they had each seen the other three at different times, but it was the first time since college days that all four women had been together at once. Now, in the semidark, their eyes darted, sizing each other up, observing the augmentation and subtraction of the years.

Lu was bustier, an inch more mid around the riff. Her voice seemed lower for such a tenor face, a face still strikingly pale and freckled. Blair looked younger, more feminine than the others, still soft-eyed and soft-spoken, as if not yet exposed to life. Sybil was leaner, even a threatening slimness in the lips, not so much an aging as a paring down. They were aware of extra random pounds, looser thighs, and more wrinkles among them, except for Kate, who retained an eerie physical near-perfection.

Lu tossed an ice cube at her. "Anything lifted yet, Kate?"

"Nope." She had already unzipped her jumpsuit. "Who wants to inspect for nips or tucks?"

"Oh, for Christ' sake." Blair laughed. "Put it away."

"Grab your chair." Sybil hip-checked Kate, moving things indoors. The night was cool, and she built a fire, then rolled in a trolley with booze and mix. "No more margaritas. Everybody's on their own."

The four of them sprawled on the living-room floor in front of the fire, passing bottles of gin and rum, smelling the mildewed tapestry behind the sofa, a homey odor, comforting. After a while Kate disappeared and came back in jeans and a sweatshirt.

"I hate those damned parachute clothes. I hate dressing like Bette Midler every day. I wish to Christ Beverly Hills would get sucked into a void." She made a dry martini. "Here's to all of us being together. Twenty years through thick and thin."

Lu moaned, "Don't get excessive."

"Why not?" Kate swallowed the martini in three gulps. "You're the only friends I've ever had. I love you guys. Even though around you I feel so very previous. Former Brooklyn beauty queen, former honor student, former—"

"Oh, cut it out," Blair said. "Be your old, obnoxious self, Kate. Brag. Tell us about your kids."

"The twins? Well, Nora's sleeping with a semi-black, and Justin's become a drug cadet. Once a year when they kiss me good night I feel as though they're trying to get the gold out of my teeth." Kate slowed down perceptibly, looking around at each of them. "And Walter's screwing a teenage starlet."

Lu shook her head silently.

Blair raised her glass to Kate. "Welcome to reality, kiddo."

After an awkward moment or two, Sybil rolled over on her stomach and reached unsteadily for the rum. "Kate, how come Walter never got you into the movies?"

"God knows he tried. Everyone thought I'd be a natural."

She looked down, ashamed. "But I have this ego thing. I can't take direction. I blew every role Walter got me. The last one was that big-budget Mexican movie with De Laurentiis. I was on a boat near the Baja coast. All I had to do was point off the bow and yell 'Sharks! Fucking sharks!' "

The three of them looked at her.

"How could you mess that up?" Lu asked.

"Thirty-three takes, and every time the director yelled, 'Action!' I would point off the bow and yell, 'Farks! Shucking farks!' "

They rolled on the floor, laughter growing until it was out of control and tears streaked their faces. Kate kneeled before them, her back to the fire, and pointed in the distance as her eyes grew huge.

"Farks! Shucking farks!"

Again the raucous laughter.

She looked so pathetic and lovely, Blair reached over, tried to hug her, missed and fell, her blonde head landing in Kate's lap.

"Reminds me of an actor in one of my plays." Blair smiled. "He brought the house down about twice a week when he blew his lines and said the situation was clitoral instead of critical."

Lu came back from the kitchen with a jar of olives and a big joint. They sat before the fire and passed it around, all four tugging hard, getting very loose.

"You shouldn't have stopped writing, Blair." Kate stroked her hair. "Your last play was near brilliant, I thought."

Blair sat up slowly. Sybil and Lu locked eyes, waiting.

"Why did it take three years for you to tell me that?" Blair asked. "Why didn't you say something the night of the play instead of picking my brain about the abortion?"

"I didn't understand the play that night." Kate shrugged, embarrassed. "For weeks I went over and over the dialogue until I realized the whole thing was a takeoff on *Othello*."

Blair's nostrils fluttered. "No kidding."

"I wrote you a long letter about it."

"Yeah." Blair laughed. "Well, I didn't have the foresight to read it before I tore it up."

"And the check you never cashed?"

"I used it to blow my nose."

"Why?" Kate cried. "Why did you do that?"

"Because," Blair said drunkenly, "I didn't need your handout, a little gratuity for my all-night recitation on a dead fetus."

Sybil looked down.

Kate stood, tears running. "What did you think I left the check for? So you could pay your rent and keep writing. I didn't understand most of your plays, Blair, but I knew you were near to writing something important. I would have supported you for the rest of your life."

She swept her hand across the mantel, taking a flower vase with her. It found its own path, arced, then shattered on the floor. "You know, you three," Kate pointed at each of them, "always made me pay. I never understood it."

Sybil drained her glass. "You had too much, Kate. We had to beg and hustle for grades, steal textbooks for classes. Girls used to leave me cigarettes in the smoker because I couldn't afford to buy them. You squandered everything. I thought you were wealthy, the way you dressed. Then I learned your Irish father and your Sicilian mother worked in a Brooklyn shoe factory to send you to Bryn Mawr."

"But then," Kate looked around, "why did you let me be your friend?"

Lu sucked on her lip in the silence and then answered, "Because you were funny and smart and beautiful. It was a gift to be with you, Kate." She crawled across the floor and took Kate's hand. "And in the end you were a very giving and moral friend. Just short in the sensitivity department."

Kate looked across the room at Blair, girlish and golden in the firelight. "Don't hate me, Blair. I was always so proud of you."

"No one hates you," Blair whispered. "I love you, I suppose. And envy you. I just didn't want your money. I don't believe people should be bought."

Sybil thought of the yellow Jaguar outside and of Blair's friend Tom. Maybe not bought, but leased.

Lu lit another joint, dragging deeply, exhaling smoke rings. "I always had this theory about Kate's dropping out and getting married in her junior year. You see, she had so much potential, smarts, looks, she could have succeeded at almost anything. We all knew that. So she chose marriage, the one thing she wasn't sure of succeeding at. She was always perverse that way."

Kate stretched full length on the rug, feeling

dizzy, thick-tongued. "Marriage," she whispered. "Eighteen years in a crypt."

Sybil nudged her. "At least you had kids."

"Hah! They had me. Raising twins damaged my brain."

They were in a circle now before the living-room fire, booze and grass leveling them.

Suddenly Blair clapped her hands. "Let's play 'Waiting for the Doughnut!' Lu, how many times have you waited for the doughnut?"

Kate sat up, confused. "What's the 'doughnut?' "

"Those home-pregnancy tests." Blair made mixing motions with her finger. "You pee in an eye-dropper, then mix it with this solution, and if the brown doughnut-shaped circle forms, it means you're pregnant. Lu?"

"Two times." Lu looked at the ceiling, as if counting. "Well, two and a half."

"Half?" Blair frowned.

"One time it turned out I wasn't pregnant." Lu hesitated. "But the guy scraped me and charged me five hundred dollars anyway."

They booed, disgusted.

Sybil looked across the group at Lu, half-laughing, half-sad. "Remember the first one?"

"In college." Lu nodded. "That rich politician from Philadelphia. That was before the days of the doughnut tests. We sat in a restaurant waiting for the results from the lab. Hell, I knew I was pregnant. He ordered breakfast for me, asked me how I'd like my eggs, boiled or scrambled. I looked at him and said very slowly, 'Fabergé.' " She laughed. "After the abortion he bought me an emerald ring. Then dropped me."

Blair sloshed her drink, spilling most of it. "Kate? None. We all know I've had two. An early one and the marathon. Syb? With you we lose count."

Sybil threw back her head, the fire pulling her cheekbones out of the dark fog of hair. "Four."

"Sybil!" Kate yelled. "I only know of two."

"Honey, you've been three thousand miles away."

"You could be the mother of four?" Kate gasped.

Sybil held up her hand. "That doesn't include that one of the abortions was twins."

Blair counted. "Eleven kids among us. We could have started a revolution or something."

They studied each other for a long moment, faces stark as pencil sketches.

"Let's forego these meaningful silences." Sybil stood, stumbling. "Dinner is kitchen cacciatore . . . I mean chicken. Who's hungry?"

As she made her way to the kitchen, the phone rang, startling them. Sybil talked for a few minutes, then hung up and looked at Kate.

"My agent heard from Walter again. There's a police bulletin out on you."

Lu raised her fist. "Right on!"

"His bimbo called the police. Showed them what you did to the apartment. Why didn't you tell me you slashed all their clothes and furniture?"

Kate shrugged. "I said there were a lot of feathers."

The others laughed.

"The LA cops have photos of your house," Sybil continued. "The garage part looks like it was insured and burned. That's arson. Plus they found the fish, and bullet holes in the walls."

Blair and Lu turned quiet at the bullet holes in the walls; they had missed that detail.

Kate flicked marijuana ashes and dragged hard. "Well, they can't trace me. I used a stolen credit card at the airport."

Intrigued, Lu leaned toward her. "Where'd you get that?"

"I live in never-never land, remember? All you do is dial a number—instand cards, instant identity."

They placed bets on whether or not Walter would find Kate, and, seated around the table, the fire blazing in the background, they brooded soddenly over the food, then attacked it.

After a while Blair raised her wineglass. "A drink to Sybil's last book, *Live Burials*. To all three books, her way of not cracking up."

"Hear. Hear."

"And screw the reviewers."

"The character who showed up at her ex-husband's party as a birthday strip-a-gram, was that supposed to be me?" Blair asked.

Sybil smiled. "It was all of us. All the angry broads who marched in the seventies and in the eighties are the drooping backlash."

Kate put her glass down, unsteadily. "Dammit, Sybil, I just never understood why the reviews were so negative. Your heroine is funny, brainy, risk-taking—"

"Yes, but the critics said she was too arrogant." Sybil pushed back from the table. "Funny, isn't it? Men write about characters with too much hubris. Conrad, for instance, Euripides, Goethe. A man writes it, it becomes a classic. A woman writes it, they call it heresy."

They raised their glasses.

"Today's heresy, tomorrow's norm!"

"Speaking of heretics," Kate looked at Lu, "what about you?"

"What about me?" Lu's tan, slanty eyes blinked alert. "My profession is a trade requiring solitude. I live with my head in the clouds. Not unlike Sybil."

"You're thirty-eight, Lu. When are you going to land?"

She laughed softly. "I land. I mix with the human population a few days at a time. Haven't I flown for ERA? And the nuclear protesters?"

"But as soon as you get tired of the human race," Sybil argued, "you take off."

With stoned precision, Lu speared a chicken leg with her fork, absorbed in a hanging tendon. "Sometimes I think I should quit flying, come back to earth. Then I think, why? So, I'm detached from things. So, I don't get involved with crowds. Sometimes I have conversations with cold stiffs when I'm stuck in holding patterns." She shrugged. "So what? I get to play eccentric, no one expects much from me. Life is kept simple."

Kate shook her head, slurring her words, "You know, you always scared me. Don't you like reality?"

Lu leaned toward Kate, teasing. "You think that credibility warp you're living out there is reality? Where grandmothers carry Lugers? And Rosemary's Baby mows your lawn?"

"But Lu," Blair pleaded, "don't you ever get just plain lonely?"

Lu sat back. "Yeah. Terribly. But every time I meet a nice guy, he acts threatened or makes me feel that a woman piloting a plane is in bad taste. So I stick to one-night stands, bar-stool cowboys with the depth of a stick of gum."

They sat quiet, staring at her.

Then Kate banged her hand on the table. "Blair's with a guy five years younger than she is, who won't even let her live with him. We won't mention Sybil's friend. And Lu ricochets from stranger to stranger." She looked around at them. "Is this what you guys marched for?"

"At least we marched, while you were out there overconsuming on Rodeo Drive." Sybil tapped her arm, slightly drunk. "Besides, you're the one who's ended up with a twenty-five-year-old who drives a cab."

Blair shook her head and smiled. "I can't imagine Kate with a cab driver. What do you talk about?"

"Well, surfing, motorcycles." Kate grinned. "He's got a Harley-Davidson he calls his hog. I have a little trouble understanding him, though. I mean, he mangles his th's, as in dese, dém, and dose."

Sybil nodded. "A linguidental fricative."

"My sista was on dis Hollywood game show onct." Kate exaggerated his speech pattern. "She was Queen for a Day. She won dis boat."

"Oh, Kate."

"We took six-packs to the beach last night," she continued. "I got loaded and said, 'Oh, your sister was Queen for a Day? I was a dyke for a night.' It went over his head."

Sybil looked at her. "Were you?"

Kate stuck her chest out defensively. "Yes. Once with my maid. I wanted to see if I was missing anything."

The others leaned into the table, riveted.

"Well," Lu egged her on, "how was it?"

Kate arched her back so that her buttocks were thrust against her chair. Then she shoved her hands in the air as if pushing something away. "Boring!" She frowned. "I felt like I was embracing a Barbie doll. Little thin arms, hairless. I went down on her and God, you really miss that male appendage." She drained her glass and refilled it, and in the silence looked around. "How many here were dykes for a night?"

Silence.

"Oh, come on," Kate shouted. "You guys were bra burners, the trailblazers of the seventies."

Blair raised her hand hesitantly. "I was a dyke for a month."

Sybil revolved her head with exaggerated slowness, like a rusty mechanical toy. "This is turning into a distinctly illuminating night."

"I never told you," Blair whispered, "because I was ashamed. I hurt the other woman. I was lonely, I just wasn't gay."

"Sybil, what about you?" Kate smiled, mischievous.

"Hmm, almost. There was an architect once who reminded me of Kirk Douglas. I fantasized about her jaw between my legs, then realized it was Kirk Douglas I wanted, not a woman. Anyway, she looked temperamental around the edges."

They turned to Lu. "Well?"

"I know I'm supposed to be the group kink." Lu shook her head. "But my fantasies run more to humping a male corpse at five thousand feet. Of course I'd have to be plenty stoned. But getting a hard-on for pudenda? Sorry, guys."

Blair leaned forward eating out of the cacciatore bowl with her fingers, her blonde bangs varicosed with red sauce. "What about straight lovers?" she asked. "How many men have you had, Lu?"

"Who keeps score? I don't know. Seventy, eighty maybe. And you?"

"Oh, thirty, thirty-three," Blair answered. "I kept track for a while, then lost interest." She licked her fingers. "What about Sybil? She keeps a list."

Sybil stood, tilting toward the kitchen. She came back with another big bottle of red wine, fruit, and cheese, and swept the dinner dishes aside sloppily. "Dessert. Use the same forks, please."

"Screw dessert," Lu yelled. "Show us your list."

Blair grabbed a peach. "Just give us numbers. Honest numbers."

Sybil turned and stared at the fire for a while and then turned back. "I kept a list since high school. Just before I got married I tore it up." She laughed a little and shrugged. "After I got divorced I wrote out the list again. There were about ten guys whose names I couldn't remember." She paused. "Altogether, including the ten names I forgot—but I can still see their faces—two hundred and three."

She said it without a sense of headiness. The others were silent. They had been talking minor leagues.

She looked around. "Is that a lot? I met a woman once who'd had over eight hundred men. And I met a man in Lisbon who claimed nearly three thousand women."

Blair's skin breathed awe. "Still, Syb, that's a helluva lot. Course you've traveled abroad much more."

Lu piped up. "How old the first time?"

"Sixteen."

"How many at once?"

"Never more than one. But one summer, in a week, five."

"Most intense screw?" Lu persisted.

"A weekend on magic mushrooms."

"Most outrageous locale?"

Sybil laughed. "You'll like this, Lu. An airport runway outside Atlantic City. We were so bombed, we just pulled the car off the road, climbed a fence looking for bushes, walked in circles, finally just fell down and started screwing our brains backwards. Just as my date climaxed, they hit the airport lights. A plane was landing on top of us."

They laughed, still awed.

"Of two hundred and three," Blair said, "how many men did you really love?"

"My husband." It echoed, sad. "And Will."

"In what approximate percentage did you experience orgasm?" Blair continued. "Ten percent? Five?"

Sybil threw her hands up in the air. "Jesus, Blair. Half the time I didn't even know what I was doing. You remember us in our twenties. I think up until about two hundred I was just trying to get it right. Who was thinking of orgasms?"

"OK. When was your first orgasm."

She looked down, embarrassed. "With Will."

"Holy Jesus. All those men, the waste!"

Sybil amended it. "Except for masturbation, of course."

Lu staggered around the table and hugged her. "Oh, honey, no wonder you love Will. Does he know you keep a Pecker Memorandum?"

"Good God, no."

They were suddenly aware of Kate, silent all this time.

Blair pointed at her with her fork. "Your turn. How many?"

Lu pirouetted in circles away from the table, landing on the sofa. "I gotta lie down for this one. I know it's in the thousands."

Kate looked at them, a half-smile enigmatic in the firelight.

"Well?" they chorused.

She changed expression. "This game is in bad taste. Don't you guys keep anything for yourselves?"

Sybil stood and threw a plum at her. "I knew it. Good, old, stingy-mouthed Kate. You did the same thing in college—sleeping around every weekend, alternating Walter with those Haverford drips, and summers screwing half of Cape Cod. But you were too virtuous to share it with us."

"Come on, Kate." Blair shook her arm drunkenly. "This sucks."

Lu stared at her from the sofa. "You haven't changed one bit, Kate." Then she got up and moved behind her, tilting the wine bottle over her head. "Look, we understand," Lu whispered. "You were loose in college, and you've been loose ever since. Just because we were faithful in our marriages doesn't mean a damned thing. At least you held yours together for eighteen years. How many?"

"It's none of your business." Kate tried to push the bottle away from her head.

Lu tilted it dangerously. "Come on, Kate. I saw all those Hollywood types drool over you when I stayed with you last year. I knew you were dishing it out. What are you hiding? Were you into groups? Donkeys?"

Blair flicked cigarette ashes into her wine, then drank it. "Honey, it's LA. We understand."

"It's my business, not yours." Kate waved her hand, ending it.

Lu turned the bottle upside down, pouring wine over Kate's head, holding her still by her windpipe. Kate screamed and struggled while the others watched. Satisfied, Lu dropped the near-empty bottle and walked away. Kate jumped up, following her, swung her around, and slapped her face hard. Blair grabbed Lu's arms from behind, holding her back.

"Damn you, Kate. Goddamn you," Blair shouted.

Kate pulled on a sweater, hair plastered down on one side of her head, part of her face and neck mottled purple, like a birth defect.

"Where are you going?" Sybil yelled.

"A walk," Kate cried drunkenly.

"Why don't you take a walk into the ocean," Lu cried, "and do us a big favor, you fraud. Do you know what friendship's about? It's about trust, reciprocity. You fly east looking for moral support, but you give nothing back. Blair's right, you're a damned ghoul."

71

Kate cried harder, bumped into a wall, found the door to the patio, and staggered out.

Through the window, Sybil watched her running across the lawn past the hedges. "She's headed for the beach." Then she ran upstairs and grabbed blankets off the beds. "We're going after her!"

Downstairs, Lu yanked at a brandy bottle. "Not me." She took a large swig. "And I'm not staying in the same house with her either. I'm going to a motel."

Sybil ran down the steps and grabbed her arm. "Listen to me. She needs us. Do you know what she left out there in LA?"

Lu swayed back and forth. "A dead fish and two scorched cars. Life in tinsel town."

Sybil's voice got softer. "Walter told my agent they found bullet holes in the headboard of Nora's bed. And Justin's."

The three of them stood quiet, looking at each other.

Then Lu shook her head, as if clearing it. "Jesus Christ."

"Well?"

Blair grabbed a blanket. "Let's go."

The night was damp and foggy, giving the moon a submarine glow. Wrapped in billowing white blankets, the three of them moved across the lawn Indian file, like a ghost continuum. They mounted the dunes and stood searching. Before them the beach spread clean and huge, the Atlantic Ocean a gray frenzy.

"Kaaate?" they yelled back and forth.

As far as they could see, left to right, there was no one. They looked again.

"She's in."

"Where?"

"There's her head."

The dull moon threw shadows as waves arced and plumed. Her arm stretched skyward.

"Kaaate!"

They started running, tumbling, sliding the dunes, blankets unfurled. The moon gifted them with another shot of her arm, and it was OK. She wasn't drowning but waving. A drifter, bedded down in the crevice of a dune, snug from the wind's way, looked on. He saw three women undressing as they ran, flinging things out, away from their skin—little silk trapezoid panties and bras like figure eights—until they sprang naked, arfing and baying into the sea.

"Kate, you bitch, you scared the hell out of us!"

They surrounded her in the dim light, hugging her, treading water, watching for the waves. A small boomer headed in. They joined hands, shrieking, and dived into the face of it; it had enough force to drag them back out. The next three waves were middling. They heard the last one approaching before they saw it.

"Oh, Jesus."

Lu broke and tried to swim for the beach, but the awful undertow pulled her back. The wave fell upon them and took control, separating them, plunging them down and over, so there was no bottom, no sky, just churning, and then legs and backs grinding on rocks, the gritty ocean floor.

Sybil thought she was drowning and panicked, swallowing salt water in pints, it seemed, screaming for air. The wave finally hissed out and left them exhausted, like dead roots. Finally Kate rose on all fours and crawled to dry sand. From a distance Blair appeared, swept down-beach; she gathered blankets and clothes, opened the brandy bottle, and suckled it.

Now they sat huddled cross-legged inside their

blankets, Kate sharing with Sybil, like three white mounds erupting from the earth. Still sodden, unco-ordinated, and not focusing, they had reached that point in a long night of drinking where alcohol was no longer a source of pleasure but an addiction.

"Lu, am I really a fraud?"

"No, Kate. That was drunk talk. You just have more of a sense of privacy than the rest of us. We're like three Ancient Mariners without the sense or taste to stick to strangers."

Kate thought a minute, then turned to Sybil. "I have to know, does two hundred and three include blow-jobs?"

"Yes. Including everything."

"Blow-jobs," Kate repeated mournfully. "Last year I asked Nora if she was still a virgin. I knew she wasn't. She said she was more into giving head. And getting head. She blows and gets blown. It was all so androgynous, I felt sad. Whatever happened to those old-fashioned, eloquent words *we* used?"

"Yeah." Lu whispered, "They had such . . . gender."

They were silent again, feeling old. Then from the depths of her blanket, Lu's low voice exaggeratedly boomed out across the sands. "Cunn . . . i . . . linnng . . . usss!"

Blair picked it up, a wolf howling for her mate. "Fell . . . a . . . ti . . . ooooo!"

"Soddd . . . o . . . mmmyyy!"

Each of them bellowed out now, loud and long and mournful.

"Bes . . . tial . . . ityyy!"

"Cop . . . ro . . . phil . . . iaaa!"

"Nec . . . ro . . . phil . . . iaaa!"

"E . . . jac . . . u . . . laaaaa . . . tion!"

Much later they staggered home, a white line waving in the foggy night. The house was cold and damp at 4:00 A.M., the candles gutted. Sybil revived the fire, and they slumped before it in the dark, still suckling the brandy bottle. A log caught, the warmth pushed out at them, and they felt the giving-in of exhaustion as heads drooped.

"Two," Kate said.

They looked around at her.

"Two what?"

She stared at the fire. "Two men in my life. I've only ever slept with Walter. And the cab driver."

"Kate. Oh, Kate."

"You see," she cried, "I've never measured up to you guys."

They surrounded her, hugging her.

Blair staggered out to the Jaguar, jangled the car keys, and decided no. She crawled into Sybil's bed, baritoning, "Anyone for dyke for a night?"

"You wish." Sybil rolled over. "Don't hog the blankets."

The house settled down. They heard Kate flush the toilet and slide into bed. Just before unconsciousness took them, Lu shrieked out from her room.

"Farks! Shucking farks!"

A chorus of tired, helpless laugher, and they slept. Wild spenders, spent.

Chapter
5

ON SATURDAY morning, Sybil swayed down the steps to the ringing phone, shuddering at the dregs of the night before. Broken glasses and half-empty liquor bottles drooled on the living-room rug. Dead joints pocked a bowl of cacciatore sauce. Mountains of cheese hung petrified to plates, like maps in relief. And everywhere squashed fruits were scattered like small, burst human organs. Over all of this, the sun shone brilliantly. It was one of those mornings she would rather imagine than live in.

"Sybil?"

"Hi, Will. Talk soft," she whispered. "My brain feels like poached squid."

He laughed. "Was it a good or a bad night?"

"A time warp. Four college girls still trying to outdo each other. What . . . day is it?"

"Saturday. And I miss you, woman."

She smiled, imagining Will in a city full of beautiful, young girls, missing her.

"Listen, I've got news, Sybil. Big news."

"What?"

"I'm up for a TV pilot."

"What!" She sat down slowly on the stairs.

"Yeah. They're looking for a guy my age to play a

son. My agent thinks my chances are outstanding. If it gets good ratings, it goes into a weekly sit-com."

"God, Will, that's wonderful. When's the audition?"

"A week or two. They want to start shooting in September." He was silent for a minute, and then his voice changed. "Sybil, do you know how much money I'd make on a regular show?"

She was quiet, distracted by the sudden change in his voice.

"Did you hear what I said?"

"Yes, Will, I did."

He was trying to tell her something without saying it, and it confused her. "I want you to do something for me in the next week."

"Anything."

"I want you to think about us. A lot. And I want to have a long talk when I get out there next weekend. OK?"

After Sybil hung up, she sat there groping for the connection between what Will had said and what he'd left unsaid. But she was too hung over, and the conversation left her feeling ill at ease.

Later that morning, Blair drove over to Tom Fairmont's house, a small, rented saltbox six miles away from Seth Lane in East Hampton. Through his kitchen window, Tom saw her pull into the driveway in the Jaguar. He winced. Driving that thing, he always felt like an embarrassed sperm inside a thundering yellow erection. He fantasized seeing the car in accordion pleats, humped by a tractor-trailer. How to tell Blair? he wondered, going out to meet her.

Fairmont was about six feet tall, manly but not muscular, with a slight paunch. Looking older than thirty-three, his hair was a reddish brown streaked with gray, the eyes gray nicely notched with brown. A sparse beard and mustache approximating a Vandyke hid lips too thin and crooked teeth.

Dressed in the role of a struggling writer, he was wearing old sneakers, ratty jeans, and a flannel shirt so faded it looked like it was inside out. A far glance at Tom gave you one of those middle-aged types slouching toward crisis and premature ejaculation. But when he smiled, his big, straight nose stood out, his wide forehead seemed to expand, and there was a given intelligence, making him almost handsome.

He saw Blair was still half-inebriated and weak, and put his arms around her. "Hi. Looks like it got a little drunk out last night."

She leaned on him as they walked back into the house, and slumped against the refrigerator while he poured juice.

"How was the reunion, and how's the runaway wife?"

Blair shook her head. "The cops are looking for her. You know, out there the word 'fire' means devastation."

He shook his head slowly. This Kate sounded beautiful and unplugged, suited to the environment she had just fled.

"What did boy Will think of her?"

"He's not out this weekend." Blair studied Tom closely. "I thought you were impressed with Will when you two met?"

"I was. But no matter how you cut it, he's still a boy."

"I'm beginning to wonder about that," she mused. "He's very definite about things. I mean, he seems to know what he wants."

Sun through the windowpane caught blonde down on the fleshy spoon of her cheek. Blair crossed and uncrossed her ankles absentmindedly as she talked, and Tom heard the linen shorts shh-shhing between her thighs. His erection was immediate. He poured some vodka into the orange juice and handed her the glass.

"Here. Hold this a minute."

As she took it, he picked her up and carried her to the bedroom.

He always had the same sensation with Blair, a soft, blind thing climbing him, reminding him of blonde caterpillars snuffling bark, the undulations of their journey from the larva to the moth. For only when she tired of suckling at him and moved up to his face, mouth to mouth, eye to eye, and he turned her on her back or she straddled him, did she blossom, blonde hair fanning out like wings.

It was the only time Tom ever saw her hair down, and the shimmering abundance of it and the generosity of her movements always made him come soon, sometimes not waiting for her, not considering her pleasure at all. She did not seem to mind; it was enough for her to be next to him, to feel the pulse of a man lying beside her as she slid down into sleep.

Two hours later Blair nudged him gently, and his eyes opened.

"It's three-thirty," she said. "I have to show some clients a house at four."

He kissed both cheeks and ran his hand along her side. "Let's make a picnic basket later, sail over near Gardiner's Island, and have dinner in the sunset."

She stretched her arms around him. "Oh, if only every day could be like the weekends."

Tom got out of bed, frowning. "Blair, we see each other on Wednesdays, Saturdays, and Sundays. I need," he squeezed his hands, verging on a bad mood, "space. Why do you make me feel that's a handicap?"

"Because you're broke," she argued. "You play

the stock market like a blind man chasing shuttle-cocks. And you're trying to write a first novel. I just want to be near you and take care of you."

He reached for her hand. "I know, honey, but it's too much. The car, for instance."

"You said you liked vintage cars."

"There are types of vintage cars, Blair. But that's not the point."

"What is?" she cried.

"That I'm scared to talk to you." Tom shot his arm out, shaking his wrist. "I mention I lost my watch. The next day I find a brand new Rolex hanging from my toothbrush." He pointed to his stereo. "I say I like Pavarotti. You lay three operas on me."

Blair turned her palms up, as if offering them for examination. "But I make all this money in real estate. Why not enjoy it?"

His voice had a growing edge. "Because I can't return the gifts. I feel like a whore."

She sat on the side of the bed, staring down at her palms. "It sounds like you're tired of me."

Slowly and deliberately, Tom crossed the room, slamming his fist down on top of the bureau. "You're not listening, dammit!"

Blair moved to the bathroom and stood under the shower, wondering why she always ended up with men who wanted options, not certainty, men who were attracted to her because she had that look, cool, blonde, distant, as if she could live without them. Hah. What their attraction and her needs showed was only the ambiguity of the times.

The same thing had happened with her ex-husband, Paul. Attracted by her seemingly emancipated, free-wheeling lifestyle when she was sleeping around New York with the stamina of the new girl in town, he had chased her relentlessly until she married him. Within two years he wanted out.

"I run into friends," he had complained. "One's moving to Paris, one bought a Maserati, one just survived a myocardial infarction."

"Paul, what are you saying?"

"I'm saying, Blair, I feel so stifled, I even envy a friend's heart attack. I don't think I want to be married anymore."

She remembered sinking into a chair, her voice sounding like a faulty recording. "Then why did you marry me? I thought you loved me."

Her husband's expression was like a surgeon explaining to a patient how he had amputated the wrong limb. "You played hard to get. I suppose I loved your inaccessibility."

When she ran into him a few years after their divorce, Paul was more expansive about their marriage. "You were a good wife, Blair, just too clutchy. Toward the end I felt this suffocation right out of Poe."

Now she stood in the shower thinking how often she caught Tom looking at her the same way, like a man needing oxygen. Yet she couldn't stop herself. Inserted in each gift she gave him—the car, clothes, jewelry—was a didactic little reminder, like a pill in a dog's breakfast. See how much I love you. See how much I can give.

Tom brooded in the kitchen, pulling down coffee cups, remembering their first year's anniversary when he gave Blair an illustrated *Lysistrata*, leather-bound and rare. The next day she arrived with her suitcase, ready to move in. A dozen roses, they were engaged. Frightened, he had resorted to joke cards and utility gifts like salad spinners and meat thermometers. Still, he could feel her sitting there, waiting to spring.

Now she walked into the kitchen in those tired, pink shorts and halter, and something touched him.

She was a lovely woman and more, a kind of hero. For she had given up the act of writing and elected to stand aside, in the role of support.

Tom crossed the kitchen and put his arms around Blair, hugging her tight. "Relax, honey. We've got time. All the time in the world."

At four o'clock Blair pulled up to a huge, empty beach estate and saw her clients waiting for her on the porch. The man and wife were both pale and tall, with extended necks, like swans mated for life. They were wealthy but not showy, driving an old Mercedes with dented plates, and looked too earnest to be just browsing, but Blair didn't think they would like the place.

It was one of those stone-and-brick, ten-bedroom *belle époque* elephants on the ocean, with an acre of marsh and pond between the house and the beach. A long driveway snaked through another acre of lawn approaching the house. Besides the fact that the basement was rotting, the upkeep alone would take a fortune.

While the couple toured the place, their Doberman sniffed Blair, whining.

"We have three grandchildren." The man smiled. "We need a big place, but not this big. Interesting, though." ·

He was white-haired, sixtyish, and fit, and he seemed to be talking to Blair's crotch. She had changed from shorts to a simple sundress; nevertheless, she looked down as if her genitals were showing and pushed the dog away, while the wife moved to the other room, oblivious.

"It's been on the market forever." Blair chatted uncomfortably as the dog sniffed her again. "They'll have to bring down the asking price, I'm sure."

He went down to the basement and knocked

around for a while, then returned. "Needs a good deal of foundation work." He smiled at her crotch. "Don't you think?"

Did he move closer?

"I think with my head, Mr. Carson. I'd appreciate it if you'd address that."

He blushed and turned away. They made another quick tour of the house, the man uncomfortably close behind Blair as she climbed the stairs to the second floor. As they walked outside minutes later, a patrol car drove up.

"Oh, hi, Miss Heywood. We wondered who was around. Didn't recognize your car."

The cop got out and stretched his legs, smiling at the couple. Blair's eyes fell on the man's holstered gun, and something struck her. While she stood, distracted for the moment, the Doberman pumped her behind with his nose, whining again.

Embarrassed, Carson called his dog and pushed him into the back seat of the Mercedes. As he and his wife slid in, Blair moved to their car, handing her card in through the window: *Dune Realty, East Hampton, N. Y., Blair Heywood, Licensed Real Estate Broker.*

"I'll see you on Monday," she said. "These other two listings can be shown then. I think they're more your size."

"Fine." Carson smiled, eyes working the area below her waist.

She felt like throwing rocks at the car as they drove away, thinking of Carson and past clients flirting, sometimes touching, giving her their unlisted numbers in Manhattan. Was this her ultimate destiny, she wondered, hawking overpriced real estate to geriatrics with hard-ons?

Then she turned back to the cop, a pot-bellied

ectomorph, and looked at his holster again. After a
minute he moved to his car.

"Take care now." He waved as the patrol car slid
down the drive.

Blair stared at the ocean for a minute, then headed
the Jaguar toward the carriage house.

Pulling into the driveway, she saw Sybil on the
lawn, white beach-shirt spinnakering out behind
her, head thrown back, watching chevron formations
of geese honking overhead. Blair stared at her long
legs and arms and thought of a carving on the prow
of a ship. She had the kind of beauty certain women
don't know they possess, needing distance, the full
proportion, to be understood.

Sybil Wade wasn't a conventionally pretty
woman: her height almost manly, cheeks too high,
jaw too firm, hazel eyes too intense. Her dark hair
seemed a metaphor for herself, refractory, unsettling
to most people, so that she was often described as
stunning, striking—words that made her sad, she
said, for they described a weapon, not a woman. And
yet for her friends there was so much endearing
about Sybil: humor, generosity, and the adolescent
awkwardness of tall women.

Once, during a book interview, pressed for a self-
description, Sybil had said she saw herself as a female version of the Marlboro man. After that Blair
was always struck by the cigarette ads: a cowboy, a
horse, the landscape. Alone, always alone. She
dropped her head to the steering wheel, loving Sybil
for her frailness, her strength; then after a moment
she honked the horn and slid from the car.

"Where are the others?" she shouted.

"Flying." Sybil laughed. "Both hung over as
hell."

Blair stretched her arms wide. "Can you see through this dress?"

Sybil turned her around slowly. "No. Why?"

"This client, Carson. He stared at my groin all afternoon, even when he talked to me. His Doberman kept sniffing and whining like he wanted to mount me."

"Were you with Tom earlier?" Sybil asked.

"Yes. But I showered."

"Doesn't matter. Your hormones were probably still jazzed up. The dog smelled sex. Dobermans are especially sensitive to jism, and Carson probably figured you'd just had intercourse or wanted to."

Blair shook her head. "I can't deal with these well-bred middle-aged mashers anymore. Maybe I'm too friendly or something."

Sybil looked at her, frowning. "It's not your attitude, Blair, it's your clothes. Blonde pigtails, white ankle socks, the old man's Lolita fantasy. You're thinking of commissions, and they're thinking of you sitting on their laps."

"Hmm," she mused. "Maybe it's time for my wardrobe to grow up."

Inside the house Sybil threw a newspaper on the kitchen table while she iced tea.

"Look at this damned thing," she said. "Something's happening to the English language. I can't read it."

She had underlined scores of phrases and words in an article on the divorced population of New York City.

"What is it? Computer talk? Astro babble?"

Blair looked at the paper. "I think it's called future gab."

"OK, define these words." Sybil jabbed the page with her finger. *"Up front."*

85

"That means honest."

"One-to-one."

"Personal. Exclusive."

"How about *situation,* as in,"—Sybil squinted as if reading a foreign language—" 'is the *situation operative?*' "

Blair frowned. "I think that means is the relationship working."

"Support group?" Sybil asked.

"Friends."

"Pair-bonding?"

"Hmm, marriage." Blair answered slowly, unsure.

"Amenable?"

"Available."

"Trade-up?"

Blair shrugged. "Dunno."

"Where one is coming from?"

"One's motives. One's reasoning."

Sybil mugged like a street youth. "Where one *is at?*"

"How one feels."

"Interface, as in 'to avoid depression one has to interface with networks.' " She stabbed each word as if killing ants. "My God, what's a *network?*"

Blair sat back, giving up. "I don't know. *Suck-face* means to kiss."

Sybil gently lowered herself to a chair beside the table. "Blair, am I nuts? I'm trying to write novels on the heroics of the human condition while the English language sounds as though it's being preempted by space jocks with denture fixations."

"Just keep writing, kiddo." Blair laughed. Then she looked down, brooding over her tea. "Umm, the reason I stopped by . . . Sybil, do you still have that gun here?"

"The thirty-eight? Yeah. It's upstairs under my bed."

"Is it loaded?"

"Well, what good would it do empty, Blair? The big house was burglarized in March, and I'm here alone most of the time. When we found it in the closet, Will cleaned and loaded it. And I know how to use it."

Blair stared down at the floor, unable to raise her eyes. "Why don't you let me take it over to my house for a while?"

Sybil leaned over to her. "Hey. What is it?"

"I'm scared," Blair whispered.

She lifted Blair's chin like a child. "Of Kate?"

"For Kate."

She leaned back in the cockpit, cocooned in electric blue, as Lu winged the Cherokee out over the Atlantic Ocean, paralleling the long, narrow spit of Long Island—patchwork cornfields, clapboard cottages, hedged estates, and Montauk Highway snaking in between. Then Lu swung over to Gardiner's Bay and pointed down.

"That's Gardiner's Island. The owner still has the *droit du seigneur.* He can shoot anyone who trespasses on his land."

As soon as she said it, she bit her lip.

Kate sighed, oblivious, and relaxed; then after a time she turned to Lu. "This is some life. I always wondered why you didn't fly for Pan Am after passing all the flight tests. You'd have been one of their first female pilots."

Lu shrugged. "Well, I suddenly realized it would have been the infinity of a nine-to-five job except with wings. All I'd do is strap myself in and stab buttons according to a voice from the control tower."

Kate studied her. "Flying corpses isn't much of an improvement, is it?"

She let that sit a minute, then answered. "Racking up airtime requirements for the flight tests, I got hooked on solo flying. It's another dimension. And after two thousand hours flying mostly stiffs, I got to like the company."

Kate laughed as she always did with Lu. It was easier than trying to fathom her.

"Anyway," her voice was suddenly soft, "I always felt if I misjudged, I wanted to go as a single, lowercase crash, instead of dragging four hundred boobs down with me in a major airlines disaster."

It was a delicate subject, her loss of nerve in that period in her past, and Lu preferred to leave it in her past.

Kate sat up, suddenly attentive, her violet eyes huge. "I wouldn't mind crashing, a real splashy ending, as long as it was fast."

Lu shook her head. "That's your problem, Kate. You always go for flamboyance, always trying to live up to your looks."

"What does that mean?"

"For instance, the average wife might face a husband's cheating with a breakdown, or maybe catch him *in flagrante,* and take him to the cleaners." She pointed her finger at Kate. "You blow away a fish that's a work of art and try to torch Mandeville Canyon. Now you're on the run for arson, like a character out of a Didion novel. Beautiful, ergo, loony."

Kate looked as if she had been struck, then dropped her head in her hands. "I didn't plan it, I swear. I just went blind." After a while she looked up. "How would you have handled it, or the others?"

Lu thought for a minute, slicing the Cherokee into a U-turn, lingering over little beach hamlets. "Cheating husband. Let's see. Sybil would have recorded everything before she split, then someday turned it into a novel. Blair would have cried a lot and tried to patch it up."

"What about you?"

Lu giggled. "I'd have probably machine-gunned husband and bimbo, then tap-danced on the wing of my plane. But not the fish, Kate. The poor, witless fish!"

They laughed until their faces were flushed like young girls, then Lu headed the plane back to the landing runway.

"One thing more," Lu said slowly. "Do you hate your kids that much? Bullet holes in the headboards?"

Kate sighed, confused. "One day they were little cannibals draining the milk from my breasts. The next day they were these pimply, pot-smoking humanoids. The only time they talked to me was when they couldn't find the TV genie. Then that 'support system' crap started."

"Suppose they were home when you shot up the place?"

Kate looked at her. "I wouldn't have shot my kids, Lu. I got home from Walter's love nest that day, and there wasn't anyone to break down in front of. So I took it out on the house." She held her neck back, resisting, as they lined up with the runway, nose down, and descended. They taxied in and sat silent as the propellers sputtered and died. "Am I in trouble?" Kate made circles with her index finger, pointing to her brain. "Did I crack up in LA?"

Lu leaned over, giving her a good, long hug. "No. You cracked open, the best thing that could have happened."

"What do I do now?" Kate cried. "I'm a cipher. I feel as if my whole life is a write-off."

"You take long walks on the beach. And let your

friends worry about you." Lu shook her arm gently. "And you cut out this I-don't-measure-up crap. OK? We've all been wives, Kate, but you're the only one who pulled it off."

"Pulled what off? My husband's screwing someone else, and my kids treat me like I'm not their type."

Lu sighed, hung over and exhausted. "Look. Sybil writes novels no one buys. Blair pushes overpriced houses with rotten foundations. And I move bodies around. It seems to me you're the one who's successful. You're the one who raised two kids, even if they are monsters. Will you think about that?"

Kate nodded vaguely as they climbed from the plane. "I wonder where Walter fits into all this."

"That's what your walks on the beach are for." Lu glanced over at her. "And should you consider that middle-class retreat called divorce, be careful, Kate. There's a lot to be said for the solitary life, the pursuit of transcendence, and so on. But nights are very, very long. And they have a way of turning into years."

The sun had inched down, and far to the east a patch of lavender was already eased with stars.

As they strolled arm in arm toward Sybil's old black Dodge, Kate had one more thought. "What do you think about Sybil and this Will?"

"Frankly, I'm tickled pink."

"Oh, come on, Lu. He could be her son, it's . . . immoral."

Lu laughed out loud. "You're committing adultery with a twenty-five-year-old, Kate. What about that?"

"That's different. I'm not in love with him."

Lu stood still. "You mean sex is now immoral only if you fall in love?" She looked up at the sky. "Oh, Lord, please deliver us from these screwball ethics. This is not what we marched for."

Kate flung her head back, concerned. "I just don't want to see Sybil hurt. Why would a guy that age be fooling around with her? I mean, he's got to be kidding."

"You'll see what I mean when you meet him." Lu grinned wide. "You get the feeling he's definitely *not* kidding."

Chapter
6

RIDING THE Hampton Jitney on the Long Island Expressway to Maidscott, Will's heart thumped. It was that way when he wasn't with Sybil for a few days. When he saw her, there would always be that moment of suspended breathing: Had she changed, found someone more exciting, mature? Then he relaxed. There was this Kate Castaldi in from Los Angeles. He would now know Sybil's three oldest, closest friends, and that was some kind of declaration on her part, wasn't it?

Will sat back, feeling confident, remembering what had happened at his gym a few nights back. After a workout and a shower, he was dressing in front of his locker when someone noticed Sybil's book jacket taped to the door. A photograph on the back of the book jacket showed her in a white shirt and glasses. A couple of men gathered around the picture.

"Who's this, Will?"

"My girlfriend."

A black bartender moved in close, studying Sybil. "That ain't no girl. That's a woman."

"Yeah, well, she's older than I am. She writes novels." He looked around at the group, half-joking, half-serious. "What do you think?"

A big, professional iron-pumper shouldered his way through the group and looked at the picture while the other men stood back, waiting. "This really your woman, Will?"

"Yeah."

"How old is she?"

He took a deep breath. "Thirty-eight."

The iron-pumper went over her slowly. He was impressed and wanted to impress the others. "Very . . . classy. A certain attitude, ya know?"

Will stepped back, flushed, as the men gathered around for another look at her, then looked at him, nodding. He waited, tense, for a delayed reaction, some comment on their age difference, but it wasn't mentioned. That had pleased him very much indeed.

He smiled now, thinking of Sybil, how sometimes her attitudes were masculine—a smoldering intolerance of whining, passive women, a confusion about ordinary domestic things—as if she had switched genders for added stamina. Other times she was like a schoolgirl: blushing and shy and so vulnerable he felt he could almost see her nerve ends glowing under the surface of her skin. Thinking of her brought to mind the remarkable life of the oyster, changing back and forth from male to female throughout its life, the only living organism that created a precious gem.

She stood straight against the Dodge as the jitney pulled up. Will stepped off the bus and loped toward her, tilting a little, the boots she gave him for Christmas still pinching. Cautiously, she searched his features as she moved to him, looking for the first sign, a hesitation in his glance, a giveaway: he had gone back to the city, compared her to the thousands of younger female faces, and realized how long she'd been out in the weather. But no, he grinned and hugged her almost with relief, and they walked back to the car.

"Tell me about the script!" She slid her arm around his neck as they sat in the front seat. "Have you seen it yet?"

For a moment Will's face was blatantly young, forgetting in his excitement the hooded look of maturity he was cultivating. "I've got a copy with me. Sybil, it sounds like it was written for me. Same physical type, same personality." He laughed. "It also sounds a little bit like your friend Kate, about a runaway mother. Her son finds her working as a blackjack dealer in a gambling casino, and they set up house together, trying to work out their separate love lives. It's a great script."

They sat there grinning, full of expectation. Then, as Will wheeled the car down Seth Lane, Sybil filled him in on the doings at the house. Lu was in and out, flying the Boston–East Hampton circuit, taking buyers and brokers back and forth before the big Labor Day horse show. Kate was still hiding out from her husband, sleeping with a surfer named Bruce who drove a cab.

As they pulled into the driveway and crossed the lawn, Kate came around from the patio in the back of the house. Will stood paralyzed, trying to take in the figure in a white bikini, all curves and breasts and nothing waist. His eyes climbed to her face like a small boy's, staring at the heart-shaped mouth, the violet eyes, and the voluminous wavy, black hair, reminding him of that *National Velvet* movie star before she became plump and camp.

"Uh," Will floundered as Sybil introduced them, "I feel like asking for your autograph."

She smiled, strangely speechless. After standing

there for a moment, Will went on inside with his suitcase. Kate looked down, and the grass at her feet stood up momentarily, as if her look produced static.

Sybil touched her arm, steadying her. "Shocked?"

"For Christ' sake," Kate whispered. "Justin looks older than that."

"You're exaggerating as usual." Sybil shook her head. "Anyway, when you talk to him you'll see how mature he is."

Kate moved closer. "Is this for research or something?"

"No. I'm not that hard up for material."

She stepped back, confused. "God, I thought this stuff was only going on in Hollywood."

Sybil's expression had the energy of a smile, but it was something else, something a little sad. "Welcome to Hollywood, Kate."

Later in the day, while Kate painted her toenails and Sybil lay nearby reading a book but not reading, Will filled them in on the TV pilot, how they were still casting for the lead role of the mother, and it was slowing down his audition. He was tense. There was something else on his mind, and he glanced at the women now and then, working up to it.

"So you two met in college?" he asked.

"Well, yes and no," Kate answered. "We were in different dorms on campus. We really met one summer, waitressing at Cape Cod."

Sybil laughed. "Waitressing my eye! All you did was lie around on the beach, subsidized with checks from home."

Kate looked down, shaking her head. "My God, I never knew what my parents put up with until I had my daughter."

Will studied her, trying to imagine Kate as a mother. "Does your daughter look like you?"

95

"Looks like and sounds like," she sighed. "And makes me feel old."

"Sorry, Kate," Sybil grunted. "Beautiful women don't get to complain."

"But I don't feel beautiful. I feel terminal." She looked over at Sybil. "I see you and the others. You're like young girls, full of sex and vitality and crazy plans. I'm just a housewife from Brooklyn with this face tacked on as a joke."

Will moved closer to Kate, suddenly very attentive. "Do you regret having kids?"

She shook her head no. "It's just that I wanted more from life than I seem to have." Then she eyed Will in a superior way that said, Don't get chummy, I don't approve of you. "Why the sudden interest in my kids?"

He exhaled importantly. "Because. I'd like to have a child. With her. I want to marry her."

Sybil stared at the end of Will's finger pointing at her. She looked at his face to see if he was joking. Kate sat still as a fixture while nail polish dripped from the brush to her toes.

Will suddenly pulled Sybil to her feet. "Let's go for a walk. It wasn't supposed to come out that way."

She staggered along the beach beside him, in shock. "You're not focusing, Will."

"I have focused, Sybil. And I've made a decision." He took her by both arms and held her still. "I'm in love with you. I want a child with you. If we start planning now, we can get married and have a kid next summer. You don't have that many years left."

Sybil stared at him. "Have a kid with you? You're still a kid."

He blushed, furious. "Am I? Is that what you've been fucking for almost a year?"

"Will, I'm sorry. You've hit me with this so suddenly." Her hands went slowly up to her face, as if to make sure she was still there. "I only meant I'd love to have your baby if I were—"

"Twenty-five with three bestsellers behind you. You know, I don't think you want reality, Sybil. You want nice, neat plots like your novels. That's not the way it is. Life's messy, it's uneven; you have to make it work with what you've got."

She stared at him, thinking how he was just beginning his career and his only steady income was from the bookstore, and how her income from her books barely kept her together.

"How could we make it with a child? It would be insanity."

"I don't understand you women." He shook his head slowly. "You're supposed to be so independent, tough, like pioneers. But the bottom line is you still want guarantees, afraid to gamble on life."

The idea that what he was saying might be true or half true made her draw back slightly. Then she leaned toward him. "Will, do you realize when you're thirty, I'll be forty-six?"

"And when you're eighty," he argued, "I'll be sixty-four. Big deal."

He turned away and stared at the sea for a while, then looked back at her, desperate and running out of arguments. "You know, I'd rather think you don't want a child that badly or you don't love me that much. I'd hate to discover you just don't have the guts. You and your hotshot friends. Maybe you're all phonies."

Sybil looked down, thinking how she and her friends were not hotshots, not phonies, just confused, struggling women who had perhaps won more points than they could handle.

She reached out, holding his arm as if for balance.

"I love you so much, Will. But I don't know how to handle what you're asking me right now."

His lips went white with frustration. "Look, you either want things or you don't! Love's very simple."

He was so persistent, she felt her head beginning to pound. Slowly, she pulled him down on the sand and sat on her knees facing him. "Look, sometimes I do think of marriage and children, but maybe I long for those things in the abstract." She shook him a little, as if to wake him. "Try to imagine me with a child, running a house, while you struggle as an actor. When would I find time to write novels?" She sighed. "Love's very complicated, Will. It's decisions that are simple."

He suddenly grabbed her shoulders, pulling her face to his. "Sybil! Do you just want to write books and dry up and grow old alone, like Victoria Grant?"

She dropped her head, confused and miserable.

He cupped her chin, pushing her head back up. "Don't you want to create something with another human being while there's time?" Then he asked softly, "Do you ever think how short life is, how soon we're going to die?"

"No," she lied, something she seemed to be getting very good at.

For there were nights she bicycled alone through the lanes of Maidscott and East Hampton, staring at big, old homes full of light and the silhouettes of people leaning together. Even the cars parked close in the driveways gave the impression of animal warmth. Sometimes Sybil stood under trees at the end of a drive, watching smoke bloom from chimneys, smelling food, hearing the sound of humans with shared blood, sharing meals. Then she would peddle home to the unfurnished carriage house and stand in the doorway, staring at a typewriter and a blank page, and wish she were dead because half of her felt dead already.

"No," she said. "I don't think of dying. Only dying of failure."

Will stood slowly and pulled her to her feet so their eyes were level. "Listen to me. Please. In September we'll have been together almost a year. If I get that TV pilot, I want us to get married."

Sybil's eyes went huge as if magnified under glass. "Why, Will? Why do you need this?"

"Because I love you." He looked out at the sea again. "Because it's degrading to feel I'm just a temporary thing in your life."

With their heads hanging, they walked home so slowly two workmen setting up Roman candles on the beach for July Fourth fireworks looked after them, wondering if they were peaceful or very tired.

The week following July Fourth, Sybil left Kate at the carriage house and took the jitney into Manhattan for acupuncture treatments. In the past few months, her migraines had started again. She had first experienced them in the second summer of her marriage when she and Stewart had taken a beach house. Lying around on weekends, trying to read, she would be aware of Stewart clearing his throat in the next room, wanting her but not wanting to advance and be rebuffed.

And she would lie there, wishing she were another woman, someone who still wanted to make love to him. Suddenly the printed words before her would recede and then advance faster and faster until the whole page danced, and the pain in her left temple shot through her eye, leaving her sweating and nauseated.

Sometimes the migraine attacks came after an argument, Stewart complaining she had used his toothbrush, changed their favorite brand of wine, bought the *New York Times* at midnight Saturday instead of the next morning (after all, it was the Sunday *Times*). The blinding headaches usually occurred after such discussions when Sybil realized he interpreted these small spontaneous acts as treasonous, signs of revolt.

Or they came after fights over his obsession with receipts, tax deductions for everything, every restaurant meal, every purchase, even a bottle of mouthwash. One night Stewart bought her a bouquet of roses, then asked the florist for a receipt.

"You make me feel so damned deductible," she whispered.

On the way home in a cab, Sybil ate the roses one by one while he watched, silent. (It was two years after their divorce before she could look back and finally acknowledge it was Stewart's income, with the help of his tax deductions, that enabled her to write her first novel.)

By the third year of her marriage, the migraines came randomly, for no reason. She popped Ergotamine and codeine the way other people swallowed aspirin, feeling the "aura" preceding the migraine attack itself. During this warning period she would feel a deadening of senses, an unfocusing, as if she were drunk. Sometimes the aura receded and there was no attack, or unexpectedly, when she had almost forgotten it, it would bludgeon her, the full migraine assault.

At times, when the attacks occurred strangers helped Sybil home. Stewart would enter their building and find the porter cleaning the hallway where she had been ill and the elevator man in their apartment wrapping ice cubes for her head. After a while, when the marriage went bad, she looked forward to the migraines, a refuge, taking herself into herself.

Now they were back, usually occurring when she was trying to work.

Dr. Soong pinpricked her with hairlike needles in her legs, hands, and neck, then she lay still in the dark, listening to a male patient groan in the next room. When the Oriental assistant came to remove her needles, Sybil asked about the man next door.

"He have pain," the assistant whispered. "I afraid to remove needles, too scary."

"What's wrong with him?"

"Impotent. No make love. Dr. Soong put many needles."

Sybil's mouth felt suddenly dry. "Where does she put them?"

The assistant bent over, staring at her with huge almond eyes. "Down there. In crotch." She giggled. "Look like pincushion in his lap!"

"My God."

"Scary for man. Many patients with problem. Work too hard, drink too much, stress."

As Sybil paid her bill in the reception room, the man appeared. He was a big, handsome Broadway star, an Emmy winner in his late forties. Walking down Park Avenue, she thought of the Broadway star and the frailty of men in their late forties, then directed her attention to Stewart Thornton, her forty-six-year-old ex-husband, standing on the corner of Park Avenue and 61st Street, waving. In the last phase of their marriage he had been impotent. Now he wore the enigmatic smile of a happily married man.

Over Japanese lunch their conversation was relaxed but careful, because many things they thought of mentioning bordered on topics that must not be touched.

"You got my note?"

"I did. Thank you, Stewart."

"I thought *Live Burials* was terrific. Forget what the critics said."

"Recognize anyone in it?"

He laughed, handsome and gray-templed. "Yes. The bedroom scene where the husband and wife fight over the air conditioning."

"I used to wake up beside you," she smiled, "feeling frostbitten."

"I remember I was going through that period of heat flashes. I don't have them anymore." He frowned. "Christ, Sybil, don't tell me our marriage failed because we disagreed on the room temperature."

She shook her head hopelessly, remembering the previous decade. "People got divorced for funnier things in the seventies."

They pushed sushi around their plates, tense in their effort to be casual.

"How's your son?" she asked. "And your wife?"

"He's wonderful and exhausting. Ann's taking a few years off from her job so we can have one more."

He looked down, than at her. "How's your life? I know you're working on another book."

"Oh, I'm seeing someone. Ahh, he's younger—"

"I heard. Seems to be the trend today, doesn't it?" He dropped his napkin and smoothed back his wavy hair. Some habits did not change. "Course there's the flip side. Ran into an old college roommate recently. He had an affair this winter with a sixteen-year-old waitress at a ski resort."

His voice had gone brisk, not really wanting to hear about her love life. The small talk was beginning to tell, and they both fidgeted.

"Sybil, I've got to get back to the office soon. Is

there something . . . well, I know you didn't call me just to have lunch."

She cleared her throat. "No. I wanted to ask you something. I seem to have trouble remembering." Her eyes roamed the ceiling.

He leaned forward. "What is it?"

"Stewart, was there a reason we didn't have a child? I mean, did we ever discuss it?"

He sat back as if she had struck him. After a few seconds he recovered. "I begged you to have a child, don't you remember?"

She shook her head, sad.

"I wanted it very much, Sybil. You didn't. You said children were so . . . continuous."

Her eyes closed momentarily. "Jesus. Was I ever that glib?"

"You said," he looked away, "children would stunt our marriage. I think you meant your growth."

"I see."

It occurred to her he was still in love with her in the way men love a woman they never understand.

"Maybe you were right, Sybil. You needed to do more important things."

Her eyes teared, but she ignored it. "I have one more question. You're the only man I've ever lived with. You knew me so well. What I need to know is—oh, God."

She started crying. He reached over, handing her a handkerchief smelling of the same cologne. She patted her eyes and looked at him.

"Stewart, do you think I'd make a better wife the second time around?"

After a few more seconds, he answered, "Yes. You'd make a wonderful wife."

"How can you tell?"

"Because you sound ready."

She sighed. "I know I was difficult, but was I giving, I mean, thoughtful?"

"You were wonderfully thoughtful and generous. You just didn't want to be married." He smiled, looking older and tired. "Remember those gold links you gave me one Christmas? You walked all over Manhattan looking for the right design. And that antique traveling clock? I knew you had to sell some of your own jewelry to buy it."

He shot his cuffs, another habit unchanged.

Sybil stared. "You're still wearing them!"

Looking down at the cuff links, Stewart smiled. "Well, my wife's not as extravagant as you; she's sort of stingy in the gift department. She gives me kids instead."

It came out wrong, but they left it alone.

They hugged briefly in front of the restaurant, and Sybil walked quickly away. He watched her loping across the street against the light, legs abnormally long, high-buttocked, head held at an angle either proud or absentminded. Turning a corner, she looked back and saw him standing there, and they both waved, knowing somehow this was their last meeting.

She headed up Madison Avenue, crying again into the handkerchief, not so much for love—that time was long past—but for two people whose life together had not been fully realized. A marriage of the early seventies, when women marched for the infinite, husbands stood on the sidelines, and divorce became an art form.

Casing her reflection in shop windows, Sybil slowed down after a while, thinking about her friends, reviewing their lives. She herself a nonselling author; Lu a small-time aviator; Blair a real-estate salesman; and Kate—who had hoped to be something famous, an actress, the President—a housewife who shot fish and torched cars for inner definition. Each of them anemic versions of what they had set out to become.

Yet all had this in common: Each woman had been given shelter before she grew into her freedom. A man had nurtured her along the way. Sybil was supported by Stewart while writing her first novel. Lu chalked up air time while her husband George paid the rent and gas for the plane and went around bragging about her. Blair's husband may have slept with other women, but he fed and clothed Blair while she wrote her first play, and he sprang for the rental of the loft for a reading of that play. Even Walter had given Kate almost eighteen years of loyalty, two children, and a Beverly Hills showplace.

Didn't the men deserve something lavish in return? Sybil wondered what would be appropriate, and the most magnanimous thing she could think of was what three of the husbands already had: Freedom.

That evening, riding the bus back to Maidscott, she smelled a man's cologne and realized she was still carrying Stewart's handkerchief. Unfolding it from her pocket, she looked down at the initialed linen, expensive and fine, like his clothes and the antiques he had collected and arranged so fastidiously through the months and years of their marriage.

She smiled, remembering his obsessive orderliness, shoes lined up according to color, ties hung according to width, even his monogrammed undershorts folded with the initials up. Then she thought of Will, who smelled of Ban and didn't own a bathrobe. His one-room apartment was a collage of T-shirts, jogging shorts, and track shoes with the tongues stuck out like things of enormous thirst, all flung intemperately, as if a locker-room crowd had evaporated, leaving only their clothes.

And yet. Where Stewart had grown to resent her work and made her feel there was something immoral about writing, Will couldn't seem to learn enough about it. He asked her questions no man had ever asked her. What did she wear to write in? Did she use both sides of draft paper or just one? Did she use a thesaurus? Where did she sit to edit? How often did she get up to stretch during a working day? On and on. And when she moved out to the carriage house for the summer, he asked her the same things all over again. She was puzzled by all the questions until he finally explained how it helped him imagine her when he wasn't there.

She thought of Stewart again, leaning over her manuscripts, dripping sweat, using her notes to wipe up food. And though she realized it had never been intentional—he was too caring and well-bred—it was the thoughtlessness of it she had found hostile. Whereas Will moved around her study like someone in a chapel, quietly, almost reverently. With all the sensitivity of an artist, he never dared read a page in her typewriter or on the manuscript pile unless she offered it. He never even touched a pencil on her desk without asking her.

And on days when she had pushed herself beyond the point of being rational, when she flew around the apartment screaming she didn't have it, she was without talent, a phony, a bluff, Will would exert a little muscle, shaking some sense into her.

"Yes, you *do* have talent. You do. But, Sybil, no writer has it . . . every day."

When she was calm he would make her talk about plot structure, characters, where her writing had bogged down. And it was this touching respect for her work, his bossiness, his sometimes hurtful honesty and care that frightened her, for she saw how strong, how supportive he could be for her.

Now she stared out the window at the ruby-strung nightlights of traffic ahead, wondering how this summer, this affair, in fact her whole life, had gotten so out of control. She suspected Will was just too much man for her, offering her too much. Then she closed her eyes and tried not to think, because the only alternative to life with Will was life without him.

Chapter
7

LU LEANED BACK, relaxed, as the small Cessna 152 hummed. Beside her, a horse vet from Boston named Hoyt Biddle squirmed around looking east, then west, like a weather vane in wind.

"Nervous?" She smiled at him.

"Little." He frowned. "I'm a simple man. Like to keep one foot on the ground."

"Hmm, a vanishing breed. Why's a simple man like you flying down to the fancy Hamptons?"

"I've got a fancy osteopath cousin who wants me to look at a brood mare for sale. He's got a jumper in that Labor Day horse show, so I'll be back for that too."

In a plaid flannel shirt with a No Nukes button, dancey blue eyes, and salt and pepper hair, Hoyt Biddle was fiftyish, stout, with a rural man's confidence that made him attractive.

"Don't worry." He laughed. "I steer clear of the fancy crowd. Just mingle with the animals."

"A lot to be said for animals. They don't talk back, except lap dogs." She kept up a smooth patter, trying to calm down her passenger. "My husband once bought me a toy terrier. Ferocious barker."

"What happened to it?"

Lu grinned. "One day it saw a roach or something and had a heart attack. I found it stone-cold dead. I was running out on a flight assignment and didn't have time to bury it, so I stuck it in the freezer."

He looked sideways at her. "Uh . . . the freezer?"

"Yeah. Unfortunately, my husband brought a client home for drinks that evening and reached in for ice cubes. When the dead dog fell out, he wet his pants."

Biddle sputtered, then shook with laughter. "Still married?"

"Nope." She smiled, half sad. "Divorced on grounds of irreconcilable differences. Plus he got me on about four counts of mental cruelty."

He laughed again. "Mental cruelty? Tell ya, men today don't know how to treat you high-spirited women. I know what I'd do with you."

"What's that," she flirted.

"Take you over my knee and give you a good spanking first, then throw you down and give you some good loving, then chain you to the kitchen stove where you belong."

She didn't respond to that, but by the time they had landed in East Hampton, Biddle was still flushed, had half a hard-on, and worked up the nerve to ask her out for a beer.

"Thanks." She lied. "But I'm involved with someone."

"Poor bastard." He grinned. "Hope he can handle the mental cruelty."

Lu's expression had turned cool, and in the silence Biddle noticed her staring at his No Nukes button.

"This sort of thing interest you?" he asked.

"Sometimes." She nodded. "I've done a lot of aerial protesting over Boston and Cape Cod."

"You get some free time, you should give this horse show some buzz business. The Long Island

Lighting Company's expanding a big nuclear plant down here, town called Shoreham." He spoke slowly and distinctly because the issue was important to him. "The locals want to stop expansion, get the plant inspected by local officials, and stop illegal deliveries of additional uranium fuel before there's a meltdown and they blow sky-high." He leaned in, checking Lu's interest. "I'm officially here for the osteo's jumper, but I'll be agitating with buttons and pamphlets."

"Maybe I'll look into it," she said.

"You should." He smiled. "I'll call you in Boston with the details. OK?"

They shook hands, and Lu watched him walk away with the unconscious swagger of a manly man. Then, in the sultry evening breeze of the East Hampton airfield, she hosed down her wheels and sat back in the grass, squinting at the Cessna shimmering in the sun, as if already longing for strips of flung-out tar, takeoff points. Like her, it looked unnatural grounded.

Lu closed her eyes and wandered back to yesterday, a quick hop up to Portland with the body of a fireman-conventioneer who'd had a cardiac arrest in a twenty-four-hour porn-movie house. He had been dead for eight hours before the management found him, his fly open, fingers rigor-mortised around his penis.

Flying him home, Lu had wondered how it would seem finding a woman like that. A devotee of the porn idol John Eveready and his nine-inch flare, found dead, eyes glazed, fingers frozen in her labia, while the cinematic bobbin shuttled slowly back and forth showing Big John in an Eternal Come. Picturing the woman, Lu laughed out loud. But imagining a man dying that way, alone in a sleazy theater smelling of semen and piss and Hershey bars, seemed unutterably sad. She could not figure out what the difference was except that the woman would have been there out of mutineering showiness. Regardless, Lu liked the idea that she could still feel sympathy for the male gender.

Taxiing down the runaway at the Portland airport on her return to Boston Lu had seen, off to her left, a single-engine, two-seater put-put with a woman at the controls. On the ground, a man was bent over the propellers, manually winding them through to lubricate them before takeoff. He had reminded her of George, her ex-husband. Spinning the propellers through before Lu revved the engine, George's expression had always been one of potential horror, as if the propellers were meant to prune his balls.

Once a mechanic told her he had heard George throwing up in the men's room before takeoff after learning a man had been decapitated by propellers. Nevertheless, George had loved flying with Lu. He was proud of her. No matter what nature came up with, sudden crosswind gusts, a storm, she always landed like a dove, once she decided to land.

Back in the sixties Lu had soloed after her first twelve hours of instruction. After a few more hours, she just plain sailed.

"You've got the natural feel of a fighter pilot," her instructor observed. "Too bad you're a female."

For a while she was infatuated with "stalls," back-pressuring the control wheel, climbing too sharply until the engine coughed like a lung victim. The plane would shimmy. The voice from the air-academy flight tower would get extremely agitated, lifting in pitch.

"Why are you doing that? Level off. Level off."

It was her first realization that she didn't like following instructions when she was at the wheel. She would smile, in perfect control, push the nose down, the throttle up, and accelerate, watching the wings suck up the horizon. Finally the tower caught on. This woman stalled for fun. When she landed, the instructor pounded over to her, his face stippled with fury.

"You. Don't fly this school no more."

She got her private pilot's license from another flight academy, then quit her job selling space at *Fortune* magazine and worked for a freight corporation flying checks, plane parts, and Fotomat film. Then she, married George Landis, an architect in Boston, and decided to fly commercial for a major carrier.

"Why do you want to do that?" he asked, astounded.

"Do you realize out of forty thousand commercial pilots, not one is a female?" she asked.

George stared at her. "Honey, I was hoping for dimension, not information."

Racking up required air time, she flew for morticians, winging corpses home in tiny planes just big enough for her and the casket. When the major carriers began hiring women pilots, Lu passed the test for Pan Am but overnight changed her mind. The responsibility for so many human lives was just too big. One day she showed George a business card: *Lu Camp, Flight Services, Inc.*

"Who's he?"

"Me." She smiled. "I've rented space at one of the flight shacks over near Logan Airport to fly charters."

George looked at the card again. "Lu Camp. Sounds like I'm married to a drag queen."

"Well, George, a group of tycoons wouldn't hire a

pilot named Lutheria Campbell to fly them cross-country, would they?"

He took a lot of ribbing from his friends but fielded it humorously. "Wake up, guys. It's the seventies. Today, cops have tits and plumbers wear Maybelline."

By 1974, Lu had set up a cot at her flight shack, expanding into tie-down space, sightseeing rides, flight instruction, and a few rentals. Besides a Cherokee Six, with removable seats for flying coffins, she bought a new Cessna 152 for short-distance single charters. George was even humorous about the way he asked her for a divorce.

"What have I done wrong?" she asked, bewildered. "How did I let you down?"

He studied her lovely, freckled face, the long, tan eyes and wild terra-cotta hair, and felt his parts hanging useless from his groin, like overripe fruit. She hadn't slept at home for two weeks.

"You passed the written part of marriage," he said, "but you keep flunking the physical."

"I've never looked at another man, George. I've always been faithful."

"I know, honey, but what you're faithful to isn't me, it's your flight schedule."

A few years later she ran into him in Las Vegas. She had flown a croupier out from the East Coast and was locked in combat with a one-armed bandit when she heard his voice behind her.

"See that wild redhead? She defies gravity for a living. I used to be her husband."

She turned around, grinning. "Hello, George."

"Hi, Lu. How's life on the runway?"

They chatted mindlessly while he inventoried her: still nice-breasted, slim-hipped, in a wrinkled jumpsuit, sneakers, and Smilin' Jack sunglasses. And she inventoried his date in pearls, crepe de chine, and high heels that made her walk like a Chinese laundress.

By then Lu had paid off her bank loan, she was operating in the black, and her flight services had become known in the northeast region. But her flight shack was now furnished better than her apartment, and as time passed she seemed to have less and less reason to land.

Now she stood up, stretching in the sun, and headed for Sybil's house, thinking briefly of the horse vet, Hoyt What-was-his-name. Attractive but the type of man she avoided like bad squalls: unbudgeable, middle-aged throwbacks. They kidded around and flirted a lot, but there was always a division line between what they said and the look they gave her. Lu suspected men like that really did believe women should be spanked, fornicated, and chained to a stove.

She had met a few pilots like that and learned to dodge them, for when they discovered that she too was an aviator, something happened to their bed manners; they turned rough, as if trying to get even. After that Lu stuck to one-night stands, approaching escape velocity with bar-stool pickups who had no grudge to bear.

End of July weather was humid and cloudy in Maidscott, accelerating the tension mounting between the women. Lu arrived from the airfield to find the others lying around on the beach sabotaging each other.

"I think I figured it out, Kate." Blair slicked lotion slowly on her legs. "The problem with your marriage was vanity. You just had too large an ego for motherhood."

Kate's cheeks flushed red. She flung her head around so her black hair stood out in waves as if starched. In a swift motion she kicked sand at Blair. "That's right, Blair. You should have had my kids, and I should have written your plays. Maybe one of us would be a success."

Blair's soft, brown eyes grew hard. She opened her mouth, then closed it.

Sybil suddenly stood and walked toward the ocean, tired of the interminable female bickering. Kate came up behind her.

"Sorry, Sybil. We've sort of descended on you, haven't we? Are you getting any work done these days?"

"Not much." She slid her arm around Kate. "How are you holding up?"

She lifted her sunglasses and looked at her. "OK, but . . . I miss that son of a bitch and those kids."

"If it's still there, don't throw it away, Kate."

"I just can't forgive him, that's all. I want to make him really suffer."

"I'm sure you'll think of something."

Sybil waded in and dived under a wave, wanting to clear her brain. Conversations were beginning to repeat themselves. Even Kate's story was getting redundant. She floated on her back, thinking what each woman needed was a wise, old matriarch, someone whose lap she could curl up in, like a small girl who had lost her way. For it seemed to Sybil they were all part of an invisible parade of women beginning to suspect they had marched their way into an ideological cul-de-sac.

She could not, for instance, remember the last time she had heard a woman say she was happy. The word seemed excessive now, as if it had slipped down in the English lexicon and shared the same rung with greed. She swam around with her theory for a while, then came out of the water and took a long run on the beach, thinking of her friends.

Lu, Kate, and Blair were each in their way boring, neurotic, intelligent, selfish; in short, tenderly human. And what they shared after all these years was probably the highest form of love, a feeling of equity and trust, without the treacheries of lust. In that sense they were probably more faithful to each other than they had been to the men in their lives.

Twenty years ago in college they were drawn to each other by intelligence and humor and a hunger for life's events. Now they seemed drawn back together out of confusion, still curious about life, still game, but not knowing how to continue. They were edgier now and fought more among themselves, having to prove more. In the long run, Sybil knew the woman's decade would work itself out; like all revolutions it had a built-in self-correction mechanism, whether it took twenty years or fifty. But in the meantime, with the loss of men, the breakdown of marriages and affairs, women meant more to each other; there was more at stake between them now.

A man and his dog approached. The dog ran up to Sybil, barking playfully, nipping at her heels, then trotted on, leaving paw prints like racing dinner forks. The man looked friendly, but as they got closer, he dropped his eyes shy, perhaps disoriented by her height, and moved too close to the water. A small wave slapped his left side, and Sybil ran on, thinking how hard it was for men and women to be civil these days. Even a simple exchange like "hello" seemed loaded.

After an hour or so, she swung back on the beach, running toward the house, seeing lights on, and deeply grateful for her friends but progressively edgier. She needed to get down to work and serious decisions.

Upstairs, Sybil showered and held one of Will's

T-shirts up to her face for a minute, missing him, then slipped it on. As she headed downstairs, the phone rang in the kitchen.

Lu talked for a while, then hung up. "That was my assistant at the flight shack at Logan. Walter's been calling there from LA."

Kate frowned. "He knows I'm with one of you. I don't have any other friends."

"Well, he can't reach me," Blair said. "My number's unlisted."

"And this house is listed under the owner's name," Sybil said. "You know he could find you if he really wanted to, Kate. Maybe he's just letting you cool off."

"Or maybe he's hoping I'll flip out on the East Coast, too, so the general consensus will be to have me committed."

No one spoke, and in the silence Kate looked up at Sybil's T-shirt. "What's THE HUNGER?"

"A punk-rock group. Will took me to see them at the Garden."

"You and twenty thousand teenagers." Kate laughed. "God, Sybil, next you'll be chicken-hawking."

Blair made a face. "What's a chicken hawk?"

"Those old men who cruise Sunset Strip picking up teenage boys."

The others laughed, and Sybil let it slide.

"Who's chef tonight, and what's cooking?" she asked.

"I am." Blair waved lettuce at her. "Fettuccine, osso buco, and Pouilly Fumé. That cheap wine you've been serving tastes like it was aged in aluminum."

They sat down and passed food, and Sybil stared out the window, remembering a night in Little Italy when Will had ordered osso buco, eating round and round the bone, saving the delicacy for last. Then he plunged in his fork and lifted it slowly, unsteadily, pointing it at her.

"Would you like my marrow?" he had asked solemnly.

His marrow. It was so poignant she had almost cried. She started to tell the story now, and thought better of it. The others were already into the wine and getting careless.

"Listen." Lu smiled. "When you and Will go out, do you have this compulsion to cut up his meat for him?"

"Very funny." But somehow it wasn't.

"Seriously, Sybil, have you told your folks about this relationship yet?"

"Relationship." Sybil put down her fork. "That's another one of those bloodless words. I'm having an *affair.* A love affair. Relationship sounds, for Christ' sake, like I'm balling my cousin in the merchant marines."

Her voice had a mean suggestibility, but they ignored it.

"Speaking of balling," Kate said, "last night Bruce and I went dancing, and this middle-aged guy came right up to my face and called me a surf baller. What's a surf baller?"

Lu put down her wine and flapped her arms like wings. "It's an East Coast chicken hawk!"

The others shrieked, banging their glasses on the table.

Blair leaned over and tapped Sybil's arm with her knife. "You know, all you'd have to do is string these conversations together, and you'd have a bestseller." She hesitated. "God knows you could use one."

Sybil sat back. Nothing was sounding right this evening.

"Blair's right," Kate piped up. "We'd all love to

see you make it, Syb. Go for something commercial this time, instead of another soul-searching woman's book."

"Yeah. Your characters are getting too rigid." Reckless with wine, Blair pulled a rubber band off her pigtail and snapped it playfully at Sybil's arm. "As a matter of fact, sweetie, so are you. You treat conversations like rough drafts. I mean, someone asks you a question, you don't react, you edit the question."

"I'm sorry," Sybil stuttered. "I didn't mean . . ."

Kate pointed at her with a forkful of drooping pasta. "Everyone has a limit, Sybil. Try to relax a little."

"Relax?" Lu sat back, laughing. "Sybil doesn't even have a television in her apartment, did you know that? A real Victoria Grant wanna-be."

Sybil's eyes dropped as if infatuated with something in her lap while they talked around her.

"I think maybe she *should* marry Will and have a kid," Blair said. "Take some time off from writing and get back in the human race for a while."

"Of course," Lu cracked, "marrying Will and having a kid would be redundant, wouldn't it?"

They laughed, banging their glasses again.

With a slowness and deliberation of movement, Sybil pushed her plate away and drank down a glass of wine. She poured another glass and looked at it a while, then drank that down and looked around the table.

"You know, guys, I think I've had it. I'm supposed to be working out here this summer. I haven't worked. I sit here day after day, listening to all the sad crap of your lives, and then you criticize my cooking, my life-style, my lover. And now my writing?"

She pushed back her chair and stood up, trembling.

"I want to know what the . . . fuck you want from me. I've tried to be a good friend, but this isn't friendship, it's a vendetta."

They sat shocked, looking up at her.

"Don't talk to me about inflexibility." She pointed to Lu. "Look at your life. You don't even have one-night stands. You've got them dressed and out the door before they're through ejaculating."

Lu stood, making a move toward the patio door.

"I'm not through!" Sybil grabbed her arm and dragged her to the sofa, pushing her down. "You have the gall to criticize my work while you spend your life flying around with corpses because that's the only kind of human you can relate to. Occasionally when you fly a live body you get to live vicariously, find out where someone is going, why, for how much. Then you drop them off feeling sorry for the poor suckers because they depend on other humans."

Lu put her hand up defensively; Sybil pushed it back down.

"What happened to the girl who wanted to fly commercial airlines and take responsibility for hundreds of lives? You're a cop-out, Lu. Tell me, how much power do you feel now, playing delivery girl to a bunch of morticians?"

In the silence, Kate stood up. "I have to go to the john."

But Sybil eyed her so ferociously, she backed down so that her arm, with a certain flourish, landed in the salad bowl.

"And you, Kate. I'm sick to death of this soap opera you're dragging around. It's the most attention you've had since the twins were born, and you're so dazzled by your situation, you don't even know if you're in pain."

Sybil leaned toward Kate as if the floor had suddenly tipped.

"I think you're rude, spoiled, and going through life as an imitation human. You hate your kids, you hate your husband, and you probably wish you were ugly so you'd have an excuse for being such a gaudy failure."

Kate kept shaking her head, as if she wanted the scene to go away.

"All that potential," Sybil whispered, "and at thirty-eight all you've accomplished is turning your home into a bomb site. And you criticize my personal life?"

The light was gone, and in the early evening only the bulb from the kitchen and the candle on the table illuminated the scene, throwing weird shadows on them all. There was no sound except for Sybil's breathing. Unsteadily, Blair stacked a few plates, rose, and headed for the kitchen.

Sybil caught her at the kitchen door, knocking the plates from her hand. "You make me the saddest."

"Don't, Sybil, don't."

"You sold out, Blair. For what? So you could hawk overpriced houses and support some guy you're not even sure loves you. You have to buy your time from him. For one Jaguar you get guaranteed weekends. For one Rolex watch you get every Wednesday night. You're so lonely you practically live here."

Blair clung to the doorway, paralyzed.

Sybil moved closer to her. "And you have the nerve to lecture me about ambition, knowing my limitations? Listen," she started crying, "I may be desperate and broke and in love with someone young enough to be my son, but I didn't sell out for sports cars and Swiss watches. I may not be a bestseller, but I'm working, Blair. I'm working!"

Sybil blew her nose on a dish towel, fighting for control but crying harder. "Twenty years ago I was the one in the group everybody leaned on. But no one

121

ever asked me if *I* was OK. No one ever knew how frightened I was. You know what's funny? Nothing's changed!" She pushed through the patio door and disappeared in the dark.

The candle on the table guttered and died, and there was only the dim, jaundiced light from the kitchen filtering into the living room. Lu lay sprawled on the sofa as if struck by sleep, but her eyes open, wandering in thought. Kate was folded at the table, her head in her arms. Blair sat in the kitchen doorway against the jamb. Vagrant moths traversed the screens, eyeing them. An hour passed, maybe more.

Sybil sat on the sand a few feet from the ocean with her head on her knees, cried out. Timidly, Kate walked up beside her and wrapped a sweater around her shoulders. She stood still a moment, her hand on Sybil, and then walked back to a dune and sat with the other women until dawn, watching her silhouette against the sea.

Chapter
8

SYBIL SAT UPSTAIRS in the carriage house with a calendar, counting the days until September. There were three weeks left of August, and she wondered if she would make it. The place had turned into a halfway house. Every few hours the driveway exploded pebbles as Bruce roared up on his hog looking for Kate. The phone shrilled regularly with Tom looking for Blair, Sybil's agent relaying calls from Walter in LA, and Will arguing with casting people.

Right now Will was banging around down in the kitchen, distracted by the television pilot, terrified he would get the part, terrified he wouldn't. He'd had one audition and then a callback for a second. If he didn't get it, he would collapse on her, then a few days later bounce back with that awesome enthusiasm of youth.

Sometimes he exhausted Sybil, making her wish he had about ten more years under his belt so he could understand how time made the bounce-back slower, the punches less sure. She looked at the calendar again—September twenty-one days away—and thought of the TV pilot and his marriage proposal, and she put her head down, thinking of the awesome emptiness of her life before it contained Will.

After a while Sybil sat up and brooded over a page in her typewriter, the germ of a new novel, and it made her sad. A few lines moved her unexpectedly. One line of dialogue made her laugh out loud, then she sat back embarrassed, remembering she had written it. But mostly it just wasn't good enough. Her character had flesh but no heart.

She sat back, wondering how writers like Victoria Grant handled characters that wouldn't come to life. Did Grant ever abandon books, just throw them out and start all over? That seemed immoral. You had to have a certain amount of allegiance to a story, a faith in its completion.

She ran her hand across a shelf and pulled down a book of Grant's essays, *Origins of Voice,* and found a chapter on writing fiction. Marked passages read:

> The author's obligation is not to charm the reader but to filter out contrivance and pretense, to search for and find the truth of the author's experience. . . .
>
> Don't create characters for their oddities. Create real, natural people as you know them. Their actions, if true, will be odd enough.

She flipped through pages worn and underlined until she found what she was looking for.

> When you feel you are no longer writing for yourself but for the critics, you have lost your way. Go back and begin again. Begin a dozen times until what you have to say rings true.

Sybil studied the passage, then reread the page in

front of her. She zipped it out of the typewriter and wadded it into a ball.

Her first two books were written for herself, and people had found them funny. What went wrong with *Live Burials* was that she started writing for the reviewers. Now she could feel them looking over her shoulder again, ambushing her at every page. The new book was about a woman so disillusioned with life she withdraws, becomes a mute for six months, paring herself down, cutting her lashes, her hair, her nails, restricting her intake of food. Then she has her cat spayed and declawed and feeds it meagerly, a sort of slow suicide *à deux.*

The book was supposed to be about isolation, but in places it read funny. If it was funny, fine, but there were problems. Would a woman who voluntarily quit talking sometimes cheat, have conversations with herself? Sybil could not decide, wondering if reviewers would find the whole story implausible. What was the point of a book about a woman who quit talking? Who cared? Suddenly the fatuity of writing another novel that no one would buy defeated her.

She slumped, staring at the scalloped typewriter keys. A whole new chorus of names to invent, a theme to sustain like an unbroken yolk through five hundred pages, a cleverness, an appealingness of character that readers would find entertaining, not puzzling or anxious-making. The thought of doing it all again made her sick.

Sometimes she wished she could just write for herself, plug into a theory and run with it, let it take her nowhere as often happened in real life. There was something immoral about writing fiction, having to create a plum premise, a finale, a punch line for every story, so readers could feel they had learned something, gotten their money's worth.

Sybil hated creating characters she would ulti-
mately desert, people she came to depend on for company, people she even conversed with in the streets,
like a woman leaning toward *prima facie* lunacy.
Her books, she felt, were finally abandoned, never
finished, never good enough. She would simply, out
of exhaustion, let them go. And when she heard
other writers say they had finished a book, she felt
they meant they had simply run out of grist.

Most of all she disliked the publishing events,
press parties where her agent slowly guided her
around the room as if she were retarded, introducing
her to publishers who dressed French, reviewers
with *recherché* names, and the paid-off ghouls from
the columns. Terrified, she would freeze her cheek
muscles in a rhesus grin so that conversation around
her suddenly did not include her.

Pulling herself together for these things was like
facing extermination squads. When *Live Burials* was
published, Sybil pulled a no-show for her own book
party, getting as far as the lobby of the hotel where
the party was held. Then she saw three publishers
who had turned down her manuscript jawing in front
of an elevator, on their way to a meeting, another
party, surely not hers.

She slid into a phone booth, turned her back to the
lobby, and stayed there for two hours, a petrified
woman in a black sarcophagus, the phone to her ear
as if plugged in to the hum of the universe. At inter-
vals she called the suite where her book party was in
progress, hearing the laughter and chatter of normal
people, not her. She pictured her agent searching for
her, his face going pale like a trout belly, eyes
extruding like grapes behind his tinted aviators. Finally he was located and came to the phone.

"Jason?"

"Sybil, where are you?"

"I can't make it."

"Listen, broad." He tried to sound tough, but he was a kind man. "This is your third book. You're not a dilettante. Get the fuck up here."

"I can't." She began to cry.

"The air is full of talent." He was talking to someone behind him, then brought his mouth back to the phone. "Sybil, a lot of important people are here."

"Why?"

"I dunno. Your publisher's PR woman has heavy organs. My point is, your absence is being observed. Intensely."

"What does it matter?" She cried harder. "They'll bury it anyway."

"Where are you? I'll come and get you."

"I'm sorry, Jason. I just can't."

After a few seconds, he breathed out. "OK, I'll handle it, honey. Know what I think you should do?"

"What?"

"What any self-respecting author does when he finishes a book: Go out and get laid."

She drifted up Park Avenue in her party suit, lost in soliloquy.

"I'm driven. Ruthless. I have assertiveness down pat. My mettle is male, yet I didn't have the guts to show up at my own book party. Why?"

An older man passed her and looked back, sad, wondering if it was booze or drugs. She cruised Will's bookstore until he closed, and carped the diem by going home to make love.

As she had with her first two books, when *Live Burials* was published Sybil sent a copy to Victoria Grant, expecting never to hear from her and expecting right. When she arrived in Maidscott in June and realized how close by the woman lived, one day on a whim she drove over to the estate. It was a huge, murky, stone Tudor with turreted roofs and a

gazebo where the old woman supposedly sat sometimes, reading verse at the top of her lungs. Sybil left
a homemade banana cake and a note in her mailbox
asking if she had had time to read *Live Burials.* A
few weeks later she got a response:

"Stop trying to hustle me. I am no longer famous. I
cannot help you. P. S. I prefer carrot cake."

Delighted, she left a carrot cake in the mailbox.
Since then she had had no response from the woman
and wondered what she would say if she ever did
meet her. Probably she would ask her the one question every young writer asks: How did she, Sybil,
know if she had what it took to become a major
writer? How did she know if she would ever be better
than mediocre? What were the clues?

For the hundredth time she sat back wondering if
she *was* good enough, if she should do something else
for a living. But writing was all she had ever done—
first magazine articles, then novels—and the problem with that was she did not know what other work
was like, except housework, something she had dab-
bled in during her marriage. Her thoughts drifted
back to that time.

It had been soothing, therapeutic work scrubbing
pots, polishing floors until her arms were charley-
horsed. When Stewart came home and found her in
the kitchen whipping sauces venomously, he always
knew with a sense of intestinal gloom that she was
having trouble writing. For in this mood, when she
turned her frustrations to cooking, curry dishes for
instance, it was diarrheic in effect. He would be eating a meal and feel his stomach rumble, waiting for
the tines of the fork to curl.

Still, she suspected, he liked seeing her there. The
kitchen wasn't her element; it gave her a vulnerabil-
ity not evident when she was at her typewriter. It

was only when Stewart realized she wanted writing more than the marriage that he turned away. And so, it seemed, did her parents.

The Christmas after her divorce, Sybil went home to visit them in Bucks County, Pennsylvania. When she stepped off the train her mother backed off from Sybil, as if she had something contagious.

"Stewart was a good man," she said. "I just don't understand what's wrong with you women today."

Her father had stared at Sybil's wild hair, satin bomber jacket, and eternal cowboy boots. "What's wrong is that they don't want to grow up."

In the car driving home from the train station, he looked at her in the rearview mirror. "You take after your grandmother, Sybil. All she wanted to do was write poetry and wear funny clothes. You will remember she died in a mental institution."

"Do you think," she asked softly, "Grandma had a breakdown from writing poetry or from having seven children in eight years?"

"I don't know." He changed the drift. "I do recall we buried her with all her original teeth."

From the back seat she stared at her parents. A mother who devoted over forty years to tending a twelve-room house, three children, and a small-town dentist husband. And a father who had spent his life searching for the heart of darkness in people's root canals.

Still, she envied them the sureness of their roles in life. She watched her mother doing what mothers had been doing for centuries—cooking, cleaning, providing—and Sybil wondered: Could every generation before now have been wrong? She helped her father skim dandelion wine agitating down in the cellar, while he discussed his dental cases with her, and she saw through the eyes of his patients that this was an important man.

And later in the day, watching them stomp up the lane together with fresh milk, Sybil thought of her mother and father in their bed at night, the warmth of a back against a back, a hand in a hand during moments of fright; deep and simple satisfactions they had shared for forty-five years. After that holiday it was very hard getting back on the train for New York. She left feeling homesick for a way of life she suspected would not be part of hers.

Now she sat in the carriage house wondering how her parents would handle Will. A few months back she had written them that she was seeing someone a little younger than she was, and one night her father had called, deep in the dandelion.

"How much younger?" he asked.

She made a joke of it. "Well, Daddy, he's old enough to vote."

Yet Sybil suspected, after an initial abhorrent resistance to Will, they would accept him more easily than they could the picture of their only daughter tripping old and age-flecked and lonely down the arches of the years.

Lazily, she pulled open a drawer, looked down at her famous list, 203 names, and thought again of her mother, a virgin when she married her father, kissed once by another man. Sometimes Sybil forgot the list for months, once for a year. But when she was sleeping around a lot in the sixties and seventies, she made entries every week, panicking when she misplaced it.

The list represented order in her life: a name, a date, a summing up. For years she had filed it under Correspondence, then moved it to V under Vital Statistics, with her birth certificate and her passport. Back in the sixties she had kept it hidden, sex still having a certain venereal cachet. In the hanging-loose seventies it was shared with friends, a decathlon graph, she the diva of the pole vault, the broad jump, the javelin throw. In the eighties it became a breviary of the phases of her past life.

Occasionally there were no names. Blond with yacht, 1978. Black with German shepherd, 1969. She wondered what promise had been broken, what faith had been breached, why she was crying on an empty street in Greenwich Village at four in the morning, when the young black walking his dog took her home to East Eighth Street for tea. She stayed with him for two nights and remembered not so much the lovemaking as the shepherd's arfing when fire engines cruised by, and the soft wetness of the dog's nose when he nudged them, needing a walk. Three weeks later the young black called to tell her he was going to Vietnam.

In fact, Sybil seldom remembered the sex at all. What came back to her were surroundings, incidentals. The pathologist with the shoulder mole who sleepwalked. The guitarist with one leg. The bartender with tatoos who carried a gun. The stranger in Athens. The stranger in Rome. The lawyer on Wall Street who could not come. The Texan who took her to a three-star French restaurant and ordered Blue Nun. The ex-convict's scars. The cashier's green eyes. The songs of the drummer in Cyprus. Sometimes she did a double-take. The drummer in Cyprus?

The Jewish tin exporter with the Nazi general overcoat, the original loops for the gun holster, and the swagger stick still intact, the sleeve still showing the outline of the swastika. He was quick to point these details out to strangers. This was a man of lofty IQ who spent his weekends holding his kidneys for Werner Erhardt, who could only come when he plugged up his ears and closed his eyes, a padded cell ejaculate. Sybil slept with him twice out of sheer awe.

Sometimes she looked at the list wondering why. What had been the point of all those men? Maybe, as a tall, shy, plain girl in the sixties, sleeping around had been a way of showing she was someone of wild hypotheses, unfettered by small-town norms. And when the seventies came she seemed to fit right in with the rhetoric sex of that era. Still, at times Sybil wondered if somewhere, on some man's list, she was remembered as a girl with transparent bravado who did not seem sure she was doing it right.

Now and then she thought of destroying the list, but to forget a name meant one two-hundredths of her would expire. She noticed something else in the past few years. Each time she read the list she read it with more concern for the fates of some of the men. The guitarist who made the mistake of needing her more than she needed him—did he find a better girl and settle down? The overweight lawyer, the ex-con with the weak heart—did their health hold up? Did the young black survive Vietnam?

This solicitude for former lovers, their health, their fate, paralleled another growing concern. Sybil began studying the handwriting of friends, the way it changed. Some writing got stronger, but with older folks, her parents, the letters trembled and diminished as if the fountain pen had grown too heavy. This led, of course, to concern for the health of her parents, aunts, uncles, abandoned years ago when she was off to see the world. It occurred to Sybil from time to time that this growing concern was the beginning of the end of youth, that she was approaching maturity, the time of looking backward in order to anticipate her next move.

She looked down at the list again, a big demarcation line between the number of men she had slept with before her marriage, one hundred and eighty, and the number of men after. She was probably mindless and more fun in the sixties and early seventies, but as her desire to play dissolved, so did the playmates. And, as she had said, up until the marriage she was probably just trying to get it right.

With Stewart she cried in bed, something she had not done with another man, because she got perilously close to going over the edge and wanted to so badly. Near the end he asked her if that was why the marriage went bad, because he could not make her come. She had wished the reason for their breakup was that simple.

"A climax isn't that important," she said. "I can achieve that alone."

But maybe that was the problem; she always came on her own, afraid orgasm with Stewart would equal dependency on him. She would lose control, stop writing, become a yawning, satisfied wife. And so she held back and let the marriage go instead.

The phone rang. It was Blair. "Hi. What are you up to besides counting the days till September?"

She let that slide. "Right now I'm reading the list."

"Oh." Blair was silent for a second. "The famous Pecker Memorandum. How do you feel when you look at that thing?"

Sybil laughed. "As though I served as some kind of Klondike for men working the liberated-woman trade."

"For Pete's sake, why do you still keep it?"

"It's my history, Blair. If I throw it out, I'll forget the first time I smoked a joint, the first time someone read me Baudelaire, the first time I went down on a man, or that I dyed my hair blonde in 1968 and drank martinis in 1970."

Blair made an impatient sound. "You know, there's a human failing called memory fatigue. We all suffer from it. Why do you have to record everything, Sybil? You act as if life's only important when you can take notes on it."

Her mind flashed back to Blair's abortion. "I don't write everything down. Some things are just recorded on my nerves." She glanced down at the list. "Maybe someday, if I marry again, I'll throw the list out."

Without missing a beat, Blair asked, "Does that mean you'll be throwing it out in September? You know, you could do worse than marry Will."

Sybil pulled the phone away from her head and looked at the earpiece as if it were faulty. "I don't believe this. A few nights ago you were all making fun of him."

"I think we were . . . jealous." Blair paused and went on softly, "Sybil, when was the last time a man proposed to you? Or any of us?"

She arched her back, trying to think of a quick, funny response, but nothing came.

"Well," Blair said, "guess I'll get back to the old tapper. I found this ancient Remington at a tag sale. Course, after three years, I can't even remember how to work the margin release."

Sybil was so excited, she stood up, knocking her chair over. "Blair, what are you typing? A play?"

"Who knows?" Blair laughed. "I'm just rooting around on the keys."

She hung up, smiling, picturing Blair rooting around on the keys, timid at first, then clattering along by rote.

Will's heart hammered over her so violently, she saw the hairs on his chest vibrating. They had begun making love slowly, but his propriety in not rushing

134

her made her hot soon, and finally she drew him inside her, watching his foraging. Sometimes Will wished for another pair of eyes, so he could see himself tunneling into her and at the same time watch Sybil watching them make love, her pupils so big they were uncanny.

Their sex seemed frantic lately. They would start slowly, then accelerate like runners going for a second wind and then a third, neither of them wanting release. Inside her, he forgot about the act of love and was only aware of the two of them racing like competitors, toward what? It scared him because it was mindless and yet not really physical.

Her breathing hoarse, Sybil would move faster and faster, like hunted game in sparse land, and he would keep up with her, as if they were running away from climax, not toward it, as if real consummation was some frontier of almost absolute indifference. Will watched his sweat flowing onto her face and breasts, and his vision was blurry and his head pounded. When he thought his heart would burst, he stopped, withdrawing slightly.

"Sybil, what are we doing? What are—"

"Don't, Will! Don't stop. . . ."

She leaned her head forward, eyes criminal and wide as if, if he stopped, she could kill him, and pulled him back into her. He clasped her buttocks firm as oak and stayed with her while her mound shook and shimmied like a small mad dog. And finally she came, her eyes wild, holding on to him desperately with her nails but not aware of it. With a loud groan he collapsed on her, their bodies sticking together like wet pelts.

But his cock was still plank-stiff, the tension contained in a huge cramp.

"Hold my balls, honey, my balls. . . ."

Gently she worked her hands under him and

cupped his testes, stroking them with the tips of her fingers. Exhausted but out of control, his body lunged again and again, as if it were trying to get deeper into her, a final stitching together. And then things went black; a cold coming washed over him, man's little death.

The rest was rote; he lay on her, but lightly, his face buried in the pillow beside her head, thinking how orgasm was almost secondary to that other thing they had shared, that mindless racing. Then he fell on his side and gathered her close, and they lay quiet, listening to their breathing, like runners at the tape. Sybil's wet lashes slowly unstuck, and her hazel eyes went over his face minutely, every inch of it, like someone memorizing it. She looked so sad, he leaned up on an elbow.

"Honey, what is it?"

She shook her head, smiling. "Nothing." Then she threw herself against him. "Oh, Will."

He folded her close in his arms and, exhausted, she slept.

For a long time Will lay awake, hearing occasional moans from the other women asleep in the house. And he thought of Sybil as she had looked on the beach earlier in the day, coaching him for his callback. The wind had come up, scattering the TV script, and Sybil ran circles, long legs kicking out, trying to anchor pages. Finally, she jogged back, waving the soggy sheets of dialogue, and spread them on the towel, pressing them down to dry. Will had studied her, touched by her concern, and more.

Her hair was dried out by the sun, her nose and patches of her arms were peeling, as if she were trying to shed old skin. Her eyes wrinkled when she smiled. She was no longer young compared to girls he knew, and when she had suddenly gazed up at him from that kneeling position, she looked so vulnerable he had leaned over and hugged her, confusing her.

Now he drifted into a half dream, and Sybil was suddenly floodlighted in his brain, her face tired and drawn from being so absolutely independent and self-supporting. In slow motion she turned to him, collapsing on him, telling him she couldn't do it alone anymore, she didn't *want* it alone anymore. She clung to him, exciting him, and he jerked himself awake guiltily, as if from a wet dream. He listened to her even breathing beside him and lay back down again, turning things over and over in his mind.

For the past four years, since striking out on his own in New York City, Will had felt he was on the verge of life, that he was continuously in the process of becoming something important and complete. But he couldn't seem to achieve that last stage. He had known hard work, frustration, rejection, had been to dozens of auditions before getting his first TV commercial, had read for scores of Off-Off-Broadway plays before landing a small role in a production that closed after four performances.

So he felt a sense of accomplishment the first time he had signed his Screen Actors Guild card and cashed a royalty check. But he still did not feel that progression he kept waiting for, that sense of completion. It was similar to his first climax with a girl. He had always thought when he experienced that, he would be a man. Will was fourteen when it happened, and all he felt was that someone had pressed ice cubes on the small of his back. He went home, took a shower, and woke up the next day, still a boy.

He had the feeling he could go on like that for years, maybe at forty-five winning a Tony or an Oscar and still feeling as though he were only on the *verge* of completion. For a long time he convinced himself it was a professional deformity, the actor's frustration, like a lawyer's skepticism or the odium of politicians. And then he met Sybil and understood he had finally achieved the last stage of development, a sense of emotional rounding out.

For the first time in his life Will experienced a gentleness and concern, a keenness of perception for the feelings of another human being. It was so strong, at times he felt almost fatherly toward her. He now had this sense of being able to dig down in himself and find a hell of a lot going on, things *he* could rely on, as well as Sybil. Whether this new facet of Will, this newly discovered or newly developed depth, was simply maturing and would have happened anyway was up for grabs. All he knew was, having met Sybil, he was no longer the man, not the same with his colleagues or his family, not the same alone.

Of course sometimes he felt the last thing he needed to slow him down was to fall in love. He only had so much time in his life to absorb all the culture and knowledge that luckier people were exposed to from childhood, and unluckier people never even missed. And he was in a hurry to prove to the world he was capable of some future distinction. But Will suspected he would always be the kind of man, young or old, who grabbed at possibilities rather than security. He was on his way to somewhere—he felt it—and he wanted Sybil to share the possibility of that future. He was making room for her, and it was enormous.

He sat up in the dark and lit a cigarette. He was making room for Sybil Wade, but he wondered, was she making room for him? At times like this, thinking of their future, he resented her writing because it stood between the two of them. Even when she wasn't working he had the awful feeling she wasn't concentrating on him. Some part of her was always busy rewriting or recording, as if he could never really get to her, as if she was always in a crowd.

Sometimes he fantasized just seizing control of her life, telling her exactly how many hours a day to work and when to stop, when to pay attention to him. Ha. Another wet dream. Until some fine day when Sybil had proven herself to herself, she would always have to know that at any hour of the day or night she had what it takes.

She was that kind of woman, and she inspired him because that was the kind of man he wanted to be. For the hundredth time now, he thought of the alternative to Sybil, girls his age who talked out of the sides of their mouth, sabotaged each other at auditions, and thought discipline and character were words for older actresses who had never known real success.

Sybil turned in her sleep, and he opened a curtain so the moon fell on her face. He stood over her, wondering what did the rest of the world know about them, thinking their only common language was the jargon of lust. What did it know about the comfort they gave each other, the pep talks, the courage needed for each day, trying to stay one confident step ahead of all the other talented actors and writers in the world?

Looking ahead, he could think of nothing sadder than a woman like Sybil dying childless, leaving nothing behind but printed words. His thoughts spread to Lu and Blair, women squandering their best assets—not talent, but beauty, spirit, youth. His attitude was male; maybe it was wrong. He was too young to know all the answers, but he knew this: He did not want to lose her, and he wouldn't.

He slid quietly into bed and took her sleeping form in his arms. Remembering their no-holds-barred sex and the strange way she looked at him afterward, he felt a constriction in his throat. Sybil's lovemaking had a desperation about it lately, and the way she studied his face was desperate too, as if she were trying to memorize it for a future when he might not be there.

He did not like this thought. He blinked in the dark and thought of his parents, because whether or not he got the television pilot, he was going to tell them about Sybil. And he wondered how his mother would react when he told her he was going to marry a woman younger than her by only two years.

Chapter
9

ON A MONDAY MORNING, after dropping Will at the jitney, Sybil stopped at the post office for mail and found a note from Victoria Grant inviting her to tea. For the next twenty-four hours she gave Blair and Kate her fullest attention, but heard nothing and saw nothing, drifting around with the senseless ease of one drugged.

Tuesday afternoon she sat in the Dodge, whipping and stroking the gearshift, stabbing at the gas pedal, begging it to start. Nothing happened, of course, until she remembered to turn the key in the ignition. Arriving at the gates of the place and finding them open, she drove slowly up the dirt road toward the mansion, with a feeling of driving into the lost past. Though it was a bright day, the place seemed overcast. An ancient whippet-like housekeeper opened the door.

"Hello, I'm Sybil Wade."

"Oh, it's you."

The housekeeper frowned, as if the name were long known, then hustled her down a hall, jangling keys in a way that made Sybil think of house arrest.

In a dim study, a fire blazed. The room was crammed with dusty, ornate furniture, sepia photo-

141

graphs, hundreds, perhaps thousands of books. Sybil stood before the fireplace terrified to the point of chill. Then she realized that, in spite of the fire, the house had the temperature of late autumn. The door opened, and Victoria Grant stood there, propped on a cane, flamboyantly old.

At eighty-five, she was a small woman, but when she sat down and they were eye level, she seemed much taller than Sybil. She was wearing a white wig that did not fit; perhaps from years back when her skull was larger. Her face was a congestion of vertical lines, like minutely pleated pink silk, but her eye sockets were deep, with a dearth of flesh as if she had had cosmetic surgery, which she hadn't; the woman was too vain.

Her clothes were outlandish. A fox shrug surrounded her shoulders, eternally cannibalizing itself, teeth devouring tail. Under that, an ancient hunting pink with mildewed buttons, a man's dress shirt with ebony studs, and a faded, floor-length taffeta skirt that dragged as if with tremendous undertow. Grant was wearing a huge emerald ring and her medal from the American Academy of Arts and Letters. It wasn't the outfit of an eccentric as much as of a brilliant, aging woman dressed as if to make up for lost clout.

She had the arch profile and the continuing disdain of one who had been remarkably beautiful, but now the eyes were glaucomic and cloudy and gave her a look of kindness.

"Sit there." She pointed to a chair beside her near the fire and studied Sybil. "Persistent, aren't you?"

"Yes." Sybil dropped her eyes.

"Don't do that," she snapped, head nodding with a slight tremor. "I loathe coyness. Aren't you a woman of the times?"

"I suppose." Sybil smiled. "Whatever that is."

Grant's famous cheekbones stood out amazingly, another reminder of her formative looks. But she had the big, gnarled hands of a buccaneer, weathered and ruthless, and when she bent her fingers over her cane, the knuckles grew like hunchbacks.

"Well, what do you want, young woman? Some morsel you can take away and chew on?"

Sybil inhaled, as the housekeeper slipped in with tea on a trolley, stared at her for a minute, and left. "I've always hoped to meet you. I wondered if you'd ever had time to look at any of my novels I sent you."

Grant shook her head and waved at piles of books stacked on the floor, overflowing from the shelves. "Authors send me books from all over the world. I don't read people I don't know. My eyes are going now."

"When you can, who do you read?" Sybil asked softly.

"The people of my generation." Slowly, Grant poured tea. "We had a sense of what was clearly valuable and what was not. Today, so much is neither. And the classics, of course."

"What women?" Sybil relaxed a little, leaning forward, accepting a cup of tea.

"Yourcenar, Welty, Bowen. Woolf, when she's not being a drip." She pointed her finger suddenly. "But don't fall into that disgusting feminist attitude of denigrating the men. No woman writers have given us the genius of Schiller and Goethe, Chekhov, Stendhal, Camus. And the black sanity of Kafka. Females still have to get rid of a lot of fatty tissue."

Sybil responded slowly because she was trying to memorize every word Grant spoke, every gesture. "Do you think it will ever happen?"

Grant shook her head. "Not in my time. Or yours, my dear. Maybe never, unless we switch glands with the men." She looked hard at Sybil. "What do you read besides the classics? How are women your age educating themselves?"

"I try to read all the good writers." Sybil felt suddenly shy. "Updike, Oates, Lessing, Mailer, Styron."

Grant nodded, almost impatient. "I dip into those youngsters now and then. They sound traumatized, if you ask me. You read one line of some of those writers and know all they have to say, all they will ever say. One day they stub their toe, and they write about that for the rest of their life."

She sucked on her teacup for a while, then carried on.

"That Didion girl. 'Fear is an arrangement of fifteen amino acids.' All her stuff sounds like that. Like she wasn't kissed enough in the cradle. And that Percy fellow. He wrote a beauty of a book, *The Last Gentleman*. But he keeps dwelling on the same question: 'Does one knock after a shot?' At some point you have to answer the question and get on to the next thought."

With great concentration she watched her trembling hand bring a small cake to her lips. She chewed for a time.

"And those two firecats, Hellman and McCarthy. Embarrassments. If they can't write anymore, instead of backbiting each other they should let their teats drag in the dust and go back to drinking or gardening."

Sybil laughed, delighted.

"That's why I don't make public appearances anymore," Grant said. "I just go out in the yard and bay at the moon."

"People would come in the hundreds to hear you talk." Sybil put out her hand, but remembered who it was she thought needed comforting, and withdrew it.

"No, my dear. They'd come to see if I still had my

teeth. I'm a bewilderment to the literary world because my legend preceded my death. That's not supposed to happen. Most people probably think I'm sitting here sucking figs and estrogen, defecating behind my sofa like Somerset Maugham."

She stared into the fireplace as if alone, and Sybil leaned closer. "All of my contemporaries read you. I always go back to your books when I'm lost. We don't have many heroes anymore."

Grant responded mildly, "That's gratifying to hear. Otherwise old age is just a doddering leprosy." She pursed her lips, tough again. "But I'm not gaga yet. I still maintain a clumsy access to thought."

She had never married, never had children, only a string of lovers throughout her life, each of whom she had outlived. Now she pointed to the closed door, the housekeeper crashing around in the hall outside.

"Wilma keeps me alert, my oldest living friend. We play chess every evening. She's like a barracuda. Sits here waiting to castle my knight."

Sybil noticed her tea was cold as she sipped it, knowing she would soon have to leave. Grant was staring past her, the way people do when they're weary.

"Is it silly to ask if your life has been happy, Miss Grant?"

"Yes, it's a silly question. Happiness is a coma. If you're working hard, you don't have time to worry about whether you're happy. The best part of my life was the creating. And a trip to Sri Lanka once. It was Ceylon then. The man in my life at the time had died or left me—who remembers? I couldn't work. So Wilma and I packed our bags, headed for Ceylon, and laughed our way around the world. It was glorious, and after six months we came home, and I was able to work again."

Grant nodded toward the sound of the housekeeper. "Never underestimate friendship. Go back to the Greeks. They understood it."

Her thoughts eclipsed each other, another sign of fatigue.

"Now there is no travel. My pleasures are simple. A glass of sherry, a sweet, good music, a few hours a day to read. The rest of the hours of each day and each night spent trying to understand what it is I already know." She looked at Sybil. "Why did you send me your books?"

Tears sprang up. Sybil blinked quickly, and they dissolved. "I've written three novels. Some reviews were kind, some were awful. They don't sell well. I feel guilty. Maybe better writers aren't getting published because I am. I've wondered if I'm good enough to keep writing."

Grant shook her head. "You sound very young. Brush up on your Plato and Emerson." Suddenly she yawned, surprising herself.

The housekeeper appeared as if by remote control, and Sybil fidgeted, waiting to be dismissed.

"Write down the titles of your books again." Grant handed her a pen. "Maybe we'll dig them out of the mulch and have a look."

She waved at Wilma. The woman hobbled across the room and helped her to her feet. Sybil stood slowly, trying to slouch so she would not have to look down at her. But Grant refused to look up and stared at a point somewhere near her shoulder. She did not extend her hand.

"Thank you so much for today," Sybil said. "May I visit you again?"

"Perhaps. When the time is right."

Sybil backed toward the door of the room, and as she turned, following Wilma to the hall, Grant added in a small voice, "And don't forget the carrot cake."

* * *

In the late afternoon, Sybil sat typing notes on her impressions of Victoria Grant, as Kate pulled up to the carriage house on the Harley-Davidson with Bruce. Through the window Sybil caught his ram's-fleece, sunbleached hair, the pouty lips and blank eyes, a surfer saving his focus for the sea. His muscled shoulders gleamed in the sun as he U-turned in the driveway and took off. Kate slammed into the house, rabid, her thick black eyebrows arched like bat wings.

"Can you believe it?" She was holding her arm in front of her like a club. "Bruce's eighteen-year-old ex-girlfriend attacked me. Said I strut around the beach like I was one of earth's greatest hits. I smacked her and told her to act her age." She caught her breath. "Do you know what she did? She bit me!"

Sybil laughed out loud. "You told her to act *her* age?"

Kate looked at her for a long time, then sat down slowly, staring at the bleeding teeth marks on her arm. "Look, I'm having a little period of insanity, OK, Sybil? I know I'm just an ego trip for Bruce, but the kid pays more attention to me in an hour than Walter did in a year. When Bruce screws me, he actually looks at me."

Sybil crossed the room, leaned down to Kate, studied her arm, and spoke softly. "In all fairness, Kate, weren't there times Walter was probably afraid to look at you? You're a woman of violent mood swings."

She nodded slowly. "Come to think of it, a lot of times my responses to Walter weren't really responses. I was just relieving aggressions. He'd come home and say, 'How was your day?' and I'd want to hit him in the mouth."

Sybil tipped a bottle while Kate flinched, studying the bubbly erosion of peroxide on her bite mark.

"Funny, the perspective distance gives you." Kate sighed. "I see now I blamed Walter for the fact I never accomplished anything extraordinary."

Nursing the bandaged arm, Kate slowly climbed the stairs and lay down, thinking of her husband. She tried to imagine life without him, and her eyes filled. As far back as she could see, Walter was beside her, her marriage had been her childhood. But motherhood had been old age. It seemed she had missed the transition in between.

Kate drifted off now, dreaming of her kids. It was shocking to her how instantly, how deeply she loved the twins, for she had planned to love only one child and wasn't a woman who made fast turns. But they grew too quickly, and each year she had lost more control.

As she fired the latest in a string of cooks, Walter would come home and find her grinding out some sad meal in her fur coat, with no time or thought to remove it when she came in from shopping. Sometimes she sat down to dinner still wearing her lynx—with egg or honey, something glutinous, matting a sleeve—and Walter would study her.

"Kate, why not take off your coat?"

She would stare pointedly at the twins. "I didn't have time."

When they were six she let the cleaning woman take them home for a weekend, and for three days and nights Kate slept the sleep of the dead. On the fourth day Walter brought the twins home.

"Do you care," he asked, "that all she fed them was root beer and Chuckles? They threw up in the car."

"Care?" She turned on him. "Do you know what it is to have them hanging on me day and night for six years? Did you notice my nap lasted seventy-two hours?"

"Kate, we can afford the best mother's-help in Beverly Hills. Why do you try to do it alone?"

"Because," she cried, hands shaking, "you have to explain things to help. How can I explain when I have trouble finishing a thought?"

Besides, mother's-help made her sound deficient, a mother but only fractionally. And there were times Kate knew she was a mother completely.

When the twins were seven, she waited for them outside their school one day, talking mindlessly with a neighboring mother. And then the woman caught her attention.

"My boy came home last week penniless. Candy, he said. That's where his money goes every week. One night I went through his pockets. Kate, do you know what I found? Acid, speed, poppers, sleeping pills." She pointed to the school yard where the children played. "They're selling that poison right here. Teenagers are dealing that shit to our kids."

Something in Kate's face made the woman step back. Kate's eyes swept around, measuring the size of the children in the yard. It was a grade school, but some of the boys milling around were teenagers. She lost her vision for a minute and concentrated on her sense of touch, rummaging in the trunk of the Mercedes until a tire iron bulged cold and heavy in her hand.

The neighbor shouted behind Kate, but she was gone, lynx coat flying open, running beside the school yard fence until she reached the open gate, yelling to the twins. Other children screamed, jumping out of her way. The tall boys, the teenagers, seemed to dissolve. Looking up, the twins saw her coming, the tire iron raised. Justin began to cry. Kate flooded over them, her hair, her perfume, her fur, gathering them to her. The tire iron pressed into Nora's little back.

"My God. My God," Kate whispered. "Are you all right, honey? Honey?" She looked from one to the other.

They nodded, dumb.

"Did those"—she looked around—"older boys offer you anything? Candy? Drugs? Did they give or sell you anything?"

"Hershey kisses." Nora dug in her pocket, frightened. "My best friend gave me some." She pulled them out soft and deformed, silver-covered chocolate blobs.

Kate hugged them both to her, shaking. They stood against her, feeling confused and important.

A yard proctor approached. "What's wrong, Mrs. Castaldi? What is it?"

Kate stood, glaring at the man, and spoke slowly. "You allow teenagers to sell . . . drugs to these children."

"We try to keep them out," he explained.

"How?!" She pointed to a tall boy just sloping out of the yard.

She caused enough commotion for the school to hire a security guard. Still, every day at different hours Kate cruised the street, staring at the school yard from her car, the tire iron beside her, looking for boys who were too tall, too old. There were times when she had been a mother completely, but those times had diminished in proportion to the twins' growing up.

At the Maidscott Beach now she gazed wistfully at families, women and husbands building sandcastles with their kids. Since the twins were infants she could not remember their being together at a beach or in fact anywhere. Was it her fault? Had she frightened her family away?

Now she wondered what it had been like for Walter the past few years, coming home at the end of the day to a wife perennially rehearsing for war. And to kids who camped out in the house, skateboarding to meals and afterwards Hondaing off into the dusk, uncaring, entirely uncaring. If they had been a family, it was only in the sense of people sitting over meals, moving their jaws together. These images came to Kate in a fitful sleep, a sorrowful summing up.

Around noon the next day the phone rang, and Sybil picked it up on the second ring, expecting Will. "Hello?"

For a moment there was no sound except the static of long-distance, and then a female voice.

"Sybil?"

"Yes. Who's this?"

"It's Nora. Please don't hang up. Is my mother there?"

"Ahh, how'd you get this number?"

"Well, it's summer. I figured you'd be out at the beach somewhere. I spent about forty dollars calling bookstores out there, asking if they knew you. The store in East Hampton said they knew the house you're staying in." She paused. "I said I was your niece, and there was a death in the family, so they gave me the name the house is listed under."

Sybil smiled. "Aren't you a clever girl, Nora."

"Don't worry. I didn't tell my dad. Can I speak to her?"

"Honey, I honestly don't know."

"Please. Just let me hear her voice."

Sybil looked through the screen door at Kate, stretched out on a chaise sunbathing, her perfect head twisted slightly as if experiencing a cruel solar tug to the brain.

"Kate?" She waved the phone. "It's Nora. LA."

Kate sat up and looked down at the grass for a

while, then staggered to the shade of the patio, adjusted to the light, and reached inside for the phone. "How did you find me?" She listened a few seconds, then answered. "Brilliant. Does he know where I am?"

"No. Listen, Mother, I'm furious with Daddy for cheating on you. I just wanted you to know that."

"Oh, really." Kate laughed, sarcastic. "I didn't know you cared."

"Look, I know you've been unhappy with us, but I also know you've been loyal to Daddy all these years. What he did was sleazy."

Nora's voice suddenly touched her, the voice of a frightened young girl trying to sound old and wise. "How do you know I've been loyal?"

"Because you were too proud not to be." Kate snorted as her daughter continued. "I believe in genital allegiance. I just want you to know I'm on your side, even though we haven't been close."

"I wanted to be close, Nora, but you grew up. I couldn't control you."

There was a long pause as if Nora were gathering facts. "Mother, I'm not a mob. You weren't supposed to control me. You were supposed to try to understand me. Instead you resented me, the way I talked, the way I ate—"

"You only ate food I could hear."

"—the way I laughed, the way I dressed."

Kate sighed, then sat on the floor, hugging the phone. "It happened too fast, honey. One day you were a little cannibal crawling all over me. I looked down at my watch, and when I looked up you were a woman—drinking, doping, sleeping around."

Nora sniffled. "I'm not perfect. Anyway, cock teasing went out with padded bras. Look, I don't want to fight. I—are you coming home soon?"

Kate fought to keep her voice even. "You don't

need me. You've got Orinoco or Bogota or whatever the hell his name is."

"That's over," Nora said. "I caught Trinidad with another girl." She cleared her throat. "Look, I want to apologize for all that 'support system' crap. And Justin too. We were just trying to be tough. OK?"

Kate thought of her son, Justin, a small-boned, small-muscled young man with a handsome face like his father's. Because he resembled Walter so much, she had always been strongly attracted to Justin but reluctant to get involved with him. "How is Justin?"

"He's in drug therapy." Nora's voice began to sound weary. "He and some guys knocked over a gas station to finance a couple of grams of cocaine. Daddy handled it in between dragneting LA for you."

"Some family," Kate groaned. "No wonder I went berserk."

"By the way, Daddy got rid of the starlet. I think he went impotent when he found the koi fish. That was heavy, Mother. It was so beautiful."

"It was a fish."

"It was a trophy winner," Nora protested. "And the cars were classics. Don't you see—hobbies are what keep husbands faithful."

Kate laughed out loud. "Honey, that's a good theory. But I shot up the fish *after* I found your father's bimbo."

"I know. I'm just trying to understand things." Nora paused. "What will you do at the end of the summer when Sybil goes back to the city?"

Kate hesitated. "I'm making decisions."

"Are you thinking of divorcing Daddy?"

"Yes."

"Oh, Jesus." Nora began to cry. "We're all falling apart."

"You're telling me." Kate wiped her nose on her wrist. "I have to hang up now."

"Can I call you again, Mother?"

"Yes." After a while Kate walked out on the lawn and looked at Sybil. "My daughter misses me. Imagine."

Sybil slipped her arm around her shoulder, hugging her. "What are you going to do in September, Kate?"

"I don't know." She gave Sybil a piercing look. "What are you going to do?"

Chapter
10

"WHAT ABOUT your sperm count?" Will asked.

Tom Fairmont looked down at his crotch as if something were leaking. "What about it?" He leaned at the tiller, tacking upwind, and crossed his legs, suddenly defensive.

"You're in your mid-thirties, right?" Will said. "I just read that the sperm count of the average male has plummeted to an all-time low. Societal pressure, pollution, tight jeans. And you sit crouched over a typewriter all day. These things decimate the sperm."

Tom wished fleetingly they were in a rowboat instead of his sailboat, so he could smack the kid with an oar. "Will, the last time I noticed, my ejaculation was salubrious, rich as Rheingold foam."

"That doesn't mean anything," Will persisted. "Your sperm count could be as low as fifty million per milliliter. A young guy like me, it's probably a hundred and fifty million. You know, strong swimmers, healthy tails."

"So what's your point?"

"Well, don't you ever think of having kids before it's too late?"

Suddenly Tom knew the point. Blair had sent

Will. She was so desperate she used a twenty-two-year-old as a go-between.

"Yeah, Will. I'd like to have a couple of kids . . . someday."

"Man, society's getting weird." Will stood up and reached in the cooler for a beer, almost tipping the boat with his height. "People my age don't want kids because they're afraid they'll be nuclear humanoids. And people your age have put kids on hold until you're in the right mood." He shook his head. "In another decade babies will be coming out of petri dishes."

"Relax." Tom laughed. "Things aren't that bad."

Will studied him. "Know what else this article said? Fifteen percent of the women now pregnant by artificial insemination are unmarried and living alone by choice. Fifteen percent."

"Where did you read that?"

"*Time* magazine." Will shook his head back and forth. "Tell you, if I were thirty-three, those percentages would make me feel slightly dispensable."

Tom looked out at the bay, then back at Will. "Well, at your age, you don't have to worry for a while."

He seemed like a nice guy, but there was something about his responses, a real lack of muscle, that irritated Will. He was like that new strain of men the article described—laid-back types who didn't want or couldn't handle women with big demands. Maybe it was a backlash from the women's movement. In any case, men like Tom struck Will as aging thumb suckers, terrified of responsibility.

"I am worried," he argued. "Sybil says I'm too young for her. She's going to save herself for some old geezer who won't even be able to get it up, much less give her a kid."

Confused, Tom pulled back from the tiller. "Sybil? I thought you were talking about me and Blair."

Will stared at him, amazed. "Man, why do you think I've been bugging you on the phone? I'm in love with Sybil, and I want to marry her. I could use some male support, Tom. And, well, I figured you know Sybil." He saw the irony of turning to Tom for advice, but desperation gave him the selective sense of a drowning man.

Tom whistled low. "Will, I can't tell you how to court a woman like Sybil Wade. She probably doesn't need to have children. Or a husband."

Will rolled his head around, exasperated. "Oh, come on, Tom. Everybody needs someone. If Sybil hadn't been lonely, we never would have hooked up."

As tactfully as possible, Tom answered, "That doesn't mean she needs a permanent hookup." What he was trying to say was that he thought Sybil was driven, and it made her selfish, tough. But he was getting in too deep.

Will sat forward, looking suddenly old and yet so pained he was doubly youthful. "You don't think she really loves me, do you?"

Tom half-smiled. "At your age, do you even know what love is?"

"At your age, do you?"

Tom shrugged. "Probably not. Sometimes I think it's just curiosity in heat. When that's satisfied, boredom sets in."

"Is that how you feel about Blair?" Will frowned.

"No. I really respect Blair." He hesitated, wanting accuracy. "I trust her. But she smothers me."

Will reached for another beer in the cooler. "I wish Sybil could be more like that."

"No you don't." Tom shook his head. "Blair's an extreme example of the Catch-22 of modern women.

They don't want to depend on men, but they need us around to show how independent they are of us." He had chugged half a dozen beers in the sun and could tell by Will's expression he was on the verge of confusing him again. "Look," Tom went on patiently, "if a man's not around, a woman isn't independent. She's *alone.*"

Will shook his head, more and more bewildered. "Well, does that mean women need us even though they don't want to? Or they don't really need us but they want to?"

Now Tom stood up, half drunk. "Who knows? Since we've had this huge meltdown of absolutes, no one knows who's dependent on whom for what." He waved his hands around like a crazy man. "Females are so busy flagellating themselves being superwomen"—then he grabbed his crotch, jiggling it— "they come home at night to their husbands or lovers and can't remember who this guy is with his cock in his hand like a switchblade, trying to mug them once a week!"

Will eyeballed him. "Say, maybe you should lay off the beers."

Suddenly the sails caught a breeze, and the boat made an offering of its speed. The sun was a hard, gold burn like whiskey on the tongue as they skated across Gardiner's Bay.

Tom half-sat, half-fell down, and waved his arms at the bay, the wooded shores. "Life is so beautiful. Why do we have to fuck it up with absolutes anyway?"

Will leaned forward. "Seriously, Tom, haven't you ever wanted to get married?"

He looked at Will for a long time, as if he had gone to sleep with his eyes open. Then he nodded slowly. "I almost married the woman I lived with before I met Blair. She made a lot more money than I did—

like Blair, come to think of it. So she sort of ran the house. Then she started calling the shots in bed." Tom winced, remembering. "I mean, if she was on top, I knew it was Friday. If she had a heavy work schedule for nine days, then for nine days there was no sex. When she wanted sex and I didn't—I was depressed or pissed off—she treated me like I was queer. I couldn't just roll over and say I had a headache, like a woman can. So I'd climb in her and bang away, dreaming of a Seconal." He sighed and shook his head. "I don't ever want to live like that again."

By now the beer had hit Will too. "Hell, why didn't you shape her up if you loved her?" he shouted. "That's what's wrong with you guys today, you're too wimpy. You can't handle a clinging vine like Blair, who happens to be terrific, and you don't want to deal with really strong women. What are you, secret faggots?"

Tom smiled, but with effort. "I'd like to have this conversation with you again, Will, in about ten or fifteen years."

Will slowed down. "I know, I know. I'm wet behind the ears. That's what my parents said. I told them I was going to marry Sybil anyway."

Tom's jaw slowly dropped. "You told . . . your parents?"

He nodded. "My mother cried so hard, she threw up on my father. Then they called the parish priest."

"Did you have to tell them exactly how old Sybil was?"

"My mother found her books at the library." He shrugged. "Her birthdate's inside the dust jacket. Man, that priest has been bugging me all week."

Tom suddenly leaned back, laughing so hard he spilled beer all over his chest. "Oh, God, I don't believe it! This is what you call a *real* situation comedy."

Will scratched his scalp viciously with both hands, as if it was full of nits, then stood up, shaking his head, trying to clear the confusion.

"Goddamn it. I'm asking for something as normal as marriage and kids, to a woman I love. And what do I get? My folks throwing up, telling me to leave the house for good. Some guy who wears gowns and flicks holy water at people lecturing *me* on perversion. And a man I come to for advice telling me marriage is dead because there's been a meltdown of absolutes." He doubled up his fist and hit the side of the boat with it. "Won't anybody take me seriously?"

Tom looked at him and sobered up a little. "Probably not, Will. Probably not. Sit down a minute. I want to ask you something."

Will sat down and stared at him, ready for anything.

"How did you get so involved with Sybil? I mean, didn't you know any girls your own age?"

"Sure I did. I was dating this model—she was fun, pretty. But man, she was making eighty grand a year. It was embarrassing. Then there was an art student. We went around for a while, but there was no real chemistry with either of them. I never felt with any woman what I feel now."

"What about girls in your acting class?"

He shook his head. "Too hungry. We're all out there hustling, but some of those females are . . . well, you can't call them overliberated—they're just born sharks."

Tom frowned like a concerned father. "What do people say? I mean, you and Sybil together. Do they think it's a joke?"

Will straightened up. "Why the hell would anyone think that? I know three girls my age right now living with guys in their forties. Come on, Tom."

Still resisting, Tom shook his head. An affair maybe, but marriage was a whole other bag.

Will leaned toward him, his pupils huge like thumbtacks. "Look, how much more do I have to experience before I qualify as an adult? I'm a generation behind Sybil, but we grew up faster. At thirteen I was a virgin. At fourteen I wasn't. I've done grass and coke and speed. I've been arrested. I've paid for two abortions because I knew I was the father both times, but the women didn't want to get married and neither did I."

He took a deep breath, popped open a beer, and continued. "I've hitchhiked my way around Europe, I've been hungry, and I've been cold. I've worked as an usher, a waiter, and a nurse's aide. I've slept with about a dozen women. I've lived by myself for four years, so don't talk to me about loneliness. And I've thought seriously of suicide when I lost important acting jobs."

He looked at Tom, and Tom looked at him, impressed.

"I'm not always sure we have a future, Tom, and when I am, I'm not always sure it's the one we think we're going to get. But whatever's coming, I want to share it with Sybil. She taught me something acting couldn't—how to love another human." He nudged Tom's knee with his beer. "So tell me, what else do I need to experience?"

Tom still shook his head, as if dealing with the logic of a child.

Will stood and looked down at him. "You're jealous, aren't you? I've got the balls to make a fool out of myself for this woman, but you don't even have the courage to ask Blair to live with you. Has it ever occurred to you, Tom, that she'd stop smothering you if you gave her some hope for the future? Huh?"

Silently, Tom headed the boat toward the inlet

and the slip at the dock near East Hampton. They anchored it and secured the rope on the pilings; then Will turned to him.

"Thanks, Tom, for all the great advice."

"Look, Will, those are only my opinions. That doesn't mean they're right."

"OK, OK." Will shuffled his feet, looking down. "I'm curious. Do you ever get the feeling life's passing you by?"

Tom nodded and looked out toward the water. "I was hurt by the woman I mentioned. Badly. After that you retreat a little."

"How long have you been retreating?"

"Oh, a few years."

"Wow." Will shook his head. "I'll tell you, I learned a few things today. If there aren't any rules, I'm going to make my own." They shook hands, and he walked away, then turned back. "I'm going to marry Sybil. What are you going to do?"

Tom watched him walk off, reckless and undefeated.

Chapter
11

SYBIL TESTED the tires of her bike for air, then swung out into Seth Lane. Headed for Montauk Highway and a good, long ride to East Hampton, she vaguely noticed a two-tone Fiesta parked outside her driveway. When she was a block or so ahead, the driver started the car and followed her at a distance.

After a mile or so, Sybil turned off the highway again, taking the back roads along the ocean into the village. After a long day at the typewriter, she was like someone in a coma, unseeing, unhearing, until she was on the bike, speed charging the blood in her veins, feeling the hot sun then cool shade as she shot under trees, bucking potholes, yipping out loud like something untied. On especially productive days she could bike for miles.

At Georgica Beach she braked, a rush of blood pumping color to her cheeks, and watched a late-day sun riding down the sky, bathers wading with their dogs, and surfers in wet suits jockeying waves. On a big blackboard someone had chalked the surf conditions: "Today's phenomenon plays song to a rhythm analogous to an endless serenade." She laughed a big, hearty laugh, giving her tired mind over to her

body, then headed down Lily Pond Lane into town,
the Fiesta following a block behind.

While she picked up some Walkman batteries at a
cut-rate drugstore, the driver of the car sat double-
parked. After a few minutes, Sybil reappeared and
peddled the bike across Main Street, paused in
front of Dean & DeLuca, the *haute* deli where they
charged customers three dollars for a palmful of
framboises fraîches in a paper doily, changed her
mind, and headed for a ninety-eight-cent box of plain
old raspberries at the East Hampton A&P.

Strolling the aisles of the big, homely store, Sybil
waved to a cashier, a sweet-faced woman with uncanny blue hair who had read her books. The two of
them had a standard repartee: Every week when Sybil checked out with the *National Enquirer,* the cashier would point to the tabloid and yell, "Trash!"
Sybil would flash an innocent smile and say, "Who,
me?" while shoppers stared at her, suspicious.

She liked cruising the A&P because it was mas-
sive and gave her a chance to unobtrusively study
the different fauna of East Hampton. The locals were
leathery-skinned men and women, quiet and handsome in the way of farming and fishing people,
whose lack of pretension made them seem aloof.

Then there were the summer people, the season-
als, who tried to look local with faded shirts and khakis, and rundown shoes, but their checkbooks gave
them away. They were always whipping them out
with cashless ease. Thirdly were the trippers, week-
enders and day people, who elbowed through the
aisles with a fanatical look, aware of the shortness of
time. With their six-packs and Trail Mix, they jos-
tled each other in the ten-items-or-less line, slicked
with Coconut Jojoba and Quik-Tan, ahead of the
game in their lunge for the sun.

Now, as Sybil brooded over the imported cheeses,

she lifted her eyes and caught a face that did not belong to any of these groups. At the end of the aisle, fingering the yogurts, was a stocky woman in a plaid, no-press pantsuit with bell-bottoms. She looked forty-five to fifty, with a pale, pleasant face, a graying permanent gone to frizz, and cheeks immolated with rouge. She was hugging a brown imitation-leather handbag against her side like a hot-water bottle, and through the toes of her high-heeled sandals her stockings showed, reinforced at the toes.

The woman would have looked at home in one of those out-of-town bus-tour groups clustered around Radio City Music Hall during the holidays or maybe at a Sears and Roebuck in a rural shopping mall. But here in the village of East Hampton, the tony end of Long Island where people strained to blend, this woman did an awkward thing: She stood out. That she had no grocery cart and seemed to stroll the aisles absentmindedly made her seem even more bereft of locale. Yet the two times Sybil walked past her, she suddenly took a convulsive interest in whatever jar her hand fell upon.

Dismissing her, Sybil moved to the fresh produce where an aging prep in a Lacoste shirt stood eyeballing a chesty, young, blonde clerk arranging the grapes. He was a well-known news commentator who looked like a dropout from Cheever country and reminded Sybil of a character from one of her novels—one of those men who fantasized about beautiful, lusty women but married mothering little Cheeverettes because lust was more manageable as a fantasy.

He moved closer to the grape girl, on the verge of a flirtation, caught Sybil watching, and pushed his cart off down the aisle. She smiled to herself, turned, and caught an eye and an immolated cheek trained on her from the corner of the diet soda section. She shrugged, chose a box of raspberries and a handful of plums, and headed for the checkout line.

"Trash!" the cashier called to her.

Sybil laughed and waved, flipping through the *National Enquirer.* Then, remembering toothpaste, she left the checkout line and made her way toward that section. Vacillating in front of the Colgate shelf—flavored gel or regular??—she looked up suddenly. Not more than four feet away, the plaid-suited woman was staring at her with frightening vivisectional interest.

With a small intake of breath, Sybil backed up a step. They were in a deserted aisle, and rounding the corner, a clerk saw what looked to him like a female standoff. He watched, curious, as the short, older woman breathed heavily, rippling plaid. The leggy woman in wrinkled shorts turned to him, as if for help, then changed her mind.

"Ladies?. . ." He looked from one to the other, but they ignored him.

"Do I . . . know you?" Sybil asked her, half-frightened.

"Please," the woman answered but drew her shoulders up, as if saying something else. Then she stared at the clerk, dismissing him.

Alone in the aisle again, they measured each other, and Sybil recognized the face of the driver in the strange car parked outside her driveway and again double-parked outside the drugstore. It was like a match struck in the dark. This woman was following her.

"Why?. . ."

"Please. I'm Will's mother."

The shelves on either side of Sybil's head seemed to waver, as if the rows of packaged goods had been painted on curtains in a breeze. After a few moments, her tongue unclove from the roof of her mouth.

"Mrs. Leahy . . ."

"I want to talk to you."

In spite of the tacky pantsuit, she had a sudden wintry dignity that made Sybil painfully aware of herself, how sloppy she looked in a wrinkled shirt and shorts, and old cowboy boots gone at the heel. She had no sense of leaving the A&P. She put down the groceries and bypassed the checkout lines like someone walking in a fog. Moving ahead of her, Sybil was eerily conscious of the fact that Will's mother had followed her on the bike, studying her shoulders and back and behind for miles—a woman who probably wanted to strike her dead.

In the parking lot the macadam under her feet vibrated, and she realized it was her body. She kept starting to say something, then looked at Will's mother's eyes, and her sentences died under the impact. The two of them swayed indecisively, not sure what to do or where to go. Mrs. Leahy was pointedly not inviting her to sit in her car.

"Would . . . you like to go back to my house?" Sybil croaked.

"No."

In the sunlight Sybil could see that the cheeks were not rouged but webbed with tiny exploding capillaries, and thinking of cheeks, she suddenly tugged at the back of her shorts, pulling them lower. Will's mother looked down at the shorts as if addressing them. Her voice was shrill, and she seemed to be panting.

"Will described the house. That's how I knew where . . . I wanted to see what kind of woman you were."

Her handbag slid down to her wrist, and she caught it by suddenly lifting her forearm, as if warming up for a karate chop. Then she seemed to lunge at her.

"You can't marry my son!"

Sybil closed her eyes, trying to keep her balance.

"You're sucking his youth out of him. What is a woman like you doing with him except for . . . sex."

At the mention of sex, Mrs. Leahy tilted against the hood of her car as though she were going to faint, for she hadn't expected to deal so quickly with the root of a situation she wanted dissolved. Sybil stared at her for a while, wanting her next words to count for something and be remembered, and then she leaned toward her.

"I love Will. It has very little to do with sex."

Blood mounted the woman's neck, suffusing her face, and she moved in close.

"You're my age."

"Yes. Almost."

"It's sick."

Sybil backed off a step, trying to grasp the sum of this woman: narrow-minded, first-generation Irish-Catholic. But she was also Will's mother.

"We should go somewhere and talk, Mrs. Leahy. There's a pond nearby. It's quiet."

She shook her head up and down, blinking rapidly. She hadn't expected to meet this Sybil, only to look at her. But having confronted her, she felt herself revved up for a good fight or a good cry, she wasn't sure which.

Sybil spun out across Main Street, down Dunemere Lane, heading for Hook Pond, a bird preserve near the ocean. She breathed in and out so harshly, the membranes of her nose and throat seemed suddenly dry, and she had to urinate badly. She was peddling the bike at such a dizzying speed, she had the sensation of flying and realized fright was the spur. That and the awareness of the woman's eyes on her, right behind her in the car, making Sybil ashamed of the difference in their bodies.

They pulled up to a wide, lush lawn of astonishingly green grass, where Sybil collapsed on a bench and tried to catch her breath. Will's mother sat at the other end of the bench trying furiously not to gape at the clipped hedges of beach estates across the water, swans gliding in tandem, and the equal symmetry of algae floating down the pond.

There was something packed about her, a field-hand huskiness, so that her waist disappeared when she sat. Sybil realized without realizing it that she was recording her: the hair like brown and gray wires; eyes blue like Will's but watery and the lids sturgeon-red. Her lips were chapped like a child's, and just below her ear was a small, iridescent wart, its cilia catching the sun. The hands were raw, like someone deeply in laundry or the weather.

Staring at her, Sybil was confused and disarmed. She had the body of a nursing mammal meant for large broods and yet the deprived expression of a mother with an only child. Below unplucked eyebrows of a woman without strategy, her nostrils flared delicately, and she was modest in the way she kept her knees together as she sat. Sybil thought she probably carried a holy picture in her wallet and marked her prayer book with strips of lace.

"I'm very sorry this has happened," Sybil said softly, "that you're so upset."

Will's mother shook her gray head, and her hair shivered. "We don't know Will anymore. He comes home once a month, and after dinner we stare at our plates. He tries to talk, but all he knows is acting, acting. And now this thing with you."

Sybil slumped further down on the bench. Her nose was peeling, her hair needed cutting, her clothes pressing. In short, she did not look lovable.

169

She looked old and sloppy, and what she was about to say was kind of sloppy too, but that seemed beside the point.

"We didn't mean to get involved. We started out as friends, just friends, but . . ."

The woman gave her a floaty look, then tears fell, and her nose bloomed large and pink. "Oh, let him alone, for God's sake! You're just using him."

"I'm not. I've helped Will. We've helped each other."

"But why does he have to marry you?"

Sybil sat up at the sound of that word again, as if something with large jaws had bitten into her backbone. "When did he tell you he wanted to marry me?"

"This week. At first his father wanted to come out here after you with a gun. But then"—she shook her head, disgusted—"he came home from the pub last night grinning from ear to ear. His friends think Will's a lady killer, running around with someone like you. A chip off the old block, they said."

The more she talked, the more the brogue came through. Her heritage, Will had said, was Connemara, the wild west coast of Ireland, where people were hardbacked and poor and proud. Without warning she suddenly sobbed out loud, like something being slaughtered.

"He was an honor student. I wanted him to be a priest."

The woman seemed to collapse: her head down, her hands working her eyes, the plaid moving in all directions. Sybil's own eyes filled, and without thinking she put her arms around her. Mrs. Leahy let go for a few minutes, wailing, then suddenly she jumped back, as if she had been kidding or changed her mood. She stared at Sybil's hair, her clothes, her body, wanting to really insult her but knowing it was far beyond her natural scope.

Instead she pulled back and punched her hard in the shoulder. Sybil was flung back, and her mouth flew open in pain. It wasn't a jab she had been dealt but a virile street punch, and she rubbed her shoulder stupidly. Mrs. Leahy stared down at her fist, shocked, then dropped her hand in her lap and sagged again, mascara drooping from her lashes like ant doody. After a while she wiped her eyes and slid closer to Sybil so they could hear each other's breathing.

"Do you really want to marry my son? Do you really want his children?"

Sybil looked out at the swans on the water, then looked back at the watery blue eyes. "Yes, I do."

The woman stood and backed slowly to her car, sniffling, tuning up for another sob. She opened the car door and looked again at Sybil.

"If you really loved Will, you'd send him away. He's still a boy. He doesn't even know what pain is yet."

She sat in her car sobbing over the wheel for a minute, then blew her nose and started the engine. The car moved forward an inch or two, and then she leaned from the window, shouting, "In the name of Jesus, give him a chance!"

Chapter
12

BLAIR AND SYBIL pushed back their dinner plates and stared vacantly through the glass partition to the bar of Bobbie Van's, a Bridgehampton oasis for summering New York writers that managed to retain the simplicities of a small-town eatery. Through the years the low-profile atmosphere of the place had attracted big guns like Irwin Shaw, William Styron, Joseph Heller, the late James Jones. Sometimes they all dropped in on the same night at the same time, paralyzing other diners.

At the moment, Blair was oblivious to the people in Bobbie Van's. Leaning toward Sybil, she gripped her wineglass, alternately fascinated and appalled by Sybil's story. "And then?"

Sybil shrugged. "Then Will's mother drove away."

"My God. How did you feel? Can you remember?"

"Lousy." Sybil focused on Blair, a little drunk. "I was thinking how glad I was not to be her, how close I would come to killing me." She drank slowly from her glass. "I was also thinking what a good scene it would make someday."

Blair sat back, studying her. "Do you have to appropriate everything, Sybil? Think what she's going through."

"I know." She looked down at the table, and when she looked up she had tears in her eyes. "But when this is over, a good book is probably all I'll have."

"But then why did you tell Mrs. Leahy you wanted to marry Will and have his kids?"

She took a deep breath. "To give her dignity."

Blair dropped her voice. "Why don't you give Will some dignity? Why not tell him now that you don't want to marry him, you don't love him, it's run the course, and you're bored."

Sybil stood up and banged on the table, drawing eyes. "Because I do love him! Because I don't want to lose him. Because it's not September yet."

"You sound as screwed up as Tom. Sit down."

She sat down, embarrassed, and Blair leaned toward her, talking softly. "You underestimated Will. We all did. He's reacting the way we want men to. And you can't handle it."

Sybil grasped the table with both hands, as if for balance. "That's right, I'm screwed up. I'm scared to death. Sometimes I do want kids, but most of the time I don't. Except I always feel as if I'm going to be struck dead when I say that." Her eyes roamed around in their sockets. "And yet I can't have children just to avoid the guilt of *not* having them. Can I?"

"Just be sure," Blair whispered. "Ten years ago we didn't want kids because we were too busy marching. But ten years from now when it's too late I'd hate to hear you say you're sorry you didn't have a child but you were too busy writing novels."

Sybil calmed down for a minute and looked at her. "What about you? You're involved with someone who acts as though even living with you is illegitimate."

"Yeah." Blair nodded. "I'm beginning to think my taste in men is bad. That's what I think. What I know is I'm tired of outsmarting my ovaries. I'm thirty-eight. I want a family. If that's a cop-out, sue me."

They sat there for a minute, angry; but not with each other, maybe the times. They Sybil put her hand to her eyes.

"That poor woman. Can you imagine what it took for her to approach me? I wanted to tell her I was terrified as she was, that this New Wave amazon she was following around the A&P is a colossal screw-up. That we all are."

"The New Wave," Blair laughed, "who never reached the shore."

"Boy, what a summer." Sybil shook her head, exhausted. "Well, what *about* you and Tom?"

Blair tugged at a blonde pigtail, trying to look brave. "You're not the only one making decisions by Labor Day."

Through the glass partition to the bar, two writerish types were engaged in a contest of eyes for Blair, and a bald man with a head shaped like the serviceable end of a roll-on deodorant blinked rapidly at Sybil. She looked down, too tired to smile but afraid if she looked at him again, she would laugh.

"You know," Blair sighed, studying the writer types, "just the idea of starting over again and telling some stranger my life story exhausts me."

They both looked so sad, the men at the bar finally turned away.

"What about Kate? What's she going to do when you close the carriage house?"

Sybil shrugged. "Who knows? God, if only we had instruction sheets."

In her bedroom at the carriage house, Kate sat, frightened, confused.

Bruce stood behind her, kissing the back of her neck. "So you're gonna stick around?"

"I haven't decided that yet," she whispered.

He slid his big, rough hands under her arms, cupping her breasts from behind. His voice was hoarse.

"I thought you decided. I thought you were gonna stay for another month after everybody leaves."

She shook her head slowly.

"What's the point, Bruce? I can't keep up with you, surfing, drugging, motorcycles. I haven't got what it takes."

He pulled her up against his stomach, and she felt his penis hard against her spine.

"Baby, one thing you got is what it takes."

Gently, he slid down her shorts, and she leaned forward for him.

"So you're staying," he whispered hoarsely. "OK?"

Later, hearing him kick the hog and roar off into the dusk, Kate lay still, wondering for the hundredth time why Bruce bothered with her. She wasn't that good a lover. He was virile and crude in the way that attracted beach girls; there were half a dozen he could have had. But he kept coming back to Kate. He could not seem to get enough of her. She who, after eighteen years of marriage, felt yoked beyond appeal.

Chapter
13

Two weeks before Labor Day, Kate and Sybil lay on the beach watching singles jog by in mateless locomotion. Suddenly Will mounted a dune and walked fast, looking behind him as if he were being followed. He stopped a few yards from them.

"Sybil?"

She looked up, then went to him. "What's wrong?"

He nodded toward Kate. "I was out in back of the house when this cab pulled into the driveway. Good-looking man got out. About forty-five, fifty. Tall, tan. He didn't see me."

She snapped her eyes shut, then open. "Just go back and introduce yourself, Will. Tell him I'll be right there." Sybil breathed deep, looked out at the ocean for a minute, then moved to Kate and knelt down beside her. "He's here, Kate. At the house."

Kate looked up. Her eyes glittered, and her perfect mouth twisted, as if with limitless hate. "I don't want to see the bastard. Tell him I left. I drowned. Tell him—"

"Just stay here, Kate. OK?"

Walter Castaldi sat on the patio staring at Will's back, at how caringly he clipped the hedge. Kate's husband was a blandly handsome man with gray-

176

brown hair and brown eyes, a strong, perfect nose, and full Latin lips. There was a threatening double chin, though, and a looseness in the waist pushing against his linen jacket. He looked more like an actor on a lazy diet than the head of an electronics corporation supplying video equipment to the major film producers on the West Coast.

In the early sixties, Walter had been a stockbroker who bought into a fledgling electronics company, eventually buying out the owner in California and moving his family there. His good looks and success were tempered by two things: a passion for loud shirts and a nervous habit of fingering his nostrils.

"Hi, Sybil." He stood as she crossed the lawn. "How are you?" They hugged, and he held her for a minute because he needed to. "I know Kate's here."

She started to shake her head no, but it seemed pointless. "She's down on the beach, Walter. Have you met Will?"

The men nodded at each other again, then she took Walter inside and mixed a pitcher of martinis.

"How is she?" he asked nervously.

"Very angry. Mostly at herself, I think."

They moved to the patio and sat.

"Does she want a divorce?"

"I don't know, Walter. I think what she wants more than anything is to feel valuable. This isn't all your fault, you know. Kate feels she dropped the ball years ago."

"I love her so much." He looked down, wringing his hands. "I don't want to lose her."

"I know that." She touched his arm gently.

He drank his drink down in three gulps and flicked at his nose.

"I'm not here to absolve myself, Sybil. I've known you almost twenty years, so I'll talk straight. I didn't want another woman. Once or twice at those electronics conventions in Tokyo, sure they brought on the geishas. But it was just physical release. It lasted about three minutes. That was maybe twice in all the years I've been married."

He looked out across the lawn as if reading from prompter cards.

"Even after eighteen years, Kate was still the only woman I wanted. But she turned away from me. The last few years I'd lie beside her, wanting her. I mean, I was glowing in the dark, like this radioactive thing." He glanced at Sybil, embarrassed. "And she'd lie there listening to me deal with these erections. Then after a while there weren't any more erections. I'd become a castrato, dreaming she wanted to bump me off. Things got weird."

Sybil leaned toward him.

"It's weird everywhere, Walter." She nodded toward Will. "He's not the gardener, you know."

He studied Will—bare-chested, muscled, viciously young—then shook his head.

"Jesus, I'm supposed to be a smart man. I can't figure things anymore. In LA now you see ten-year-old girls wearing brassieres and high heels. Their forty-year-old mothers are wearing purple punk hairdos and short shorts and chewing bubble gum."

Sybil pointed at the punk-rock T-shirt covering her bikini, and they both laughed.

"Where are you staying?" she asked.

"At the Huntting Inn in East Hampton. I'll stay there until Kate sees me, Sybil. I don't care if it takes until Christmas."

"What about the kids?"

Walter looked down, brooding over his seventeen-year-old twins, then he looked up, sad. "Nora got accepted at UCLA for the fall. She says if Kate doesn't come home, she's not going." He shrugged. "Justin won't be going to college. He hates books. Thanks to his mother, he was frightened by words at an early age."

Sybil leaned forward, tapping his arm. "You can't blame it all on her, Walter. Some women don't have the right metabolism for motherhood, especially mothering twins."

"I've thought of that," he said. "I should have been home more often when they were young. But I was chasing my first million. Then her moods got scary. I used to make up excuses to stay late at the office."

He flicked at his nose again.

"But I'm not functioning without her. Now I don't even make it to the office. Sybil, I'll do anything. Sell my business, move back east if she wants. I can make money anywhere."

He suddenly hunched forward, half-smiling.

"You know the funny thing? Kate was a lousy housewife. Couldn't manage maids. Tried to do it all herself. Man, dishes were always greasy. Clean pots would slide out of your hands. She'd only sweep the relevant parts of the room. You know, where you walked."

Sybil smiled, imagining Kate as a housewife who tried to outsmart dirt instead of attacking it.

"And her cooking." Walter frowned. "It always tasted like she was mad at me. I love cinnamon toast for breakfast, very simple. You butter toast and sprinkle sugar and cinnamon on it, right?"

She giggled. They were on their third drink by now.

"But Kate would blanket the toast with cinnamon. It was horrible. I couldn't swallow it. Then she'd stand there cursing me, saying I couldn't eat her food because I didn't love her anymore." He looked at Sybil. "Try to imagine eating sliced suede."

When she calmed down and stopped laughing, she noticed Will staring at them from the corner of the hedges. They were having too good a time.

"Did Kate ever do anything right?" she asked, sobering up.

"Well, frankly," Walter admitted, "she was a better father than a mother. She liked fixing things—the stereo, the kids' bikes, things I should have been doing." His face suddenly went old. "And when she loved me, it was very right." He looked down and then away.

Sybil reached out and took his hand in both of hers. "I don't know what's going to happen, Walter. Kate needs time alone. But she's a damned fool if she lets you go."

He looked at her, surprised. "You're an interesting woman, Sybil."

"Why?"

"In all these years I could never peg you. Kate always had that look of latent cruelty. Men were forewarned. Lu was the dizzy one in your group. She'd try anything and fuck it up. It made her human, lovable. And Blair, always a victim. But you were always one step removed, no giveaways. I found you threatening."

Sybil smiled. "Maybe it was my height."

"No. The first time we met you were sitting down. Even then you had a certain attitude. I didn't think you liked men much."

An endless declension of high-kicking men, like 203 Rockettes, flashed through her brain.

"Boy," she said, "I sure tried."

"You're different now, Sybil. I'm allowed to get a closer view." He pointed his finger at her. "You know, you're softer."

"Walter," she laughed, "it's been twenty years. We're all softer."

She poured the last of the pitcher as Will moved in fast from the lawn.

"Oh, hello, son." Walter smiled. "Join us."

Will shook his head at Sybil, eyes rolling frantically, and pointed to the driveway.

She looked at him as though he had gone dimwitted. "Will?"

Before he could answer, Bruce rounded the corner of the house, all bronzed muscle. "Hey, hi! Where's Katie-babes? We're supposed to go hogging."

The words clung like wet hair.

Walter stood slowly, towering over the kid but seeming frail. "By Katie-babes you mean Katherine. My wife."

Bruce looked at Will, then Sybil, then back at Walter with a weird smile, like someone hiding missing teeth.

"You'd better take off," Will said.

"No problem. Nooo problem!" Bruce backed off, across the lawn. A minute later, his Harley roared, spitting pebbles.

"Katie-babes." Walter sat looking down at the patio bricks. "Is this supposed to be a joke?"

"No," Sybil said quietly. "A joke is when you make somebody laugh."

Will moved away, leaving them alone again. Walter had folded as if grown old at lightning speed, and Sybil wracked her brain, wanting to toss him a crutch.

"Do you know, Walter, in all those years Kate never slept with anyone but you? She told me you were the first, the only."

He looked up. "Really? She would never tell me. You know how she is."

She nodded in the direction of Bruce. "That's just a little insanity phase."

"Well, God knows I had mine."

"Look, go back to the inn." She stood and walked him to the cab, and hugged him. "Let me talk to her."

"Will you call me as soon as you do? I'll be in the bar waiting."

As the cab pulled away, he leaned from the window, smiling with profound inability.

"Anything you can do, Sybil. Thanks."

An hour later, Will stood at a pay phone near the beach, a block from the carriage house. "Thing is, Tom, the poor bastard's here alone. I mean, he's gonna be sitting at the bar all night waiting for Kate."

At the other end of the phone, Tom Fairmont's voice came across, faint and disinterested. "I don't want to get involved, Will."

"Come on, man," Will persisted. "While Walter was at the house, that punk Bruce showed up looking for Kate. Walter almost broke down. I felt so bad I wanted to take him out and buy him a drink, but he kept calling me son."

"So you want me to go over to the Huntting Inn and give him some moral support." Tom laughed. "You're something else, Will."

"Well, Kate's got her backup group at the house. Why not?" Will paused, then shouted into the phone. "Men used to stick together. Besides, Tom, this guy's known all of them for years. Maybe he could give you some insight on Blair."

Tom thought about that. "So how will I recognize Walter?" he finally asked.

Will grinned. "He's wearing a navy blazer and a real bright shirt."

In the bar of the Huntting Inn, on the main street of East Hampton, Walter made his way past half a dozen men in pale Lacoste shirts and golf shoes. He slid onto a stool, and for a second the bartender stared at the loud tangerine shirt under his jacket, iridescent like a construction flag. Then he looked at his sad face and smiled genially, taking his order. Walter was nursing his third scotch at about six o'clock when Tom strolled into the bar.

"Walter Castaldi? I've heard about you. I'm Tom Fairmont."

Walter stood, clenching his fist. Another Katie-babes?

"I'm Blair Heywood's friend." Tom offered his hand. "Can I buy you a drink?"

Walter pumped his hand vigorously, and they sat down.

At eight o'clock, Sybil hung up the phone at the carriage house and turned around.

"Guess who Walter's getting drunk with?"

Blair shrugged. "Bella Abzug."

"Tom Fairmont."

"What?" Kate shot up from the sofa.

"Oh, wowwww." Will feigned a groan.

"That bastard," Kate bellowed. "Over there dissecting me, pulling Blair's boyfriend into this. I want him *out* of East Hampton, out of my life!"

Sybil looked at her steadily. "Then go tell him, if you've got the nerve."

Kate stared at each of them, shaking.

Two hours later, Walter turned, half drunk, as Kate entered the bar of the Huntting Inn.

"Kate!" He smiled at her, frightened, then pointed to Tom Fairmont. "As you can see, Tom and I have male-bonded."

Kate advanced on them. "Sensational. You both look like you're ready to climax."

Walter stood slowly, reaching for her.

She jumped back. "Don't touch me. I want you to get the hell out of East Hampton. Now."

Conversation in the bar stopped, and in the silence Tom stood, moving between Kate and Walter like a referee. "Let's be civilized," he whispered.

With the unsteadiness of a man in liquor, he led Kate and Walter to a small, quiet table in a corner of the bar. Kate sat down hard. Her breathing was so loud, she sounded like a runner. In the dim light of the bar, her wavy black hair surged around her face, pulling the violet from her eyes. Her cheeks were deeply flushed, matching the natural flush of her lips, and as she leaned toward the table, the nipples of her breasts pointed out like aimed darts. Tom stared at her, wondering how a man could win an argument with a woman so beautiful.

She turned to Walter. "What do you want from me?"

He looked down at his drink and sighed. "I want you to come home, Katherine. I can't make it without you."

"What's wrong?" she smiled. "Can't you get it up for the starlet anymore?"

"Oh, boy." Tom made a motion as if to leave the table. "I think you two need some privacy."

Kate pulled him back down to his seat. "I was faithful to my husband all these years." She enunciated slowly, "He took a teenage mistress and set up a love nest in Hollywood Hills. It made the columns. Don't talk to me about privacy."

The waiter brought a dish of nuts. They stared at it as if the nuts were combustible.

Walter downed his drink, looked at Tom, and spoke slowly. "My wife hasn't given me a blow-job in twelve years. She hasn't let me kiss her on the lips for two. Is that what you call faithful?"

Tom dropped his head, infatuated with the wood grain of the table. Kate's jaw hardened as if her inlays had just fused; tears crested her lids and slid down.

"You never loved me," she whispered hoarsely. "I just fit in with the rest of your ambitions."

"That's a lie!" Walter shoved the nut bowl across the table with such force, it exploded in her lap. "I fell in love with you when you were a twelve-year-old gum-chewing Brooklyn fat-ass. You didn't even have a waist then."

He looked at Tom again, as if for support. "I was a poor Wop nothing, a nineteen-year-old go-for on Wall Street. Katherine lived next door. Weekends I'd sit on the stoop watching her sashay up and down the block, this chubby kid, talking about how she was going to be beautiful and famous. I fell in love with her then, a little fat-ass. She had such spunk."

Walter looked across the table at her. "Katherine was the first woman I made love to that I didn't pay for."

Tom's mouth fell open.

"I only went with hookers," Walter continued, "because I was waiting for her to grow up. I didn't want to care for another woman. And I never did."

Kate shook her head as if disbelieving a story she already knew was true.

"Maybe we'd have been happier if Katherine had become just pretty, not beautiful." He sighed. "People used to come up to her on the street and say, "What? You're not in the movies? You're not Miss Universe? You're just a housewife? What a waste.' "

She sat back, suddenly calm. "I never considered our life a waste. Until you cheated on me."

Walter passed his hand over his eyes, exhausted. "My God. I miss you so completely." He looked up,

185

bewildered. "Maybe I'm crazy. I even miss your vicious moods. Life's boring without you."

She looked at Tom and shrugged. "I want to be a human being. And he wants an aborigine." The scene was played. She stood. "I'm tired, Walter. I'm going home to bed. I'll see you in a few months, in divorce court."

He jumped up. "Katherine, you can't mean it."

She looked him up and down for a minute. "While I'm at it, I should tell you your taste in shirts was always strictly Brooklyn. You made fun of my cooking all over Beverly Hills, but people used to shade their eyes when you walked into a room. Goodbye, Walter."

She turned and walked out of the bar. The two men stared dully after her.

Then Walter whispered, "I blew it. Didn't I?"

Tom shrugged helplessly. "Maybe you should invest in some new shirts."

Walter looked down. "This *is* a new shirt."

The bar closed, the lights dimmed. The two men gathered close, staring at Walter's shirt as if finding a campfire warmth in the radiant, tangerine glow.

Chapter
14

SEVERAL DAYS LATER Kate opened her eyes, the whites shot through with carmine-colored veins. Slowly, as if her eyes were new organs being broken in, she turned them to Sybil, who was leaning over her.

"Did I get arrested?"

"No," Sybil whispered. "Amazingly."

"Did I hurt anyone? Damage anything?"

"Only your liver. You were on a three-day drunk, Kate."

"How did—"

"Bruce found you dancing topless in a gay bar on the highway. A men's gay bar. You told them you'd had a sex change and being female was the pits. You needed money to reverse the operation."

"Oh, my God." Kate rolled over, her head feeling like a squashed melon, and saw newspaper print on her arms and chest.

"Bruce had to wrap you in the *East Hampton Star* to bring you home."

"Sybil, I'm so sorry. I just went berserk after seeing Walter."

Sybil pulled the sheets up around her, laughing

softly. "Forget it. All we wanted was to find you in one piece."

After a couple of Alka-Seltzers she dozed off again, and Sybil sat there wondering what the next installment with Kate would be. Then slowly she crossed the hall and looked down at her desk calendar, almost a daily ritual now, wanting the summer over yet not wanting September to come. But it was approaching fast, as if the last seven days of August were counting down in seconds.

Later in the day the phone rang, and it was Lu in Boston. "I just got the whole story from Blair. How's the go-go girl?"

"Sleeping. I wish you'd get back here. Compared to the rest of us, you suddenly seem prosaically sane."

Lu laughed. "That's why I called. I'll be aerial demonstrating over the horse show on Labor Day weekend, so save me a bed in that funhouse, will you?"

"Great." Sybil sat down, feeling somehow relieved. "How's the horse vet? Still calling?"

"Yeah. But distinctly not my type. He keeps telling me I need a spanking. It's like hearing bars drop around me."

"Well, bring him to the party after the show, and we'll look him over."

"What party?"

"Oh, sort of an end-of-summer. Shoreham Shutdown gathering here at the house. Blair cooked it up."

"I'll think about it." Lu hesitated. "Ah, how's Will?"

"Crazed." Sybil paused, half-crazed herself. "He keeps getting callbacks for the TV pilot, but so do two other actors."

"I don't mean that. I mean, do you know—"

"Lu, all I know is I want peace of mind, and I want to get back to work."

"Well, good luck, kiddo. I've got a feeling Will wants a more specific answer than that. He deserves it."

Sybil hung up and sorted through her mail, thinking how her friends seemed to have moved over to Will's side. Or maybe their loyalties had not changed; maybe in rooting for Will they were really rooting for her. She stared at an envelope for a long time before she recognized Victoria Grant's handwriting.

Sybil had lost hope of hearing from her weeks ago, and so hearing from her after all seemed magical. But she felt a sense of dread as she pulled a note from the envelope. It would be sad magic, like pulling a dead rabbit out of a top hat. She read the note three times before she understood that Grant was inviting her back to tea. Then she ran outside, hopped on her bike, and went shrieking up and down the lane.

Hearing her shouts, Kate woke and sluggishly hung her head out the window as Sybil skidded back into the driveway, waving the note.

"Victoria Grant!" she shouted up at her. "Tea! Tea!"

"Oh, for Christ' sake." Kate shook her head. "If only you could get that excited about reality."

The next afternoon, a wet, stormy day, Sybil arrived at Grant's house with a freshly baked carrot cake. Wilma, the maid, looked angry when she answered the door and wordlessly led her to the study. The house seemed haunted that day, creakings and moanings in the studs and joists. Victoria Grant sat before the fire almost buried in shawls and blankets.

"Hello, Miss Grant," she whispered.

Not a word.

They sat silent, listening to the day howling outside, staring at the fire. The woman coughed a lot, sounding miserable. Old sheepskin slippers, so worn the nap was bald, stretched from under the blankets toward the fire. Sybil smelled the frying odor of hot leather soles and stared, expecting to see smoke, as Wilma trolleyed in the tea, poured it, and leaned toward her.

"You can't stay long. She's miserable today, the weather."

She sat on the edge of a chair, sipping tea, staring at the famous Grant profile anciently reminiscent of her picture on a book jacket. The woman ignored her, mewling, coughing, occasionally rocking back and forth.

Sybil finished the tea, and after fifteen minutes nervously cleared her throat. "I think I should go. I'm disturbing you."

As if Sybil's going was the cue, Victoria Grant leaned over away from her and brought two books up from the floor. Pages of Sybil's novels had been marked with strips of frazzled ribbon which, in her sudden terror, reminded Sybil of pastie-tassels worn by strippers. Slowly, Grant unfolded the shawls from around her, making a nest in her lap for the books.

She slipped the wire frames of her glasses around each ear, settling them on the almost transparent bridge of her nose, then opened a book and leaned back as if sharing it with the lamp peering over her shoulder inquisitively. She turned pages, stopping here and there to read, and Sybil saw notations in the margins. And seeing them, she tried to breathe normally, but her chest suddenly hurt; she slumped as though her back were warped.

Grant brooded over both books a long time, coughing, ignoring her tea. Finally, she closed them and sat looking into the fire. Then slowly, almost painfully, she turned her head in Sybil's direction until her eyes, hugely magnified, rested on her. With great effort she reached out an arthritic, weathered hand and patted Sybil's arm gently, repeatedly.

"My dear." Her voice was rattled, hoarse. "Keep writing. You must keep writing."

Sybil dropped her head to the mottled, gray hand. After a while, Wilma came and led her to the front door. She drove home in the rain, coming down heavy now, pulled quietly into the driveway, and curled up on the front seat until it was dark and the rain stopped.

In Manhattan, Will stood on the stage in his acting class facing a young actress who suddenly slapped her hips, exasperated.

"Please follow the script," she shouted.

"I am," Will argued.

"No, you're not. You keep calling me Sybil. This character who's supposed to be your mother, who you call by her first name, is Ethel."

She looked out over the class at the drama coach. "Can we break?"

The class broke up, and they sat down on the stage. Will lit a cigarette, embarrassed. "I'm sorry. I've got a lot on my mind."

"And by the way," she smiled, lighting her own cigarette, "when we're not rehearsing, my real name is Cheryl, not Shirley."

Will nodded. "Right. Shirley is my mother."

"No, your mother is Ethel."

"No. My *real* mother in the Bronx is Shirley." He threw his hands up in the air. "Jesus, I don't know whether I'm coming or going."

She looked at him for a minute. "Maybe you bit off more then you can chew."

His eyes narrowed, and he leaned his head to the

side. "Don't you think I can handle this pilot if I get it?"

"I'm talking about your . . . personal life, Will."

She was attractive, twenty-six, with a minor role in a TV soap opera. Lately her interest in Will was keen.

He laughed, shaking his head. "You know, Cheryl, for a year I sat next to you in this class. I couldn't get a hello out of you. All of a sudden you focus on me as though you've had your vision corrected, even offer to rehearse this TV script with me in class. You know what's funny? I know you're not attracted to me; it's my situation. Right?"

She looked down at the stage, arranging her features in a superior attitude.

"I'm fascinated by what motivates people," she said. "For instance, why you're involved with this writer. I read her book, by the way. It's not that great. So if you're going to sleep around with older women, why not pick someone famous who can help your career?"

Will looked at her steadily, without expression. Then he leaned over and said softly, "I don't need help with my career. Is that, by the way, how you get your parts in the soaps? Sleeping around with middle-aged producers?"

She shrugged. "It doesn't hurt. You've got to use all your ammunition to get to the top. I'm just saying, if this woman can't help you, why waste your time?"

Will shook his head, staring at her again as if she were deficient in something important.

"Besides," her voice got hard, "how do you know she isn't just using you for material?"

He stood up and squared his shoulders. For a minute she thought he was going to hit her. Then he slipped on his jacket and picked up his script.

"Thanks, Cheryl. Thanks for the rehearsal. By the way, when was the last time a man asked you to marry him?"

She looked at him, puzzled.

"As a matter of fact, when was the last time," he backed toward the door, shouting, "a man told you he loved you? Or even liked you?"

Out on the street it was pouring, but Will hardly noticed. He elbowed his way blindly through crowds and walked in the rain for hours, angry and not knowing why.

Chapter
15

THE FRIDAY before Labor Day, Tom Fairmont looked up at his living-room window. Someone was throwing pebbles. He leaned from his typewriter and stared through the window. Lately, Blair had been playing hard to reach. Now she stood in the yard with her hands raised in the air like a holdup victim. He threw open the front door and stopped, seeing her old beat-up VW in the driveway.

"Blair!"

"Look, ma." She laughed. "No gifts."

"Where's the yellow hard-on?"

She hopped up the steps, pigtails flapping. "Sold. I broke even."

"You're kidding." Tom started to hug her, but she stood off a little. "I've missed you. A lot."

Blair laughed softly. "You mean you noticed I wasn't around?"

He let that pass as she walked into the living room and laid something down on the table.

"What's this?" He picked up a manuscript and flipped through a hundred and twenty-five pages of dialogue. The title page read *Jaguar*.

"It's a play. About a woman trying to buy love."

"Blair, what are you up to?"

"What I should be, I guess. I sent a copy to Circle Rep Theater in the city. They want to have a reading in late fall. They think it's very funny."

"But when did you start writing again?"

"Oh, I've sort of been doing it in my head all this time."

He moved across the room, took her by the shoulders, and really did hug her this time. "I'm so proud of you. I never believed you could quit writing just like that."

She hugged him back but almost absentmindedly. "Well, you were right, Tom. Anyway, I've made enough commissions in the past three years to go back where I belong and do what I do best."

He pulled away. "Back?"

"Yes. The lease on my house is up next week. I'm not renewing."

"Wait a minute." He sat down quickly, putting his hands to his temples. "What about us?"

"Us?" Blair looked at him, surprised. "Tom, I've tried to accomplish that word for three years. Now that I know where my next meal is coming from, I've had time to develop a little perspective. I see that you and I both need a few more accomplishments in our lives. And contrary to what everyone thinks, suffering is not my favorite state of mind."

He looked up at her so pained and shocked, she sat down beside him.

"New York is a two-hour jitney ride away, Tom. I'll go back and keep my fingers crossed for your book. Maybe you'll finish it soon. And maybe you'll come to see my play."

She was throwing things at him too fast, and his mind reeled, looking for scapegoats.

"They talked you into this, didn't they? Your buddies."

Blair answered slowly. "There is no they. Just me.

195

For three years I've been like this character in a play with no lines, no opinions. Then I started writing about the car, and I saw that all the time I had lines, I just didn't say them."

They heard a fire engine on the highway. Tom watched her turn her head toward the siren, as if it were a long blast from a ship, summoning her to depart, begin again. "Oh, Blair, don't throw this away," he whispered. "I love you."

"I'm not going that far, Tom."

He looked down at the floor for a while. "Where will you live in New York?"

"I'm subletting a studio in the East Village where it's cheap."

"The East Village. Hippies. And Sybil goes back to an apartment you describe as furnished like a waiting room. And Lu sleeps on a cot in a flight shack." He shook his head slowly. "I can't understand you women. It's like you're all keeping in shape for adversity."

Blair smiled, sad. "As Lu says, you have to travel light when you're flying blind." Her soft eyes filled, and she turned away for a minute. After a while she stood up and spoke quietly. "I don't think anything in the script is hurtful or too personal. But I wanted you to read it and let me know."

Tom kept his head down, bewildered.

"You can bring it back on Sunday," she continued. "We're having a small party of sorts at the carriage house. Please come."

He tried to answer her but could not. Confused to the point of anesthesia, he tried to stand up but could not manage that either. After a minute, Blair walked to the front door and closed it quietly behind her. Through the screen she saw Tom still crouched halfway out of the chair, as if undecided whether to sit down or draw himself to his full height.

* * *

That same night Lu sat back in her plane cabin, a rosy glow in the large night sky, watching luminous red needles on her instrument panel communicate that all was well. Above the horizon, flashing strobes of occasional distant planes made holes in the black background, and below, pocks of light dotted villages tracing her route to Boston.

Flying a corpse home to Lowell, Massachusetts, she had stopped in Concord to see her parents. Within five minutes her father was lecturing her on recent newspaper photos of her buzzing a political clambake with a BAN THE BOMB banner.

"You know, Lutheria, you have a lot in common with Jesus Christ," he said. "Your motives are Christian, but you've got this weakness for publicity."

It always amazed her how quickly her father could deflate her, making her feel like one of those bit-part expendables who got strafed early on in old "Flying Tiger" movies.

"Why do you put me down, Daddy?" she asked. "If I were a man, which is what you wanted me to be, which is why you gave me a female diminutive of your name, you'd be proud of me. Your son, the aviator, the nuclear-freezer who cares about the destiny of mankind."

He looked at her critically. "Well, you're not a man. And you're getting to the age where these aerial shenanigans and personal interviews you give no longer sound rebellious, they sound feeble-minded."

"Daddy—"

"How do you think your mother and I feel when you tell some newspaper reporter you believe in possessing men the way they've always possessed women, quickly, between takeoffs?"

197

"But—"

"You've got your own business, a good income. Why do you have to paint yourself as an exhibitionist-nymphomaniac? Is this what you call Liberated?"

Lu had left the house in tears. Now, recalling the conversation, she looked out at the stars blazing beside her like white screams and let out a good scream herself. Why did she always go home expecting approval from a man who had raised her like a son and then, when she wasn't looking, changed his mind. She tried to shake him free, wishing she could relegate her father to the rest of the men in her life, just a one-night stand.

The plane merged with a cloud, and she gripped the controls, screaming over and over. As she emerged from the cloud, the moon washed the cockpit in silver light, and for the hundredth time in her life Lu wished she could stay airborne, that there was an alternative to landing.

She parked the plane in a corner of the airfield, and before she could even unbuckle her belt, felt her eyelids droop. Some nights after a flight she was so peaceful she just stretched back in the seat of the cockpit and slept. Tonight she wasn't peaceful, just too sad and spent to move. She leaned back, took a deep breath, and when she woke it was morning.

In the flight shack her assistant had left a message stuck to the hanging fly tape, saying the vet, Hoyt Biddle, had called from the horse show in the Hamptons. He was driving up to Boston on Saturday night to pick up cartons of protest pamphlets, and could he hop a ride Sunday morning back down to the horse show with the cartons? The girl had told him to be at the airfield at 7:00 A.M.

Lu groaned. An hour in the plane with that persistent middle-aged macho was not something to look forward to, particularly in her frame of mind.

Then she noticed a P. S. on the note: "He said to tell you he's looking forward to molesting you."

"The son of a bitch."

Standing in the portable shower behind her flight shack, Lu thought of the note again, and it made her so angry she snapped the bar of soap in half.

At dawn Sunday the skies were draped in wet gray, but Boston radio said their destination was clear, with twenty miles' visibility. She was topping off both tanks and hosing the caked mud off the wheels when Hoyt Biddle pulled up in the parking lot.

"Morning." His smile looked forced, as if he had stayed awake all night practicing it. "All set for the big day?"

"Morning," Lu said abruptly. "I guess." Then she turned away, fiddling with her hose.

They slid his cartons of protest pamphlets behind the seats, then she checked her instrument panel and signaled for him to board and buckle in. Watching him shrink beside her, Lu fired up the engine on her little Cessna 152. She taxied down the runway, picking up speed, rumbling between the rows of yellow lights, fifty, sixty, seventy, a slight back pressure on the control wheel.

The Cessna resisted momentarily, then shrugged off the pavement, and they lifted smoothly. Biddle stared down through the clouds as though he had dropped something valuable; his big, warped hands gripping his knees with such intensity, blue veins erupted through the skin.

"Relax. We've got good visibility ahead, and I'm a first-class pilot." She paused. "Even though I'm a woman."

He turned and gazed at her, puzzled. "Seems as though I caught you in a bad mood this trip."

She raised her voice over the accelerating roar of

the engine. "It's not a mood. It's a reaction I have when I'm around men who don't take women seriously."

Biddle shook his head, even more puzzled. "Miss Campbell, considering this is only the second time I've seen you face-to-face, though God knows I've tried to improve on that, I would venture to say you've got me mixed up with someone else."

For a while they were silent as she tracked from one navigational radio station to another, primary signposts along the route to Long Island.

Then, hoping she had calmed down, he tried again. "Well, what kind of aerial show are you planning to give us?"

Lu jerked her thumb to the back of the plane. "My staff helped me paint a couple of banners: EQUESTRIANS FOR LIFE. RIDE FOR THE SHOREHAM SHUTDOWN."

He nodded vigorously. "Great! Sounds just like what we need." Trying to keep his mind off the altitude, Biddle hesitated, then continued. "By the way, that's a pretty relaxed staff you have. Every time I call to leave a message, that fruitcake secretary calls me Mr. Diddle. And those two 'Nam vets you have for mechanics sound like they're still in Saigon." He laughed. "Say, how do you run a business like that—"

Lu horsed the plane into a sudden, vicious climb so that his head was flung back. He stayed that way, paralyzed, his face white. For a minute she felt like turning back, forgetting the horse show and dumping her passenger as quickly as possible. Then she looked back at the rolled banners, as if hearing a cry for attention. Biddle looked like he was about to wet his pants, so she finally leveled off.

After a few seconds he rolled his head toward her. "Woman, what are you trying to do!"

She kept her eyes straight ahead while she talked.

"Look, I don't need some middle-aged masher to tell me how to run my business. And I think it's really cheap of you to use the nuclear-protest movement as an excuse to get laid. Isn't that why you've been calling me? Did you have visions of nailing me right here in the cabin of my plane?"

His big hands were working, and she had the feeling he wanted to reach over and shake her.

"Listen, if you do that again," he shouted, "I'm going to take control of this plane myself. Then we'll both die." He leaned toward her. "What's eating you?"

Lu looked over at him, her eyes long and narrow. "I know your type, Hoyt Biddle. Mental hard hats who can't stand having a woman at the wheel. The only way you can feel masculine is by trying to cheapen me—telling my secretary you were looking forward to molesting me. Men like you make me sick."

In silence they cruised across Long Island South, gathering it under them. Around Gardiner's Bay the land turned prawn-colored in the morning light as Lu wheeled, got clearance for landing at East Hampton Airport, and nudged the control wheel, pointing the plane nose down.

"Cessna turning base." She continued her descent. "Cessna turning final."

Biddle stared straight ahead, as if what she was saying was in bad taste. Aligned with the runway, she sank to the tarmac, a soft landing like a leaf settling to earth, and cruised over to the parking field. For a minute, as the plane muttered itself to sleep, the two of them sat there, neither transmitting nor receiving. Then he spoke.

"I have a few things I'd like to say before I go. You seem to care a great deal about your business, so I was trying to give you advice on your staff. But it's none of my affair, and I'm sorry."

He slowed down for emphasis.

"Secondly, since we met a month back, my intentions toward you have been only honorable, though you cut me off every time I called you. Thirdly, the word molest is not part of my vocabulary. I told your secretary I was looking forward to *protesting* with you."

He unbuckled his seat belt and opened the door, sliding his boxes out of the plane while Lu sat there.

Then he looked at her again. "If there was anything aggressive in my manner today, Mzzz. Campbell, that was all bravado. You see, I'm purely terrified of flying. I admire any woman who can pilot a plane."

Before she could respond, he nodded to the folded banners in the back. "I'm sorry you troubled yourself with those. I don't think we'll be seeing each other again."

With the lethargy of one in shock, Lu watched him walk away, then leaned her head back on the seat, touching her fingers to her cheek. Her skin had the detachment of something under frost, and she thought of crying and wondered why. After a while she climbed down, slid her tote bag out behind her, locked up, and took a cab to the beach, deserted in the early hours.

She stood on the long stretch of sand, so marbled and clean it looked like private property, and kicked off her shoes, watching gulls stroll, exercising muscle over smaller birds. Then she walked the length of a jetty, kelp-softened and poised like a whale, and sat down at the end of the rocks and stared at the sea. She had been angry last night and angry this morning on the flight in. The anger was gone now, and Lu sat there trying to figure out what had replaced it.

As the morning matured, a ragged dog padded into view. From between clouds, a ray of sunlight shot him, and he suddenly froze, an amateur on a lit stage.

Lu laughed and whistled to him, and he lifted his head to the jetty.

"Hey, boy," she called, "I need a friend."

He barked once and padded on.

Chapter
16

"NORA, Your voice sounds funny."

"That's because it's closer, Mother."

"How close?" Kate asked.

"East Hampton. We're here."

Kate pulled the phone away from her head, cursing, then brought it back. "This is betrayal. You've been conning me, dammit."

"Mother, the summer's over."

"Yeah, well tell your father so's the marriage." She stabbed a tack into a wall, trailing crepe paper, dreaming the wall was Walter. "Does he think this was just some long, bad mood I've been in. Then come September, back to that House of Oz?"

"The house is for sale, what's left of it." Nora was trying to sound tough and older than seventeen, but she sounded young and raw. "We know Sybil goes back to New York after Labor Day. I want to see you, find out what you're going to do." Her voice got younger. "I've had a horrible summer. I miss you."

Kate slid down to the floor. "Are you all right, honey?"

"My brother's on probation for armed robbery and drug abuse, my mother's sleeping with a Hell's An-gel, and my bed's full of bullet holes. How can you ask me if I'm all right?"

"Why did you come with your father?" Kate cried. "I thought you were mad at him."

"I am mad at him. But he's my father, and he loves you."

"Nora, I am not going back with him." Sybil and Blair swept around her, gothicizing the carriage house with pink and white crepe paper, but leaning into the phone conversation.

"Will you come back with me?" Nora asked. "Will you take an apartment with me? I found a place near UCLA with two bedrooms. I'd do the cooking, Mother. I'd . . ."

Kate closed her eyes, touched, imagining herself and her daughter living together with no cheating husbands or lovers, no emotional freak shows. Just two functioning humans growing closer and getting on with life. But then she remembered Walter. "What about him?"

"Daddy and Justin can find their own place. You two have to work out what you want to do about divorce. But please, Mother, don't divorce me."

"Funny. I thought about it."

Blair looked at her strangely. And Kate remembered all the talk between the women about her needing time alone to find herself, the girl she had put on hold so many years ago.

"Nora, I need more time. Even living with you would be too close to your father. It would look like he was halfway to getting me back."

"Please." Nora's voice verged on hysteria. "I'm so lost, so mad at everything. We could be friends, roommates. We could talk to each other."

"Where are you, honey?"

"At that Huntting Inn place. Daddy's downstairs trying to rent a car for however long it takes to talk you into coming home. Can I come and see you? Please? Where is it? I'll hitchhike."

"Look, I want to see you too. But this is the worst time for you to come. There's a party here this afternoon."

"For what?"

"Labor Day. Ban the Bomb. Who knows?"

"Can I call you back later?" Nora begged.

"Yes. But not when he's around." Kate's voice changed. "Tell your father to go back to LA. He's got to understand this marriage is finished. I want you to stay for a day or two. I'll put you back on the plane myself."

"OK. I love you, Mother. I have to go. He's here." She hung up.

Blair stood over Kate. "Well?"

"They're in East Hampton. But cool your motor, I'm not going back to him."

"That's up to you." Blair dismissed Kate's problem, concerned with other things. "What's the story on Lu?"

Kate shook her head. "Guy at the airport hasn't seen her since the last time I called. The plane's still sitting there. A cab driver says he took her to the beach."

Sybil frowned. "I don't care where she is now as long as she materializes by four o'clock. There are going to be thirty people here expecting to meet the famous No Nuke aviatrix."

Will stomped up and down the stairs, then banged the screen door heading out to the lawn where sheet-covered tables would hold food and drink. He felt a little crazed; his mind was on the TV pilot and Sybil and their future. He knew in the next few days he was going to get a lot of good news or a lot of bad news, and right now he just wanted it over. Somehow the waiting and not knowing the worst was worse than knowing it.

Blair came and stood beside him on the lawn, and held his hand for no reason. "The last days of summer." She said it like a girl from an old-fashioned novel.

"Wow. It went so fast." He shook his head. "Like a dream."

"As you get older, Will, you begin to see it's all like a dream. Everything's ahead of you. Then one day you look around, and somehow it all got behind you."

"Man, that's depressing." He looked down at her. "Makes me want to sit back and give up."

"Don't give up. Just pay attention."

She looked so sad and lovely in the sunlight, Will squeezed her hand. "What about Tom?"

Blair sighed. "Tom is, as they say, still trying to get his act together. I've decided to go back to the big city and work on mine. Maybe something good will happen with the distance in between. What about you and Sybil?"

"Come on, you know what's going on, Blair. I'm just waiting for her to say yes. And please don't give me that crap about being too young."

He unfolded a news clipping from his pocket. "Look. It was in the paper yesterday."

WEDDED BLISS. HE'S 28. SHE'S 91. A couple in Idaho. Married two years, the copy said. Ecstatically happy, even though they had been run out of their hometown. Although blind in one eye, the wife still enjoyed sex. The photo showed the handsome young husband bussing his wife on the cheek, a wrinkled, featureless thing dredged up from a sarcophagus.

Blair burst into laughter and hugged him. "I think Sybil *should* marry you."

Will stepped back, grinning. "You're kidding."

"No. You're no worse than any other couple around. In fact, you two are the best thing I've seen in a long time. She needs you, Will. She goes too long without human contact."

He nodded slowly. "Shit, Blair, I love her so much. I'd be good for her. Sometimes she looks so frightened." He glanced down at her. "Sometimes you all do."

Blair smiled. "Sometimes we are."

Around noon Sybil looked out the window and swayed. Her lawn seemed infested with frogmen. Four or five of them fanned out around the house while one headed for the patio.

Will stopped him at the door. "Bruce."

In his wet suit, Bruce's body gleamed like muscled licorice, giving his voice menace. "Where's Katie-babes?"

"Upstairs. What's going on?"

"You're a nice guy, Will. Stay out of this." Bruce pushed open the screen door and came in, leaving the others outside, vigilant.

Sybil moved toward him, "Wha—"

"I was surfing with the guys. Got a call at the beach. Her old man's back in town."

"Bruce, her daughter's with him. This is really a family thing."

He stared at Sybil, narrowing his eyes. "Yeah? Well, consider me family." He whacked crepe paper out of his way and stood at the bottom of the stairs yelling, "Kate!"

Blair strolled down the stairs. "Why, Bruce, how very Lloyd Bridges we are today."

Then she saw the others posted outside the house and looked at Sybil.

"Katie!" he called again.

There was a groan. Feet hit the floor from her bed.

Kate appeared in a white terry robe and came down the stairs, sleepy and petulant, so beautiful at that moment she did not seem authentic. She looked at his wet suit, then at her friends, faces appearing and disappearing as the drooping crepe paper swayed across the living room.

Through a window she saw other wet suits and shook her head, trying to clear it. "Am I awake, for Christ' sake?"

Bruce's lips stretched tight across his teeth, but his eyes were big and pleading—a young man caught between an ugly mood and distress. "He's back. Your old man."

"How do you know?" Kate asked.

"You forget, my uncle owns the fuckin' cab company."

She shrugged her shoulders and tried to look uninterested.

The moment was important; Bruce used words sparingly. "So?"

Kate rubbed her eyes and put her hands on her hips. "Don't worry. I'm not going back with him."

"Fuckin' A!"

From the patio, one of the wet suits grunted. Will moved in. Sybil and Blair pulled together, and Kate looked through Bruce as if he were suddenly transparent.

"Listen," she said, "if I stay, it's not out of any duty to you. It's because I'm not a flunky anymore. Get it?"

"Don't mess around, Katie. If I find you've just been jerkin' me off all summer—"

"What?" She pushed her face at him. "Will you beat me up? Smash my face in a little?"

That perfect face. He dropped his eyes, and she softened.

"Oh, Bruce. Don't spoil everything. Look how much fun we've had."

"Yeah." He nodded reluctantly. "But why's he back?"

She looked around at the others, then at him, "Because we've been married for eighteen years."

With exaggerated motion, Bruce brought his fists together and cracked his knuckles audibly. "Well, just get rid of him. Or we'll have to help him out of town."

"Come on, Bruce." Will patted his shoulder. "There's a party here today. Let's keep the vibrations positive."

Kate backed up and stood on the bottom stair so that she was taller than Bruce. "Listen, Bruciebabes," she teased, "I want you to leave now and go home and get really slicked up for the party. You know, clean shirt and jacket. I want to show you off, OK?"

She hugged him, wet suit and all.

"Aw, Katie."

"Go on. I'll see you later."

They watched the slick broad backs of the surfers dwindling in the driveway.

"Jesus," Sybil breathed out. "Do you realize how much adrenaline was flowing around this place a minute ago?"

"Yeah," Will said. "Well, I hope they go back to the beach and surf it off."

The annual Hampton Classic horse show was spread out in a grassy meadow off the highway near Bridgehampton, a few miles from the East Hampton airfield. For the show the meadow was transformed into a kind of King Arthurian court with a dozen striped spectator and refreshment tents, ranging in size from one hundred to three hundred feet in length.

With over twelve thousand spectators, this Sunday was the big day of the five-day jumping event, the Grand Prix.

At the entrance gate, groups carried placards protesting the Long Island Lighting Company's expansion of a nuclear plant at nearby Shoreham. SHOREHAM, SHUTDOWN OR MELTDOWN. MOTHBALL NUKE PLANTS. GIVE LIFE A CHANCE. Inside the grounds, spectators wore all manner of nuclear protest buttons.

At noon, two hours before the Grand Prix, a fifteen-fence jump-off with thirty-two thoroughbreds competing, Lu threaded her way through the spectators and the tents. After walking in circles behind the jump grounds, in a maze of stalls, horse-vans, and thoroughbreds led around by trainers and stewards, she stopped a trainer leading a pony hunter.

"Where do I find a vet named Hoyt Biddle?"

The man pursed his lips. "What stable is he with?"

"Startrek, from Boston. A horse named Glorybound?"

The man smiled. "Oh, the No Nuke vet." He pointed the way.

Hoyt came up and stood behind her with his hands on his hips while she poked around his horse-van. She turned around and, facing him so suddenly, looked down, shy. After a long minute he moved closer to her.

"It's hard, isn't it?" he said softly.

"Yes."

"Well, try."

"OK." Lu frowned earnestly. "I'm really very sorry for my behavior this morning. I guess I have this . . . chip on my shoulder."

He nodded. "It must keep you busy."

"Look, Hoyt, I really want to fly those banners."

"Well, I'm damned happy to hear that. We've got

several hundred protesters counting on you. I was just wondering what to tell them."

They sat down on the lawn, smelling manure and liniment in the air, a nice smell. She threw her head back, inhaling, but eyeing him, still unsure, while Hoyt explained everything slowly and thoughtfully.

"OK. To get down to business. Now today's the big purse. Those grandstands and spectator tents will be packed." He pointed at her. "You'll have the attention of ten or twelve thousand people. Timing's the thing. And your altitude. You can't fly too low. It's illegal, and you'll spook the horses." He made kissing sounds, thinking. "I'd say you should make your first pass, oh, about five minutes before the Grand Prix. Everyone's alert then, in place. Then I'd space them every five minutes or so."

Pointing up. Hoyt waved his arm back and forth. "You'll only get away with a few passes over the field. More than that, the police copter will start bugging you." He slowed down and looked over to see if she was following. "I'd go up with you, but you know how I feel about flying and . . . well, you've probably already got company."

"I don't."

"Oh. You said you were involved with someone last time."

Lu bit her lip, hesitating. "I sort of made that up."

"Why?"

She looked him in the eye. "You seemed too cocky. It didn't appeal to me."

Hoyt thought about that, half-smiling. "What kind of man would appeal to you?"

"Oh," she looked around, uncomfortable, "someone who meant what he said. A solid, steady . . . somebody."

In the distance, crowds applauded the junior jumpers.

He leaned toward her. "I'm a solid, steady somebody."

Lu suddenly stood up, confused. "I thought you were serious. I thought we were talking about protesting."

"I am." Hoyt got to his feet. "And we were. But we finished." He took a deep breath and, holding her elbow gently, walked her in a large circle, the way he did spooked horses.

"Look, I'm fifty-three," he explained. "Widowed. I'm not rich. Not poor. Two grown sons. I don't consider myself old, though. I plan to stay young as late as possible, maybe avoid middle-age altogether and go straight from here to senility."

Lu stood still. What was he babbling about?

"In other words," he continued, "I still cut the mustard."

Then she backed away. "Are you trying to be funny?"

"No. I'm trying to court you. I've been trying since we met. It's a little hard to do on a telephone, but that's as close as you'd let me get." He leaned forward as if breathless. "At this moment I'm terrified you're going to buzz the horse show, fold up your banners, and take off into the wild, blue yonder, and I'll never see you again. I'm moving in fast because life is short, and someone else will if I don't. I know your type. Difficult. Nervous. I can handle it."

Hoyt pointed to the horses strolling by. "Been dealing with them all my adult life."

Lu looked at his big, broad chest, the gray pelt growing out of his shirt. Then she folded her arms and faced him with spread legs, like a marine, but she was too pretty, and it didn't take.

"You think you're hot stuff, don't you, Hoyt Biddle?"

He smiled. "I see I make you nervous. Know why?"

She stuck her chin out. "Why?"

"I'm a precious thing." His blue eyes crackled, and his salt-and-pepper waves stood up in the sun. "Men like me are almost extinct. Sturdy, virile, wise."

She laughed but was still wary.

"I wouldn't ground you or try to tame you," he said. "You could fly to your heart's content. I'll just keep both feet on the ground, if you don't mind. But I'd be there for your landings." He leaned close. "I'm a tender man. A good, strong lover. I can cook steaks and chops, and I don't mind doing dishes."

Lu tried for sarcasm. "What *do* you mind?"

"Unfaithfulness. Mendacity. Also, I don't hem skirts."

She laughed again, confused, because she wasn't used to liking the men she was physically attracted to. Then she looked at her watch. It was almost one o'clock.

"I've got to get to the airfield."

Hoyt walked her to a cab, holding her hand in his, and it felt safe, huge, like a catcher's mitt.

"Now I'll alert everyone to zero hour." He smiled. "When you buzz us, you'll see a beautiful sight down here, a couple of hundred pennants waving for the Shoreham Shutdown!" Opening the cab door, he gently turned her around. "If you promise to come back here afterward, I'll introduce you to Glory-bound and his owner. He took a ribbon yesterday."

As Lu slid into the back seat, he closed the door and leaned his head in the window after her, studying her white skin and red hair.

"Sorry if I came on so strong. Wild-haired women always made me act foolish. You will come back, won't you?"

She looked down for a minute and then slowly

nodded. "But I can't promise anything, Hoyt. Maybe we'll just be friends."

"OK." He smiled. "We'll start out that way. Like virgins."

Chapter
17

SYBIL STROLLED around the lawn, checking glasses and bottles on tables. She avoided the patio and the first floor of the house where drooping ceilings of pink and white festoons made her feel slightly migrainous. On an elm tree shading part of the lawn, Will had hung a huge grape cluster of pink heart-shaped balloons. Each heart was silver-lettered MARRY ME. In the breeze, the balloons danced and the silver letters shimmered in the sun.

She stared up at them, wondering, Why, Will? Everything was perfect. Why did you have to want more?

Sybil was still standing under the tree around two o'clock, wondering how she would tell him she couldn't marry him, when he pulled the Dodge into the driveway and strolled across the lawn. They stood there enlarging their awareness of the balloons by not looking up. But the silence was too loaded, and Will fled conversationally to Lu.

"Guys at the airfield said she's demonstrating at the horse show right now. Man, there's a huge traffic jam there. Some local woman led a thirty-van convoy of protesting mothers right into the show to get the governor's attention."

"Christ." Sybil frowned. "All we need is for Lu to get mixed up in that."

He hugged her reassuringly. "Don't worry. She'll be here."

A breeze came up, and the pink things bobbled overhead in an aerial lunacy. Looking up at them, Sybil backed off across the lawn.

At three-thirty the first guest arrived, a perspiring little poet with marcelled hair and lips edged in rime from sucking breath mints.

"I'm early," he protested, "but I heard there were such interesting combinations of people in this house all summer, I couldn't wait to get here!"

Kate enveloped him in red parachute-silk and dragged him off to the table set up as a bar. At four, people started drifting in from the horse show: a few artists from Maidscott, the town magician who also delivered oil, three authors from East Hampton, a dancer with a leashed macaw, an innkeeper, a man who sighted whales, and a sculptress in a dress of rotting crochet.

Tom arrived in a wrinkled linen blazer and tie, and Blair met him at the door, moving in a measured way as if no longer drawn to him. She was wearing soft, blue silk, high-heeled sandals, and her blonde hair was upswept. He handed her the script.

"It's terrific, Blair. Except I had trouble with the ending."

She smiled. "So did I."

"I've got to talk to you." He touched her arm. "I'm dead serious."

"Later, Tom. OK?"

Like polite aborigines sensing a meal, the crowd shifted quietly from the drinks to the big buffet under the balloons. Occasionally people looked up at the bobbing hearts, then looked around, trying to match the silver lettering with one of the couples, but none of the couples seemed appropriate. A tall, husky real-estate agent stared at Kate, his body bucking in mindless velocity toward her.

"Hi. I'm here alone." His eyes dug deeply into hers.

Kate recognized the overeager flush of a momentarily unattached husband. "Oh? Where's your wife?"

"Ah . . . she's on the bench today."

She looked at him with wooden incomprehension. "On the what?"

"The bench."

"What does she do for a living?" Kate asked. "Shine shoes?"

His voice went falsetto with insult and wilted lust. "My wife happens to be a circuit-court judge!"

Inside the house, Will flipped through albums and suddenly a Moog-synthesized *Firebird Suite* boomed across the patio from the stereo system. He moved back outside, slipping his arm around Sybil's waist.

"I thought we should have appropriate music for our flying guest of honor."

People stared at his arm around her waist until someone remembered to react.

"Yes. Where *is* the famous pilot?"

Sybil smiled nervously, checking her watch, while the growing crowd flowed back and forth from food to drink. The poet, orchestrating his talk with a chicken leg, spat quiche at the innkeeper.

"I'm for a total meltdown and a new human race," he argued. "We're living in the age of dreck."

The innkeeper's wife dabbed gently at the outbreak of quiche on his tie. Inside, the phone rang, and Will waved through the door to Kate. She moved across the patio and stepped inside.

"Katherine, please don't hang up. It's Walter."

She hung up, carried the phone to the kitchen, and buried it in a drawer, then turned to face Bruce, clean-shaven, in a white shirt, jacket, and jeans. Kate hugged him, and he lifted her a few feet off the floor. Behind him, two of his musclebound friends, a blond and a bruiser with a punk haircut, stood in jackets, their eyes weirdly dilated.

"You guys," she teased, "look absolutely clean-cut."

They grunted, coked-up, looking around for a few cars to lift. As Kate led them outside to the drinks and food, the innkeeper's eyes grew, and he leaned toward Sybil.

"Those young men are rough. I know them. Be careful."

More cars pulled into the driveway. People hugged, airbrushing cheeks in greeting. A man with a fastidious hairdo made a pass at the man who sighted whales. A woman wearing a beach hat, making her look like an ambulatory mushroom, slid a huge slice of Jarlsberg into her purse.

Lu suddenly materialized across the lawn in her khaki jumpsuit, hair shining copper in the late-day sun. She was flushed and lovely, and the man trailing her was flushed too, and uncertain. The small crowd turned, curious, as Sybil moved toward the couple.

"Lu, thank God. What happened to you? Where—"

"This is Hoyt Biddle." She smiled.

The other women advanced, studying him like an amoeba: a certain male integrity, a broad physique, his face strong as if carved out of limestone. But there was an odor, slightly brackish, like wet hay or . . . manure.

"Boy, did we stop the show." Lu grinned. "Over twenty protesters arrested."

They clustered around, fascinated, and Kate eyeballed Hoyt.

"Well, what do you think of this radical female pilot?" she asked.

He drew in his breath and smiled. "If she can hold her liquor, maybe I'll keep her."

Sybil dragged them back across the lawn, introducing them.

"Everyone, this is Lu Campbell, the Amelia Earhart of the No Nukes Movement."

With his arm around Sybil's waist again, Will stared at Hoyt. The man looked too old for Lu. Hoyt stared back, trying to interpret Will's arm around Sybil. In spite of their thirty-year difference, there was a similarity between them, a strong male confidence, and recognizing it, they both relaxed.

People leaked slowly in and out of the house. Will changed the *Firebird Suite* for an old Stones album, and couples gyrated on the patio. Sybil relaxed momentarily, her gaze drifting over the crowd. For a few seconds she had the drunken sensation of being alone in the world, as if she were sitting at the top of a Ferris wheel, rocking gently, able to see the crowd below but also what was beyond.

She thought of her friends and the summer just past, and wondered what was ahead for them, knowing that not much would change. They had all reached the age where habit had become intention. No matter what happened, Lu would always fly, a hawk asleep on the wind. Blair would find a man, lose him, find another until one of them took. Kate would put a newer, maybe better version of herself together and then somehow mess it all up. For herself, Sybil was sure of only one thing: There would always be the worlds she could create, more real to her perhaps, than life as it happened.

Liquor flowed. Blair waltzed out of the house with a cake, huge with rose-budded lettering: SHOREHAM SHUTDOWN. People applauded, stabbed at the cake for a while, and went back to their drinks, gaudying their glasses with frosting. Bruce's punk-cut friend studied Sybil's long legs, working up to an approach, and finally decided on humor.

"You know, I've always wondered," he said loudly. "Do tall women wear special bras?"

The crowd around her fell silent. Pulling herself up even taller, Sybil turned slowly and looked at him. "Yes. The cups are on the back."

Lu snorted her drink through her nose, and the guy let himself be sucked back into the laughing crowd.

Two men on the patio touch-danced into the house, and a few minutes later they touch-danced out the side door, embellished in pink and white crepe paper. The bartender syncopated ice and stared at the teats of the sculptress, like dull pennies breaking through rotting crochet. The woman in the mushroom hat considered a bottle of champagne, changed her mind, and copped another cheese. Hoyt Biddle slugged back a drink, fascinated, rolling his head around at the crowd.

He looked at the balloons, studied the silver lettering, MARRY ME, then gently nudged Lu, pointing up to the hearts. "Who's asking who?"

She nodded at Will and Sybil. Hoyt closed his eyes as if his vision were no longer reliable.

Sybil watched a taxi pull into the drive, saw two passengers emerge, and took Will's hand, needing strength.

"What is it?" He looked down at her, then looked across the lawn, and his stomach muscles jumped.

They moved quickly away from the party, trying

to head Walter off at the side of the house. Beside
him, Nora looked young and tragic, a perfect version
of Kate. Sybil ran to them, hugging her.

"Man, this is bad timing." Will took Walter's arm.

"She hung up on me. I've been calling for an
hour."

"Where's my mother?" Nora cried.

At that moment Blair turned from the crowd and
swayed slightly against Tom. His eyes darted to
Walter, then back to Bruce and his muscled friends.
Bruce stood with his arm around Kate's waist,
chugging champagne, small wads of napkin in his
ears protesting the babbling poet who was protesting
the human race.

"Mother!"

Hearing Nora's voice, Kate turned and was already moving across the lawn.

Bruce turned too, removing the napkin wads
slowly, his nose aimed at the house as if smelling
spoor. Watching the others push Walter in the side
door, his eyelids lowered, then slowly opened, and he
turned to his friends. "The fucker's here."

One of them squeezed a plastic champagne glass
in his hand until it crackled and collapsed. "Amen."

Walter was standing inside the house arguing with
Sybil and Will when Bruce entered from the patio
door, muscled and headless, whacking crepe paper
out of his way. The head appeared.

"Bruce," Will whispered. "No, man."

Sybil moved to him. "Bruce, please go back outside."

Walter's eyes narrowed, and he pulled himself up,
tall and paunched out of shape. "So," he expelled,
"Katie-babes."

Bruce shook the others off and advanced, hands on
hips, snorting bestially, like a thing on the last rung

222

of the genetic pool. "You keep coming back, don't you?"

"This is none of your business, young man."

"Kate's my business. She's not going back with you." Bruce flexed his muscles as if ready to spring.

"Look. She's got two kids almost as old as you. She . . ." Walter stopped, realizing logic had no place here, only reflex.

Sybil turned to Will. "Go get Tom."

At the door to the patio, Will met one of Bruce's friends. "Uh, I think you better stay outside."

With lazy pleasure and no thought, the punk-cut pushed Will widely aside.

Sybil intercepted him. "Wait. This is my house. And I'm asking you to go back outside. Please."

His hand reached out fast, so fast she knew he was hopped-up on something. He held a large amount of her dark hair, not pulling it, just holding.

"All you older bitches are so . . . polite." He smiled. "Do you say please when you want this boy to fuck you?"

He seemed to suddenly nod, a reaction to Will's fist in the back of his neck, and in the same instance, or so it seemed, he swung around almost gracefully, burying his fist in Will's stomach. Will fell backward and sat on the floor, pulling down a storm of pink and white crepe paper.

"Stop it," she screamed.

Tom evolved through the door, picked up the fire poker, and waved it at the punk-cut. "Out of here. Or I'm calling the cops."

Kate flew into the house and lunged over to Bruce and Walter. "Are you out of your damned mind?"

She looked from one to the other as if the question was up for grabs.

"I want to talk to you," Walter said, watching Bruce.

"You're not going back with him," Bruce said, watching Walter.

That age-old bolero, the male standoff, was taking place, and Kate saw it had little to do with her.

"You goddamned vain men."

She thrust her elbows into their chests, trying to separate them. Bruce pushed her half-roughly aside, like extra flesh.

"C'mon. Let him be a hero."

He waited for Walter to make a move. Nothing. He egged him on. "I screwed your wife. Good . . . and plenty."

Walter's response was a seizure. He brought his knee up between Bruce's legs and met Bruce's drooping face with a fist that had the ballistic force behind it of a husband cheated. Bruce went down in a confusion of floating festoons. Kate dropped to her knees beside him, but Walter jerked her back to her feet. As she struggled, he slapped her hard across the face.

"Is this what you left your family for?" he shouted. "So you could fuck around with this piece of plankton? Answer me!"

She swung a marble ashtray against his head. He swayed, but his skull seemed damage-proof.

"You left me first," she sobbed. "You left me."

They were both accurate, but somehow they were both wrong.

Sybil struggled to them through the maze. "Stop it. Stop it."

Blair and Lu had been working the crowd out on the lawn, trying to keep them distracted. But people slid off, curious, locomoting to the patio and the side windows. Then, at the sight of Bruce's blond friend, Hoyt Biddle felt a shot of adrenaline to the brain that almost unbalanced him. Lumbering back from the car without his jacket, looking like a cutout from a muscle magazine, the blond was fitting brass knuckles over his hands.

Following him, Hoyt pushed his way into the house, yelling back at Lu, "For Christ' sake, stay put."

It was hard to see at first—men's bodies thrashing, a woman's high heel, Will and Tom grappling with the punk-cut. Hoyt slugged it out with the festoons for a minute, getting his bearings, then dived at the back of the blond and half-missed, tackling only one leg. The guy swiveled around and came up under him, connecting brass with his jaw. Hoyt was lifted almost to his feet by the impact, then quietly sagged out of plumb.

In the corner, Kate pulled Bruce to his feet. "Please get your friends out of here," she cried. "They're hurting everyone."

He shoved his bleeding face at her and grabbed her wrist. "Who's side are you on, huh?"

Confused, she turned to Walter, slumped against the wall—maybe a delayed reaction to the ashtray, or maybe his muscles feeling the subtraction of the years.

The blond slid something across the floor to Bruce, and Kate saw his fist pull back, catching a gleam of afternoon sunlight. For a second she wondered how human skin could reflect the light so breathtakingly, a hard reflection like yellow cloisonné. Then the fist hit Walter's ear, and the ear split. She saw the brass knuckles that had caught the light so memorably, fitted on Bruce's hand as he and the blond worked Walter over.

"Stop," she whispered.

Ignored, she stepped back, almost absentmindedly, turned slowly in a circle, taking in the room, touched the purple handmark on her face, and wandered to the stairs.

Hoyt revived, feeling his jaw stupidly, trying to count the pieces. Amazingly, only the flesh was split; the bone intact. He lay there a second, shaking his limbs, regathering all that adrenaline. Then he got slowly to his feet, inhaling so that his chest expanded with the breadth of a bullishly strong, middle-aged man, and lumbered across the room, grabbing the blond by the back of the neck.

Dragging him backwards with a stranglehold on his windpipe, Hoyt spun him around and flung him across the room into a wall. Before the guy could recoup, he picked him up like a barbell, spun him around again, and flung him against a further wall. The crowd at the windows shrieked. Nora ran to the patio screaming.

"What are they doing? Where's my mother?"

Lu pulled her back, craned her neck through the door, and turned to Blair. "It's a bloodbath."

Inside, the place reeked of human sweat and mucus and blood, the floor a menagerie of pink and white snakes. Sybil crouched half-dazed in a corner. The guy with the punk-cut was down with Tom squatting over him, bleeding and wrecked. The blond, half-conscious, was swinging at Hoyt. Will seemed mounted on Bruce's back, but Bruce flung him off, still going at Walter's face with the knuckles.

"Stop."

It was such a small word, they turned and through the pink haze saw Kate on the stairs pointing the gun.

Quiet spread through the room like a virus. Only Bruce continued mindlessly pummeling. He slowed for a moment to catch his breath, and in the stillness something pounded, a heart.

"Stop." Kate said it again, as if memorizing the word.

Walter's arms flailed out pitifully, as if to embrace Bruce. This seemed to anger him; he grunted, lifting Walter to his feet.

"You won't come back again, you mother-fucker."

He leaned Walter against the wall, set his face straight, and landed a blow with the knuckles to the cheek, then pulled his arm back for another slaughtering punch.

"Kate. No. No." Sybil raised her arm uselessly, knowing the thing was done.

"I told you . . ." Kate began, then sighed and pulled the trigger.

At first the room went black, or so it seemed: a collective human reaction, eyes snapping shut as the report clove the skull, reverberating in the near-empty house. Bruce went down slowly, eyes bulging. On the floor he whinnied and wriggled, trying to turn his leg around as if curious about the pain in his thigh. Walter slid down beside him, as if curious too, but he was beyond focusing. At the sound of the shot, Nora was sucked into the house, suddenly aged.

"Kate," Sybil reached up slowly, "give me the gun."

Kate looked down at her, then pointed the gun at herself, her heart.

"Mother!"

"Back off," Kate whispered. "Everyone."

Slowly, conscientiously, they moved back. People outside scattered toward the driveway, and there was the sound of tires grinding into pebbles.

"Kate," Blair said evenly, "we love you."

Slowly she sat down on the stairs, still pointing the gun at her heart. And then she turned it around, pointing it again at Bruce, then laid it sideways in her hand and looked down at it. In the total silence her small voice was amplified, the words strung out like a record running down.

"I saw . . . a movie cartoon once. Bugs Bunny ran off a cliff. For a while he was suspended, still running, moving his legs in midair. It took him a while to look down and see there was nothing there." She fondled the gun. "That's how I feel. Everything is somewhere else. All the things you count on."

"Katherine," Walter called up to her from the floor, startling everyone, as if they imagined him dead, "this young man's hurt. We've got to get a doctor."

Kate looked up surprised, as if she had drifted off. Her eyes were huge, with the blue-black density of plums. Someone was crying.

"I feel so totally alone," she said. "Why? Why do I feel homeless?"

"Kate," Lu moved toward the stairs, "we're all homeless. This room is about homeless people."

Kate sank down a few steps closer to where Walter lay. "You know, I was faithful to you for eighteen years, but for the last eight I was cheating." She sighed, ferociously tired. "Isn't it cheating to say you're faithful when you've lost the desire?" Then she slowly shook her head. "How did I lose it? Did I misplace it? Was it stolen?"

Walter wiped his face gently on his shirt-sleeve and winced at what he saw. "You're the only woman I've ever loved, Katherine." His voice was raw, like someone coming out of surgery. "But maybe I stopped showing it."

Kate looked out over the room, from one face to the next. "Sometimes I dreamed of my husband dead. Not that I wanted him dead, but widowhood seemed more of an achievement to the world than marriage. I'm sorry."

Walter suddenly lay his head down on the floor, exhausted. She gazed down at him and ran her fingers through her hair dreamily, drifting off again.

Hoyt took a few steps toward the stairs. "Kate, honey. You don't know me, but I know guns. They have a way of going off. Would you like to hand it down to me?"

"Mother. Please give him the gun."

"No." Kate suddenly sat up straight.

"Why?" Nora pleaded.

She looked out at them. "If I give up the gun, I'll lose everyone's attention."

There was a general shifting in the room, a telepathy of fear and miserable exhaustion and yet a shivering with unspent adrenaline. There was a smell, too, of blood mixed with cordite.

"You have our full attention," Tom said gently. "Bruce could bleed to death, Kate."

She stared down at Tom, defiant. "You haven't liked me, have you?"

"I was put off by your beauty." He strained to be honest. "And a certain caustic, lazy intelligence."

"I was never lazy." She shook her head. "I was . . . I became overwhelmed. Do you know what nihilism is?"

"Yes," Tom answered. "It's what you ran away from in LA. But you're creating it right now in this room."

Bruce whinnied loud, reminding them he was still there, blood Rorschaching around him.

"Will I be arrested?" Kate asked.

"No. Self-defense," Walter croaked with Brooklyn certainty. "An accident."

Something composed itself in Nora's mind, and she moved quickly to the stairs and knelt.

"Mother, remember when we were kids—the time you came to school to beat up the drug dealers?"

229

"Yes."

"Justin's always remembered that fur coat. Every time he sees a woman in a lynx he talks about the day you saved us with your tire iron."

"Does he hate me, Nora?"

"No. He misses you. Come home. Live with me." Kate shook her head. "You'd make me feel old."

Nora looked down, weeping. "I have a feeling . . . I'm much older and more wasted than you'll ever be. I need you. Badly."

In the deepening shadows of the afternoon, sirens wailed.

Kate stood slowly, as if struck with common sense, and ceremoniously laid the gun down on the stair, surveying the room.

"Well, this is some movie," she said and moved slowly down the steps to her daughter. She took Nora's hand and knelt to her husband, cradling his face in her lap.

"Walter, can you hear me?"

"Yes," he whispered, sinking.

"I still want a divorce. I need it."

"Yes."

Nora surrounded them both with her arms, crying hard. The women gathered around Kate, and the men gathered around them. Even without the gun, she had everyone's attention.

After a while Hoyt moved casually to the stairs, removing the chamber from the gun. Then he glanced at Bruce's buddies; combat had detoxified them.

"You saw nothing," he instructed them, limping around with his open chin. "It was a drunken free-for-all. A gun went off accidentally." He picked up the brass knuckles and wrapped them in crepe paper. "Otherwise I'll have to mention these. And the crystals you were snorting, stashed in your jacket in the car."

The blond nodded, desperately agreeable, two ribs broken and a shoulder like a squash. Hoyt shoved the crepe paper bundles in the refrigerator as an ambulance and a squad car pulled into the driveway.

Two police entered through the side door, hands at their unbuckled holsters. "Holy, silent, suffering Jesus."

Their eyes worked the room, trying to find a point of reference in the human carnage, their faces going bright to dark, bright to dark, reflecting their car flasher through the windows. Two paramedics entered from the patio door, paused, and lowered a stretcher to the floor. One of them advanced, with a studied lack of shock.

"Who here is *not* injured?"

Kate rode in the back of the ambulance with the paramedic and Walter and Bruce, both men unconscious, hooked up to drip jars. Bruce's pants were slit, his leg bound; Walter's head was swathed in bandages. Lu rode up front with her arms around Hoyt, shot up with painkiller, his jaw wrapped haphazardly.

"More fun than horse tranquilizers." Hoyt smiled, then drooped.

Sybil followed in the Dodge with Nora and Will in the front seat, Blair holding Tom in the back. The police car trailed behind with the two bruisers, one crying, one in shock. Sirens screamed, and neighbors lined Seth Lane as if for a parade. As they pulled out of the driveway, Blair glanced back at the carriage house shimmering in the early evening light, a final glow presaging the shorter days of fall.

Chapter
18

AT THE local hospital, Bruce and Walter were transferred to trolleys and rolled to Emergency Receiving. Within minutes Bruce was rushed down the corridor to the OR. The others staggered in behind the ambulance, like a squad back from fresh combat. Skulls were X-rayed, and flesh was treated and stitched.

In the corridor outside Emergency, Kate sat unseeing, flanked by Sybil and Nora, her daughter holding her hand maternally, as if they had reversed roles. Lu and Blair paced back and forth in front of them as a cop approached.

"Don't say a word, Kate," Lu whispered, "no matter what he asks you."

"Miss Wade," he pulled up a chair, quiet and earnest, "can you tell me how the fight started and who fired the shot?"

Sybil looked up, dazed, only half-feigning shock. "There was a lot to drink. Two men started arguing. It turned into a free-for-all."

"Why were they arguing?"

"Marital, you know, difficulties."

The officer looked around at each of them. "Which of you is the wife?"

Sybil hesitated, then nodded at Kate.

"They were arguing over"—he referred to his notes—"Mrs. Castaldi? And did one of the men shoot the other?"

Sybil looked up. "No. I did."

"That's not true, officer." Blair leaned over, her breast brushing his shoulder, distracting him. "I did. I found the gun upstairs. It belongs to the house."

A nerve under the cop's right eye began to jump. He looked from Blair to Sybil. Kate seemed to wake up, her lips parted.

Lu moved in fast. "They're both lying, officer. I shot him. I'm a licensed pilot, and I'm licensed to carry a gun." She looked him in the eye, watching the nerve jiggle like a tiny worm under his skin. "I also fly corpses," she whispered hoarsely, as if that gave her an edge on the others.

The cop turned around as his partner came in from the squad car. "They're covering for one of the guys."

Blair recognized the partner as the pot-bellied local whose gun had aroused her interest weeks back.

He patted his stomach as it if were upset. "Well, we know the gun's registered to the owner of the house." Recognizing Blair, he concentrated on her. "Do you know it's a felony to give false evidence? You're covering up a shooting."

"Will someone be arrested?" Blair asked.

"You'll all be arrested if you don't tell the truth. If it was an accident and the guy doesn't press charges, that's another story. The owner will probably be cited for leaving a loaded gun lying around."

"Well, I did it," Sybil insisted. "I was trying to break up the fight. I aimed at the ceiling like they do in the movies. . . ."

The cop with the nervous eye looked at her as if

she were a chronic liar. "You aimed at the ceiling and hit a man's thigh?"

Kate suddenly jumped to her feet, shaking her hands through her hair as if trying to wake up. "Stop it. Stop this charade." She looked from one officer to the other. "I shot him. I didn't mean to. He's my lover. But he was beating up my husband. He wouldn't stop."

"Is this true?" The pot-bellied cop looked around at Blair.

"It's true," Kate said. "They're covering for me because I'm in trouble in Los Angeles. There's a warrant out on me for attempted arson. My daughter can tell you." She touched Nora's shoulder. "I set fire to my husband's cars, and I murdered his fish. I was angry. He was having an affair."

For a moment the cops forgot to take notes.

A doctor moved down the corridor, carrying X-rays. He paused, looking them over. "Any of you ladies need attention?"

Blair sighed. "Only internal."

Neither Bruce nor Walter would press charges. It seemed a fair exchange. The bullet hole in Bruce's thigh would heal, giving him a certain outlaw cachet with his "fellow plankton," as Walter referred to them, in months to come. Walter was kept in the hospital for two days, with Kate and Nora at his side.

In the early dawn Blair whispered, "I ran into the house because I thought those goons were probably knifing you."

"Then you still care." Tom held strands of her hair up to the light, watching them drop to his arm.

"Yes." She sat up in his bed. "But that seems inconvenient for you."

"I could finish the book in the next few weeks, Blair."

"Well, when you do, come into the city. We'll celebrate."

He took her by the shoulders. "Don't you understand? As soon as I turn the book in, I'll be ready to have you move in with me, or something."

She laughed. "Or something? Tom, you're still hung up on your options. Maybe if I leave you alone for a while you can work them out."

He shook his head slowly. "I don't believe you're talking like this after the way we just made love."

"We've been making love like that for three years," she answered softly. "And I still go home lonely afterward."

"My God." He closed his eyes, holding his stomach. "I feel like a hunk of something important is being cut out of me."

"It is, Tom. I finally figured out that I supplied what I thought I saw in you. I've been doing it with men for years." Blair pointed to herself. "I'm a valuable human. If I can remember that, I've got a real future."

He felt tears, but anger too. "How did you get so hard all of a sudden?"

"I didn't get hard." She paused. "I just got to be another year older."

Tom stood up and paced around the room in his shorts. "Blair, what do you really want? To go back to the city and write plays and struggle all over again?"

"That will do for a start. Then I want to marry and have a child. Maybe two."

"What do your buddies think of that?"

"Sybil and Lu don't need children. They're more interested in refining themselves than reproducing themselves." She paused, trying to figure it out. "I don't mean they haven't grown up. It's just the lives they've chosen need constant revision and nourishing. They have to rely on themselves for these things."

Tom spoke carefully. "Will *you* have enough left over for children?"

"Easily. Maybe I'll be a superwoman and have a family *and* write plays." She smiled. "I hope the marriage works out, but if it doesn't, I know the child will."

He shook his head. "How can you be so sure?"

Blair looked up at him with her big, brown eyes, and he noticed the whites seemed very clear and solid, like ceramic.

"Because I'm ready." she said. "I watched Kate and Nora yesterday, and I realized what I want's inside me. I just have to find a man who wants to share it."

He suddenly went down on his knees beside the bed. "Do you want me to ask you to marry me right now?"

She looked at him tenderly. His position was right, but he kept getting the wording wrong. "No, Tom. You're just not ready."

She got out of bed and pulled him to his full height because that was how she wanted to remember him.

"In any case, with or without me, I think you're in the wrong place. Bestsellers don't get written in the Hamptons. If you want solitude, try Nova Scotia. Or if you still have the guts, go back to New York."

She took a long time showering, then combed her hair and dressed, and walked slowly around the house, as if memorizing parts of each room. Watching her walk down the steps to the old VW, Tom saw her hair flowing loose and yellow in the sunlight. She shook it a little, and it billowed.

The morning was cool, an end-of-summer feeling,

and moving across the lawn she felt her skin tighten, as if alert. Blair sat for a moment with her hands on the steering wheel, then cried as she started the car, but that was all right. She fought looking back and finally did, and that was all right too. Like a cutout in the window, Tom's silhouette slowly receded as she pulled away.

Lu woke in a chair, facing Hoyt Biddle asleep in a double bed. They were in a little motel cabin back off the highway in the pines. She stood slowly, stirred the embers in the fireplace, and looked out the window. Closer to the highway, the motel's shingle swung in the sunlight: COZY CABINS. Estimating they were half a mile from the site of the horse show, somewhere between Bridgehampton and East Hampton, she sat down again, staring at him. He opened his eyes, started to smile, and felt the pain.

"Uh, good morning." He touched the bandaged jaw gingerly. "What'd they sew me up with, barbed wire?"

Lu nodded, leaning toward him with a bottle of painkillers.

"You get to pop these every few hours. If you're good." She handed him a glass of water and two pills.

Hoyt drank, lay back for a second while the codeine worked, and then managed a real smile. "Man, was I high. How many stitches did they give me, how did we get home, and did you seduce me in my sleep?"

"Twelve stitches. Sybil drove us. I undressed you as far as your undershorts." She half-smiled. "We're still virgins."

He laughed, stretching out his hand, and she took it. "Thanks for staying with me, Lu."

"I asked you to what I thought was going to be a party, not a massacre," she apologized. "Anyway,

237

your human-barbell exhibition was very impressive."

"Last thing I remember is that stretcher-bearer coming in asking which of us was not injured." He stared at her for a minute. "How's your shoulder?"

Lu looked at him, puzzled, then laughed. "Oh, the chip! I'm sure it's still around."

"Not around me, I hope."

She laughed again.

He started to tell her how lovely she was in the morning light, her terra-cotta hair all wild around her pale, freckled face. Then he felt his gray-stubbled chin and his dirty, creased hair, and decided he needed to bathe, but when she looked down, he was fast asleep. When he woke a few hours later, there was a note pinned to his pillow:

"Gone for groceries. Don't leave town. Lu."

Hoyt smiled, thought of the bath, but slipped under again. Saliva gathering in his mouth woke him. The cabin air was full of cooking as she turned from the kitchen area.

"Hi. The tub's running, and I've got steaks frying."

Lu crossed the room in jeans and a wool sweater, and handed him a glass. "It got cool outside. Jack Daniel's weather."

He took a long swig with two more pills and stood unsteadily, gathering the blankets around him as she supported him toward the bathroom.

"Man, first time in my life," he said, "I feel creaky."

"For Christ' sake, Hoyt, you were slugged with brass knuckles by a judo expert."

"What happened to the little mother-fucker?" he grunted.

"You broke his ribs and dislocated his shoulder, and probably saved Walter's life."

"I'll be damned." He sank down in the tub, pleased.

After the steaks they sat in front of the fire with the Jack Daniel's and a deck of cards. From time to time Hoyt glanced at Lu. Her tan eyes slanted down, watching him shuffle the cards, and he could smell a fragrance in her hair. The fact that she was sitting beside him in his cabin seemed a small miracle.

"Have you checked in with everyone?" he asked.

"Yes," she said. "The plane's tied down fine. They know where I am."

She had watched the sensitivity of the man in the way he laid the new fire, handling the logs, the kindling wood, like he was putting small animals to bed. And Lu decided that hiding in the pines with a horse vet was a good place to be.

"What about your friend Kate?" Hoyt frowned.

"She's staying at the Huntting Inn with her daughter. They'll all be flying back when her husband's released tomorrow. He'll need a little plastic surgery in LA. And I guess Kate has to face a judge or something out there."

He sat back, dipping into the Jack Daniel's, slowly articulating the bandaged jaw.

"You're a lovely straight-talking woman, Lu. That draws me. What confuses me is how you got in the middle of that madhouse."

She stared at him. "You've been concentrating on horses too long. What you saw yesterday is the current version of reality."

He snorted. "Honey, if that's reality, I think I'll just stay with the four-leggeds. I saw a human mushroom in full view of everyone steal the party cheese. I saw men with women's hairdos pinching each other's behinds, the boy bartender slip his phone number to an old woman, a middle-aged man almost permanently disabled by thugs with certifiable weapons, and a daughter watch her mother go berserk."

They laughed, and he shook his head. "How did the times get so weird?"

"Well, let's say it's all part of the pursuit of transcendence."

His voice got almost hard. "What puzzles me is why you women today have to pursue it with such damned apocalyptic flair!"

Lu was pleased at the show of temper. "It's good to see your underside, Biddle. You were beginning to sound like a lot of brawn with no grit."

"Is that so?" His eyes twinkled.

They made a large dent in the Jack Daniel's and played two games of poker before she felt him staring, suddenly, immediately not interested in the cards. She shivered and leaned toward him a little high.

"I have to ask you something. That first time I flew you down here, did you have an erection when you got off my plane?"

He smiled broadly. "I did."

"What did you do with it?"

He took her hand and grinned, drunk on her wild hair and white skin.

"Well, it wouldn't go away. Its mind was on you. So finally I took myself to a men's room, situated myself, and had a bona fide ejaculation."

Lu lay her head on the table, laughing, and when she looked up he was carrying her to bed. He turned out the light; the cabin walls lit up gold with the fire, and he slid in under the covers, feeling her tremor, edging toward her like an iron filing to a glowing magnet.

"I thought," she whispered as if she believed it, "we were just going to be friends for a while."

"Honey," he breathed, "I'm fifty-three. If you wait

until the dialogue is meaningful and the vibes coincide, I may be senile."

She laughed out loud, wanting this big, delightful man.

"I snore," he whispered, kissing her eyes, her cheeks, touching her breast tenderly. "But I'm a good hugger. I don't turn my back."

She slid her arms around his thick chest, avoiding his jaw, and lay her face in the gray fur, smelling like leather warmed in the sun.

Before entering her, he put his mouth on the pillow beside her ear. "Lu, honey? Are you protected? Is it safe for you?"

She nodded yes and closed her eyes, and tears came. It had been years since a man cared enough to ask.

When she woke during the night, the fire was out, the cabin air frosty. The tip of her nose was cold, but the rest of her felt snug, safe. She dug deep into his arms and chest, listened to the vibratos of his soft snores, like the throaty beat of a plane engine, and let herself go, and flew out into the realm of dreams.

When she woke again, he was sitting beside the bed, staring at her in the semidark dawn.

She sat up slowly. "Didn't I do it right?"

He laughed. "You did just fine." Winding his finger around one of her curls, he talked on. "You know, the day my wife died, I dove off a bridge and came up a stone, needing nothing. It took me a decade to understand we each need a balance, a counterweight, except maybe wild beasts, poets, and gods." He paused. "And now there's you. I was just sitting here trying to figure out how to keep a woman like you . . ."

"Keep me here?"

Hoyt crawled in beside her, putting his mouth to her breast. "Keep you. Period."

The next morning he was quiet, pensive. "I was thinking. We're both due back in Boston. Or we could stay. And agitate."

Lu looked at him, confused. "Agitate?"

Hoyt folded his arms and faced her, full of plans. "That woman, Wilma Dean, arrested at the horse show for leading the mother's convoy against Shoreham. She's going on trial next week. Disruption of the show, disruption of the peace." He paused. "I bet she could use local support: flags, pamphlets, organized protesters."

She raised an eyebrow. "And aerial play?"

He grinned. "And aerial play."

"Hoyt, is this a ruse?"

"Could be. I want to know you, Lu." He moved close and settled his hands on her waist. "I'd like to stay in this cabin with you for a while. I figure if I keep you flying, I mean flying with a real purpose, that will make you happy."

Still cautious, unsure, she dropped her head against his chest. "And what will make you happy?"

"Just having you acknowledge gravity now and then." He hugged her. "We each choose a life, honey. Mine's horses. Yours is flying. Don't let anyone take it from you."

Her mind was already racing. "Let's see, where's the trial being held? What day? How much time do we have? What's the air space over that courthouse? We could do a real anti-Shoreham air show."

"Whoa." His face drained. "Don't ask me to participate in aerial ballets." Then he smiled. "But I'll be there for your landings."

Lu walked around the room, excited. "I'll call the guys at the flight shack and order half a dozen banners. Wilma Dean will be a hero. We'll make the prosecution and the pronukes look up and weep!"

Then she gazed at him with her long, tan eyes. "And you'd *better* be there for my landings."

Hoyt looked down at his fly and it was swelling, and he felt good enough to weep himself. Then he crossed his legs, discouraging his thoughts. For the moment, they seemed inappropriate.

Sybil shrugged and turned in a sleep that was more a floating semiconscious. She opened an eye. A pink snake shivered near her face beside the sofa where they had made love.

Near dawn, she and Will had left the hospital and driven Lu and Hoyt to the cabin, then dropped off Blair and Tom at his house, and slowly headed home. Will had followed her into the carriage house, looked around, and wordlessly pulled off her dress and underwear as Sybil gently moved her hands across his bruised face and arms, wondering if his erection had anything to do with her. Some men got hard at the sight of carnage.

Now her head lolled as her eyes roamed the living room. Dried blood mottled the gray-stucco walls, rattan rugs were rippled with broken glass, mounds of ash had blown from the fireplace when the screen was thrown, and crepe paper hung from the ceiling like dead vines.

"Some ending." Will woke beside her, his eyes following hers.

He slid her dress across her breasts and hips, grunting, easing the pressure on his sore back, then put his arms around her, brushing ashes from her hair.

"You know," he said, "I had this feeling about Kate all summer."

Sybil stretched her neck toward the ceiling, then rolled her head in circles, stiff. "She'll be OK. Watch-

243

ing someone beat Walter senseless was a quick way for her to find out she still loves him."

"Suppose she flips out in LA, shoots somebody or tries suicide."

She turned to him, putting her lips to his cheek. "Will, there aren't any suicides in this group. None of us are even real tragedies, just average females fighting loneliness and trying to do what we need to do. I joust with the muse. Lu flies. Blair writes plays and dreams of marriage." She shrugged. "Kate's a little more dramatic than the rest of us. But she doesn't want to die. She just wanted to get even."

"Well, she sure got everyone's attention." He lay back exhausted, then suddenly turned his head to her. "How the hell did she find the gun?"

"That's what I've been wondering." Sybil looked up at the ceiling again. "She must have ransacked my room."

Will got slowly to his feet. "I'll check it out. How about some coffee?"

He slid on his pants and stomped upstairs while she worked her way across the debris to the kitchen, filled a kettle, and looked out the window.

"Oh, my God."

In the early morning, the scene outside looked as if a 707 had opened its garbage chute over the lawn. It was buried in plastic cups and paper plates suppurating quiche. Horseflies mooned sedulously over mounds of gnawed chicken parts, and birds pecked at rosebud hunks of cake floating in tubs of melted ice.

Dragging a huge, plastic trash bag across the patio, she slowly began collecting bottles, now and then calling to Will for help. His stomping around upstairs had stopped, and there was no response. After about fifteen minutes the bag was filled, and Sybil dragged out another bag, slowly filling it. She was back in the kitchen pouring coffee about half an hour later when she was suddenly aware of Will standing in the doorway, his face eerily distorted.

"Will. What's wrong?"

His lips moved like someone learning a foreign language. "I . . . I . . . this . . ." He looked at her stupidly, then looked down at the stapled pages in his hand. Fluids shifted in her brain as she recognized the list Lu referred to as Sybil's Pecker Memorandum.

"Will!"

"I think I'm gonna puke."

He dropped the list and staggered out of the house across the lawn. Sybil's hands flew to her face as she stared at the pages on the floor, trying to read the list through Will's eyes—all those men over the years traveling her body. She felt the chill of a sudden sweat; her mouth filled with vomit, and she swallowed it back down. Then, shaking, she picked up the pages and climbed the stairs, needing to get the lay of the room, to know how he had found them.

As soon as she got to the top of the stairs, Sybil understood. Not finding the gun in its case under the bed, Kate had gone berserk, torn closets apart and flung drawers around until she had her hands on it, lately stashed under Sybil's underwear. The list had been in a desk drawer beside the typewriter, and now Sybil stared at the empty spaces of the desk, drawers lying in different corners of the room. Then she sat down on the edge of the bed, feeling a shame so entire that the sorrow she felt next came as a relief.

In the distance she saw him sitting on the sand against a huge log, so close to the water occasional small waves slapped his legs and puddled around him. His head was down, and his arms were hunched around his knees like someone warding off blows. Approaching him, Sybil's bones felt brittle like breadsticks, and she thought her legs would snap.

"Will."

He lifted his head and looked at the sea, unhearing, his body rocking and numb, not knowing how to deal with what he had just read. Slowly he shook his head back and forth like someone whipped without knowing why. She sat down on the sand maybe four feet away.

"Will, can you hear me?"

There was no response.

She raised her voice over the surf. "There are only two men on that list I loved. My husband. And you. The rest of them . . . a lot of times I was just lonely. Some nights it was easier saying yes than no."

He put his head back down, and his shoulders shook.

Sybil tried again. "I'm so sorry you had to find it. I wish I were dead."

His head came up slowly. "The thing is"—he was crying and his voice was awful, but he wanted to finish the thought—"you kept it around. You *wanted* me to find it."

"I swear to God I didn't," she cried.

He nodded vigorously as if he was right and she was wrong. Maybe it was so.

She stared down at her fingers clutching each other, like someone praying. The waves went back and forth, and sand shifted around them, and she wished she could walk into the ocean and sink like a weight. After a while Will stood and in a kind of largo, walked to her, pulled her to her feet by her shoulders, and looked in her face.

"Now I understand what you meant when you said you were too old for me. You meant too worn out, too used."

246

Sybil let out a small cry. He stepped back as if making a decision, then stepped forward, took her shoulders again, and started shaking her. He shook her until things went black and her head pounded, and then he shook her some more, trying to get rid of the rage.

"You used *me,*" he screamed. Then he let her go so abruptly she fell, the ground suddenly against her cheek. He stood over her with his legs apart. "Tell me, was I good material? Huh? What's next on your fuck list—a fifteen-year-old?"

She was crying now and surprised herself by struggling to her feet and hitting him hard in the chest.

"Don't talk to me like that. Will. I thought of having your child. I thought of marrying you. I've given you everything I had to offer."

He pulled her face up to his, laughing viciously but still crying. "You don't have anything left to offer. What could be left?"

Helplessly, Sybil pounded his chest again until he grabbed her by the wrists. For a moment their eyes locked, and she saw Will's blue irises looked suddenly worn thin, as if with shock.

Then he backed away from her and looked down. "I feel like I should wash my hands." He turned and moved slowly down the beach, erect, almost formal, like someone at a wake.

She stumbled along beside him, unable to bear the sight of another segment of her life phasing out. "It's just a list. A record. It doesn't mean anything, Will!"

He kept walking, as if in a trance.

"I don't know why I brought it out here. Maybe I was trying to remember something. Please understand." Sybil bent over, hugging herself as if in pain. "My God, I love you. I never meant to do something so cruel."

There was no response. He was like a man whose feelings no longer had compression.

She reached out for his arm. "Don't leave me."

Will finally slowed down. "I told you I didn't want to be temporary in your life, Sybil. You don't want to marry me, right?"

"I can't. You'd begin to hate me." She stood still. "You've already begun. I need the illusion of freedom, but I need you too."

Now Will spun around, and his face, even his muscles, registered contempt. "You need. You need. What about what I need? All this time you've just been using my age as an excuse, saying I should wait until my testicles had fully descended before I thought of marriage." His voice sounded awful again. "The truth is you don't want to get married. You haven't got *room* for another person in your life. You're too damned selfish."

She was quiet because it was too late for anything but honesty.

He blinked hard, but tears gathered again. "You know what occurred to me when I read those names? That two hundred men all have one thing in common—they're all in your past." He moved his face close to hers. "And my name is at the bottom of that list. I'm just another number."

This time he turned abruptly and walked in the direction of the house. Sybil folded on the sand, feeling the seethe and suck of hysteria as he grew small in the distance, like something being painted out of a canvas. She closed her eyes trying to imagine what it was like for him, reading the list, realizing what it was, and she suddenly remembered Blair's abortion and her own sense of total violation. Like Sybil, Will had seen more than he wanted to know.

She lay back on the sand and stared at the sky for a long time, wondering what he would leave her to take forward with her into the future. And when she finally stood up again, the morning had passed, the hour was noon, her shadow on the sand was small. She walked back to the house so washed out, so depleted, she could not react when she saw Will still there.

He had cleaned up the yard and pulled down most of the balloons, and he sat waiting for her on the patio with his bag packed, looking older, as if inside him some rich pod of innocence had burst.

"I've had a few thoughts." He spoke quietly and pulled up a chair for her.

His eyes were swollen from crying and so were hers, and as he took her hand they faced each other like two Orientals.

"I'm sorry I said what I said. You're not worn out, Sybil. You've just lived longer."

"I wish to God I hadn't lived so much, Will." She cupped his hand in both of hers. "You made life seem new again for me. I never meant to hurt or shock you."

"I'm in shock, yeah. Two hundred men is quite a crowd. But what really jolted me was seeing my name there." His hand shook, but his voice was steady. "Maybe I understand a few things now. I guess I did all along, I was just hoping you'd change your mind."

He dropped his head slightly, and she watched a pale-blue vein hammering at his temple. "You know, I was sitting here wishing you could have been more passionate like Kate, then I remembered you were. You would shoot someone for me. But then afterward you'd sit down and take notes on it."

Sybil leaned closer, listening carefully, as he continued.

"I see now I've been selfish too. All I could think of

was what I wanted. Acting. And marrying you. And because I loved you so much I believed it could work."

The air was cool, but Will was sweating. He unbuttoned the top of his polo shirt, and she saw where her nails had scratched his chest.

"Who was I kidding?" He looked up at her. "You don't need an ordinary life, Sybil. You can create any kind of life you want—a husband, a family. All you have to do is put it down on paper. And if it doesn't work out, you can rewrite it."

"That's not reality," she whispered.

"I know. But maybe it's as real as you need to get." He shifted around in his chair and looked down at his lap. "I need more than that. But maybe not immediately. Maybe my needs will have to wait a few years."

She suddenly moved her hand to her rib cage, as if trying to hold something in. "Will. I'm going to be so empty if you go."

"Well," he said softly, "maybe someday you'll write a book about us."

She shook her head. "Never."

"It's OK. I'd like to read it. I bet it would be terrific." He stood slowly, reaching for his bag. "I think I'll be going now. There's a one o'clock bus." Then he touched her hair. "I know this sounds corny, but I'll always be sorry we didn't have a child together."

Her body was trembling like a tuning fork; even her teeth chattered. She felt blinded and put her hands to her face. Will lifted her slowly to her feet.

"You're going to miss me, Sybil, for a long, long time."

Fighting for control, she stumbled along beside him in the driveway, watching their feet move together.

"How will I know what happens to you?" She wept. "I can't bear not knowing."

"Jesus Christ," was all he could say.

He suddenly felt so weak, he leaned against the old Dodge and pulled her into his arms. As they held on to each other, a deep visceral response to her ran through him underneath his anger.

"Will, don't leave me. Please don't go."

He stopped shaking, and cleared his throat, and looked up at the sky. "There's only one way I'd stay. Isn't that funny? I still want to marry you, so damned badly."

Sybil stood at the end of the driveway and watched Will walk up Seth Lane, toward the jitney stop on the highway. After a while he slung his bag across his muscled back and broke into a slow jog, then eased into a brisk pace, and he kept the rhythm of the pace, heading out of the lane onto the highway.

She would never remember exactly how she felt then, or how long she stood there. She would not remember how the light changed and the shadows grew longer, or how different noises failed to attract her attention. She would realize much later, that she failed to detach herself and record these things as they happened.

Chapter
19

AFTER A FEW DAYS spent packing and shipping her life back to New York, Blair drove over to help Sybil close the carriage house. She arrived with the local newspaper, and together they leaned over the article on the court case of Wilma Dean, the leader of the No Nuke mother's convoy.

The court found her guilty of disrupting the peace, but the judge had voiced his support of a bill giving local residents the right to vote on stopping expansion of the Shoreham nuclear power plant and demanding official inspection of it. A half-page photo showed the woman smiling victoriously, holding her hands up like a boxing champ.

Behind her, a small plane flew a banner overhead, the letters black and huge against a white background: A HUMAN OTHER IS A PRECIOUS THING.

"That's Lu, that's her Cessna!" Sybil stabbed the paper repeatedly.

They leaned over, beaming, studying the picture; then they tore it out and tacked it on the wall.

Later, vacuuming behind the tapestry unweaving the satyr's chase, Blair found a red parachute-silk scarf, and they stared at the fireplace, thinking of Kate.

"Farks. Shucking farks."

Sybil drifted upstairs with mops and pails. In a closet she found the T-shirt lettered THE HUNGER, and after a while she stopped cleaning and sat down, remembering the sounds of the ocean deep in the nights with Will. When she came downstairs Blair was holding a wadded ball of pink and white crepe paper. They looked down at it for a moment, then looked around.

"For an empty house," Blair sighed, "It seems strangely full, doesn't it?"

Suddenly the air was alive with engines, at a distance, then closer. Motorcycles pulled into the driveway, and four sets of muscles sat there, white T-shirts absorbing the sun.

Blair stared through the window. "Oh, Jesus."

Sybil walked out of the house and faced them on the lawn, searching for some zoological parallel to the situation. All she could come up with was gang-rape. The punk-cut guy, with a vulpine smirk, got off his bike and came across the lawn; the rest remained inscrutable behind their reflector shades.

"Hi," he said.

She wondered how to interpret that.

After a moment she felt Blair move to her side. "How's Bruce?"

"He'll live." He grinned, then dropped his eyes. "We were wondering if . . . what happened to the knuckles."

Sybil's eyes fell on his hands, then swept to the other three bikers, then moved back to him. "They're yours. Under two conditions."

He matched her look. "What's that?"

"That you take them and leave this neighborhood quietly." She placed her hands on her hips. "But first you apologize to me."

Blair squeezed her arm, trying to pull her back,

253

but Sybil resisted. The guy narrowed his eyes, looked her up and down, lingering on her breasts and long legs, remembering his crudeness at the party. Finally he spoke.

"I'm sorry what I said about your friend." Then he added softly, "Maybe I was jealous. Him and not me."

Sybil breathed out. "OK." She left and came back with the brass knuckles wrapped in a dish towel.

He opened it slowly. "Wow, the fuckers are cold."

"What about your blond friend?" Sybil asked.

He pointed to his ribs and shoulders. "He won't be surfing for a while."

They stood silent.

"Well," he said, backing away, "it was some party."

He waved and walked off, but after a few steps he turned back to Sybil. "You know, you chicks are . . . hard to figure."

She looked at him, half-smiling. "So they say."

They watched him give the thumbs-up to his mates as he settled on his bike. A few of them kicked their hogs, revving up, but the punk-cut said something, and the engines died down. Then, like an ambush unit, they got off and quietly walked their bikes to the end of the drive.

By evening Seth Lane seemed quiet, abandoned by the summer people in the second week of September. Blair and Sybil had their last walk on the beach in the autumn air and, fortified with a bottle of champagne, plunged into the surf, immensely warm. A last sun slipping fast by six-thirty, as if not setting but recanting, a last lobster at a local inn, the two women smiling, full of memories and glad for each other. The next morning they were Pledging the fireplace when the phone rang.

Sybil looked at it, puzzled. "I thought they'd already disconnected it." She answered and spoke to her agent for a few minutes. "Jason, hi. Yes. I'll be back in town tomorrow. Sure, lunch next week." Then her body went stiff, and her voice changed as she listened. "He did? Oh." After another minute she hung up and turned away.

Blair saw her shoulders shaking and moved to her. Will?"

Sybil nodded. "He got it. He got the pilot." She fought for control but failed.

Blair put her arms around her and held on to her for a long time.

At noon a neighbor picked up Sybil's old Dodge for winter storage, and as she and Blair dragged luggage out to the VW, the phone rang again. This time it was Kate, and they hovered together at the receiver.

"Hi, guys. I'm sitting on our lanai—that's terrace to you—a block from UCLA."

"What do you mean 'our?' " Blair shouted into the mouthpiece.

"Nora and I." Kate's voice echoed long-distance. "We have a small two-bedroom joint that's heaven —no laundry, no dining room. We're painting the kitchen revolver-black."

They were silent.

"Oh, sorry about that." Kate laughed. "Anyway, the rest of the place is eel-gray. Very sardonic."

She sounded strangely serene. Blair and Sybil looked at each other.

Then Sybil asked very carefully, "Kate? Are you on something?"

"Yeah." She laughed again. "I'm on suspended sentence. The judge recommended either I go into analysis or be committed to a nice, quiet milieu with bars on the windows. I'm starting a shrink twice a week, I'm taking psychology courses at the university, and Nora and I play racquetball every night." She paused. "Incredible, huh? I can still smell pot from her bedroom, but after what we've been through, it's ozone."

Their cheeks grazed as Blair and Sybil held the receiver between their ears like kids with a toy phone.

"How's Walter?" Blair asked.

"OK. A little plastic surgery refined some face scars, and he tightened his dewlaps while he was at it." Kate's voice changed, more serious. "He and Justin are holed up at the House of Oz until it's sold. Then they'll take a place together."

"Uh." Sybil hesitated. "What about the divorce?"

"We've started proceedings. But Justin says if Walter and I don't remarry within two years, he's moving to San Francisco to join the gays. I said I hope he likes the Bay Area."

They laughed, delighted.

Kate hesitated, then asked, "How's Bruce?"

"He's going to be fine, Kate." Sybil reassured her. "You made him a hero. His friends will have something to talk about all winter."

"I sent him a card with a check. Is that tacky?"

"It's tacky if it's under five hundred dollars," Blair teased.

"You know," Kate's voice grew quiet, "He was crude, but he taught me a few things. Things I could have used as a mother. I'll probably make a better grandmother."

Sybil looked at the receiver for a moment, then finally answered. "We'd probably all make better grandmothers."

"On the serious side, Sybil, I think you should marry Will." Kate took on a lecturing tone. "I really gave it some thought. He's unique, born old, probably. You two should find a small house in the woods so you can write your novels, produce kids, and have nervous breakdowns out loud."

"What about me?" Blair piped up.

"You need a real rat. I think it improves your plays. The worse the men are, the more you can invent about them. Maybe one day you'll meet a genuine heel and write a hit."

"Oh, Kate," Blair pouted. "Is that all?"

"No, kiddo. Hold out for someone who deserves you. Tom wasn't bad. He just didn't have the metabolism for big decisions."

"Well, Mother Nature," Sybil laughed, "any advice for Lu?"

"Tell her to hold on to that new number," Kate shouted. "He's hot stuff, even if he is a little gray around the edges. And he must be pretty secure to walk around like that smelling of horse manure. Anyway, I have a feeling it's going to work."

"Why?"

"Because it's Lu's turn." She paused. "Well, I've got to go. I'm due at the Pacific. I have this standing appointment every day—two-hour walks on the beach alone. I'm beginning to like the company."

"You sound in better shape than we are," Sybil said.

"Well, I know you're not going to take my advice. You're each going to fuck it all up again, and I want in on every detail. Anybody gets desperate, take the Red Eye out here. Otherwise, thanks, guys."

Her voice cracked a little.

"Take good care of yourself." Sybil blinked rapidly.

"Yeah." Kate laughed. "Knowing me, I hope somebody takes another house next summer."

They hung up and stared at the phone for a long time, as if there were more to come. Then they locked

257

up the house and stood in front of it, storing it up for memory.

After a while Blair slipped her arm through Sybil's. "You know, there's only one thing I'm sure of right now."

"What's that?" Sybil asked.

"You and I are going to be a real hysterical duet for the next few months."

They were quiet as they walked slowly down the drive and climbed into the beat-up VW. Blair revved the engine, and as they pulled out of the driveway she looked back, and pointed to the hanging branches of the big elm. Through the rear window, Sybil saw one silver-lettered pink balloon still bobbing in the falling leaves, like a lush fruit out of season.

They turned onto Seth Lane, feeling their systems gear up for the hard rhythms of New York and the times ahead. Then they merged with highway traffic, joining the locomotion back to the city, occasionally silent, then chattering, replaying the summer, laughing hard, crying hard, now and then letting loose with a song.

Three Novels from the
New York Times Bestselling Author

NEAL TRAVIS

CASTLES   79913-8/$3.50

A woman reaches for her dream when she joins Castles, a prestigious international real estate firm, and follows her driving passion for life from the playgrounds of Bel Air to the boardrooms of New York. On her way to the top, there would be men who tried to keep her down, but one man would make her see the beautiful, extraordinary woman she was.

PALACES   84517-2/$3.95

The dazzling, sexy novel of a woman's struggle to the heights in Hollywood. Caught up in the fast international scene that burns up talent and dreams, fighting against power moguls who have the leverage to crush, she achieves fame and fortune at Palace Productions. Yet amid all the glamour and excitement in the celluloid world of illusions, she almost loses the one man whose love is real.

And now...

MANSIONS   88419-4/$3.95

Her first success—as Washington's top TV news personality—was ruined by a lover's betrayal. As wife to the young scion of the Mansion media empire, she was expected to sacrifice herself and her dreams. But if the world gave her a woman's choice between love and success, she gave the world a woman's triumph. And when real success was hers, she was ready for the man who offered her love.

AVON PAPERBACKS